THE WORLD'S EYE

Joshua Banker

REALM OF TAH'AFAJIEN BOOK 4

First Publication, 2020
Library of Congress Control Number: 2020912457
ISBN: # 0-578-72245-3
ISBN-13: #978-0-578-72245-0

For more information, including artwork, maps, updates and announcements, visit

joshuabankerbooks.com

Prologue

The war in Moa'rehnza was mercifully short. Though many an expert predicted a protracted and bloody conflict, the skirmish quickly became a manhunt for the dregs of the old regime as they fled into hiding.

While the main force of the Gendarmery, Verenigen's military force, struggled to seize a series of northern port cities, the 12th VRF, under the command of Lieutenant Marianus O'mas, trekked through the heart of the country directly into the capital city. Working with a local cell of the Moa'rehnzan resistance (known as the Nascao Das Peosseas or NDP), the 12th neared the end of their mission to remove the entrenched corrupt leadership; those in charge hoped that direct action would pre-empt years of hostilities.

The 12th's mission culminated in blood and fire.

In a spectacular explosion on the night of the Eighth of Gnosimond, 2060 BAE, the royal palace was destroyed. A rumor among the populace speculated that the Moa'rehnzan head-of-state, Carolus Res Ceosan, died in a blast of his own causing. The remaining members of the autocrat's High Council were eventually killed or captured by NDP forces, who were working with the 12th at the time. Any deposed leaders apprehended by the Gendarmery were turned over to the burgeoning transitional leadership to be held for a later trial.

Over a four-month period between Sehbienimond and

Thecimond of 2060, a Gendarmery force was stationed in the capital city of Gran'rehnza. At first, their aid was a vital asset to the NDP. While the NDP had successfully driven most of the Moa'rehnzan military out, it required a sizable armed presence to hold the metropolis. However, the longer the foreign forces remained, the more public opinion began to sour.

At the beginning of 2061, the remaining members of Ceosan's administration had either been defeated or had surrendered. Discussions between Gendarmery officials and NDP cell leaders began over the future of the country. By the end of Iefimond, a formal treaty to end the war was drafted and signed. If the NDP could establish a stable reformation government, the Gendarmery would cease its campaign and depart.

Though it required time and effort to coordinate, Verenigen's armed forces eventually boarded ships bound for Port Hadley. It would be the beginning of the following season before the last troops had packed up and departed Mercarton, the port city claimed by the Gendarmery at the first conflict.

After months abroad, the men and women who had fought in Moa'rehnza came home. Once reunited with their families, they shared stories of the conflict; soldiers told of horrific battles, waged on bombed-out city streets. The tales of violence and damage fostered resentment among the civilians. The fact that the Gendarmery, the same military force that had assaulted the southern continent, was now also in charge of local law enforcement became unbearable to many. Eventually, representatives in Congress rebranded the organization as the Verenigen Marshal Forces (VMF), hoping that disavowing the long-standing name would alter public perception. A series of marketing campaigns were deployed to shape popular opinion on the new moniker.

To a degree, this movement worked. Within a few years,

the citizenry grew, if not comfortable with, tolerant of the VMF as a law-enforcing entity.

Though a select few members of Congress and the Gendarmery senior staff knew of the mission charged to Lieutenant Marianus O'mas and the 12th VRF, none knew how unique the squad truly was. Told to handpick his soldiers for what could have been a suicide mission, O'mas stacked the deck with gifted men and women. These rare individuals exhibited abilities above and beyond those of the average person: not only were they experts in warfare, but they also possessed odd talents like enhanced strength, heightened dexterity, and the ability to heal themselves or others. These people hid amongst the unknowing.

With these exceptional individuals, O'mas was ultimately able to complete his mission.

Once disbanded, the members of the 12th went back to their lives, returning home or completing their service contracts with the Gendarmery.

Lieutenant Marianus O'mas, who had come out of self-imposed seclusion to lead the mission, once again left the service. This time, he was done for good.

There was only one place in all of Verenigen where he could establish a retreat.

The Twelfth of Gnosimond, Year 2061 BAE
Vertegarte

Never before had O'mas felt his age. He was completely spent, physically and emotionally.

His eyes were tired, and the muscles along his shoulders and hips ached. The back-and-forth sway of the steed trotting behind the trader's caravan had kinked his back. O'mas looked forward to the moment he could stand on his feet.

He turned his attention back to the forest pathway, shutting off all wandering thoughts. When one traveled through Vale Grans'tsarren, it paid to be vigilant. So many predatory animals roamed the surrounding woods that being absentminded was foolish. Oblivious travelers were often rewarded with the hasty shortening of their lifespans.

Even schoolchildren were aware of the Vale's dangers. The denizens of the valley were revered in an almost mystical way, and there was an understanding that no one should trek the area without an experienced guide. O'mas' best option for safety was to tag along behind Arbis Barger's Trade Caravan as closely as his ride would allow, though it didn't permit him to travel as quickly as he would like.

The air around O'mas was rich with the aromas of local flora. Though there was no sign of recent rain, heavy moisture hung densely in the atmosphere. Beneath the rattle of the convoy as it pushed southward was the soft murmur of woodland noises: the creaking of timber and the rustling of leaves as a light breeze whisked through the nearby thickets.

For a moment, O'mas glanced up at the distant peaks on either side of him. He was deep in Vale Grans'tsarren, a massive gorge between the Southern Hadleys to the east and the Horans to the west. Except for a trade path through the northern end that led to Grundy and the beaches of Medaveh's Coast to the south, the massive forest of old-growth trees was cut off from, not only Verenigen, but the rest of the world.

The common belief was that the war had begun here. O'mas knew all too well that it would be written that way in history books for years to come. The reality involved a more sophisticated understanding of the variables and motivations that went undocumented. To the common man, though, the Moa'rehnzan foray into the Vale had initiated the conflict in earnest.

Tucked away in the heart of the Vale was his ultimate destination, the village of Vertegarte. Surrounded by endless acres of dense, ancient foliage, the small township stood as the lone, small beacon of humanity within the verdant basin.

Whatever the dangers of the area, O'mas was resolved in his decision. He was done with the outside world. If there was one place in all of Verenigen where he could disappear, it was the Vale. Even if they found out where he was, Congress was unlikely to dispatch anyone to retrieve him. While this was technically a part of the Verenigen continent, the Vale was unofficially off-limits.

Truth be told, after his recent conferences with members of the legislative body, there was nothing left for him to say.

The post-mission briefings with "certain interested parties" had been brutally comprehensive. As O'mas detailed his operation, he spent much of his time on the defensive. Every choice he'd made had to be exhaustively nitpicked to satisfy the petty interests of old men who'd never seen a battlefield in their lives. No matter how he phrased his account, they seemed to want more information, as if a scapegoat might be found in the details.

As he'd recounted over and over, Moa'rehnza's despot, Carolus Res Ceosan, was thought to have been killed in the blast that ruined his palace. Any living High Council members were incarcerated. Some, like Jude Brandich, were now in the custody of the VMF. The rest, at some point in time, were captives of the Nascao Das Peosseas. O'mas was certain they had been executed by now.

To make matters worse, there was the matter of the Grymore Foundation. In his original orders, O'mas had been commanded to dig up anything implicating the industrialist Etremaus Grymore and his company for selling arms to the Moa'rehnzan government. One faction wanted to brand him as a traitor. If they could weaken the Grymore Foundation's influence over Trone Stenan's politicians, there would be a shift of power. Even Etremaus' purported death, since his ship had been reported lost by representatives of the Foundation, did little to appease those out to ruin the man.

Early on in his mission, O'mas had felt driven to unearth the truth. Once he and the 12th were deep in enemy territory, though, such issues seemed trivial. By the end, he was just relieved to survive the ordeal.

Now he knew that no amount of evidence would have been enough. His taskmasters had their own agendas, and everything he provided would only fuel their vendettas. Ultimately, these were people who wanted absolute answers that he could not give.

If he was honest with himself, O'mas was too worn out to care. As it was, the burden of the knowledge he had was a crushing weight.

O'mas slumped over and sighed. These ruminations were an unwanted distraction, especially now when he needed to be the most attentive. A headache began to form behind his eyes.

It took another hour for the convoy to reach its destination. Once the carved wooden gateway marking the entrance to Vertegarte came into view, O'mas could feel the muscles along his spine loosen.

He followed the train of wagons, all loaded down with various wares, into Vertegarte's central clearing. As they passed the last turn in their trek, he spotted a tall building with a maroon-tiled roof that served as the village's common house. Schoolhouse and legislative office by day, the small community's multipurpose structure often acted as a de facto meeting place.

Once they came to a stop, O'mas slipped down from his horse and led it to the last of the caravan's carriages. Before long, a man disembarked and took the steed's reins from him. He'd rented the use of the charger so that he could follow the traveling merchants along the lone roadway connecting Vertegarte to the outside world.

In truth, O'mas would have no immediate need for transportation. He planned to stay in Vertegarte for a few days. Still, there were a few loose ends he needed to tie up beyond the valley's borders. At some point, he would have to transfer his personal effects to the new residence. Perhaps he would sell his quarters in Chancel.

In time, he would visit Willem Ethvarth in Port Hadley. If O'mas wanted to formally retreat from society, it would do him good to spend quality time with the man who'd been his closest companion over the years. Despite Willem's best efforts, O'mas could not be persuaded to make his home at the Ethvarth estate. It was dangerously close to Fort Granic, the local VMF base. He'd be too easy to locate there. The mental image of soldiers knocking at the front door often haunted him.

For a while, O'mas lounged about in the dirt clearing that surrounded the town's common house. From time to time, he stretched out the stubborn stiffness in his lower back. Aimlessly, he strolled back and forth as his attention lingered on the caravan as the crew set up for the day. The merchants would sell their wares to the residents until sunset approached. If there was any local merchandise or produce to be bartered, that would be bundled for resale to other markets. After a quick repacking, the series of horse-drawn carriages would exit and retrace their original route. If time was on their side, they would arrive in Grundy, on the other side of the Vale's northern border, by tomorrow evening.

As he kicked the dust from the tops of his shoes, O'mas

heard someone calling to him. It took him a second to place the voice, but once he did, he stood upright.

"O'mas! Marianus O'mas!"

O'mas looked up to the familiar face of Cal Farber, one of the local woodworkers, as he crossed to meet the newly-arrived visitor. On more than one prior occasion, O'mas had met with Cal. At first, it had been merely to hammer out their business arrangement, but now there was a true warmth in their interactions. A sturdy, good-natured fellow with the hands of a seasoned craftsman, Cal was affable from the moment of their first meeting.

"Good to see you again," he stated, dusting his hands on his smock before offering one to O'mas. "Not so long since your last visit." There were a few wood shavings trapped in his beard that stuck fast matter how much he shook his head.

"I came empty-handed this time," O'mas noted as he clasped Cal's meaty paw. "No time to stop and pack up anything for transport. By the state of your storage shed—as last I witnessed it—I assume there was little else I could bring down until the house was finished."

This comment elicited a bout of hearty laughter from Cal.

"Too true. Good news is that we're on schedule. Weather permitting, you should be able to move in by the end of the month."

"That *is* good to hear," O'mas announced with a smile that cut across his weary face. "My apologies for the inconvenience, but I am truly grateful for your aid. I know that my moving into the village is probably not exactly a welcome event." He glanced at a few of the villagers as they passed by the pair. More than one worked hard to avoid meeting his gaze.

Cal snorted as a smile curled the corners of his lips. "Those who don't care for it can go pound sand. Sure, Trinsler and his toadies probably ain't too hot on it, but considering their history, they keep to themselves and wake up thankful every day that folks around here have better things to do than grab up pitchforks and torches."

Though Cal did not expound upon the topic, O'mas knew the story all too well. In late '59, at the onset of the war, Trinsler had served as the elected mayor of Vertegarte. When he became aware of the Moa'rehnzan incursion to the south, he'd evoked Vertegarte's Right of Protection. This act sent the bulk of the Vale'vigia—warriors trained to defend the village against both the Vale's more dangerous wildlife and what bands of raiders and marauders were foolish enough to enter the forest—to defend the southern acreage from the invading force. Rather than request aid from the Verenigen Congress, he held fast to his policy of staunch isolationism. After the worst of the fighting was over, it became clear that the Vale'vigia were almost entirely wiped out. Even now, years later, the remaining members still searched for the remains of those who'd fallen in battle. It wasn't long before he was ousted from his position by an enraged community. Now, as O'mas understood it, he lived as a pariah in his home on the western outskirts, surrounded by only a few who remained loyal.

"Still, the man-hours and supplies required for the build likely puts a strain on the—"

"You fret too much," Cal said with a dismissive flip of his hand. He then motioned to the dense copses that bordered the village. "Lumber we've got in spades. You're putting woodworkers and carpenters like myself to work. Pumping some badly needed coin into the local economy, so to say. As you can imagine, we don't have what one might call a bustlin' marketplace." He waved toward the caravan.

O'mas only nodded with a half-smile.

"You wanna see how far along we've gotten?" Cal offered as

he took a few steps to the west. "It's almost livable, if you don't mind the interior being unfinished."

"Certainly. No time like the present."

As the Gendarmery's role in the Moa'rehnzan conflict came to an end, many of its soldiers eventually returned to the communities where they had once lived healthy and whole.

In the first year, those medically discharged and sent home were hailed as honorable men and women who gave up their own well-being for the sake of their country and home. They were greeted as cherished heroes, paraded around the town squares, even though the hostilities still raged in a foreign land. As the conflict dragged on over the months, feelings on the home front began to sour. When finally relieved of their duties, the militiamen arrived to find a populace who wanted to forget that the war even existed.

Men who were not trained to cope with the horrors of battle were now emotionally scarred and incapable of dealing with the omnipresent feelings of dread. Teenagers sent off to fight arrived home without the ability to channel their rage properly. Even the strongest of wills struggled to resume the banal country life. Countless stories circulated of former soldiers who attempted to kill a family member over a seemingly-innocent misunderstanding. More than a few considered suicide to end the nightmares that woke them every night. Alcoholism and drug abuse were not uncommon.

There was a small subset of people who chose, rather than resume their original lives, to put their new skills to use. Men and women who had discovered that they were good with guns now desired to make a living by such means. Some chose to enlist in the recently-rebranded VMF. Others joined a growing number of highwaymen and bandits who roamed the countryside, often attacking the lesser-used trade routes for meager profits. Contracts with certain seedy organizations became available in some of the larger cities. Some headed for the island nation of Tir, where such employment was readily available.

A few became mercenaries, just common armed muscle hired out to act as bodyguards, treasure- and bounty-hunters. While there were official channels in Verenigen by which one could procure proper documentation, many of these would-be soldiers of fortune chose to go out on their own. Even though the work was dangerous, there was more money in jobs of questionable legality.

It was in this burgeoning trade that Kyote Kurttsen and Erich Rolde, formerly of the 12th VRF, attempted to make their living.

Chapter 01

The Twelfth of Sehbienimond, Year 2061 BAE
Trone Stenan

"Hold up, asshole! If you… stop now… I won't beat on you all… that… much!"

Kyote's breathless bellowing had no effect on his prey. He figured that would be the case. It wasn't the most persuasive of offers.

If anything, it seemed to put even more distance between himself and Gillem Jeffries as they sprinted through the debris-littered alley. It was clear Jeffries wasn't in a talking mood. Only minutes ago, the man had bolted the instant he saw Kyote and Rolde through the crowded marketplace.

Kyote doubted that Jeffries had been tipped off. In all likelihood, he was just skittish and bolted at the first sign of trouble. To Kyote, though, it didn't really matter. Even if he had to chase Jeffries across the entirety of Trone Stenan, he was going to collect on his bounty. At some point, the second-rate thief would run out of steam and give up. From what Kyote could tell, Jeffries was not exactly a fit man. He was carrying an extra fifteen kilos around his waist. Currently, his flight was fueled by a fear of being caught. That kind of adrenaline would eventually wear off.

Though the weather in the northern city was particularly lovely for the time of year, a dense layer of sweat covered Kyote's olive-hued forehead. Droplets dripped from his brow and into his eyes. He swore to himself as he frantically swiped with the back of one hand or the other to clear his vision. Strands of ratty brown hair that had gone uncut for some time trailed behind him like streamers caught in the wind.

He briefly considered casting off his canvas jacket, as if that would allow him to move faster.

It was to his advantage that the midday streets of Trone Stenan weren't particularly busy. A few pedestrians jumped out of the way as the pair rushed down the paved avenue. Even focused on Jeffries as he was, Kyote could hear the rumbling of motorcrafts on nearby lanes. He fervently hoped that none would turn their direction. If Jeffries hijacked one of the ore-powered automobiles, he could lose his pursuer in a matter of seconds. Trone Stenan was a sprawling city, one of the largest in all of Verenigen. Despite the heavy presence of local law enforcement, it was easy for someone to disappear in the densely-packed industrial metropolis. Truthfully, they'd only managed to track him down by canvassing some individuals who didn't want people looking too closely at their own enterprises.

For a fleeting moment, Kyote wished he carried more than a knife. Even the smallest caliber pistol might have allowed him to put a bullet in the other runner's leg.

Let's not kid ourselves, Kyote quickly admonished himself. *I probably would have wasted an entire clip without hitting him. And then, I'd just be even further behind.*

As the chase continued, Kyote began to feel the pounding of his heart as it beat against his ribs. He could hear his pulse thumping in his ears. His ragged breath played as a backdrop to the beat. While his vision remained focused on his bounty, everything else slowly faded. Colors blurred into a grayish mass, and all sounds but the rhythm of his own body became faint.

Kyote welcomed the sensation. It had also come to him in the heat of battle during the 12th's time in Moa'rehnza. He was uncertain what to call it: bloodlust, frenzy, or berserker's rage. In truth, he didn't care what he called it. What he did know was that it was a side-effect of his other gift, and it came in handy. In this unfettered condition, when any shackles of polite social conventions were cast aside, he moved faster and fought with more fury.

A flicker of orange flashed in the rim of his brown, almost black, eyes. This same supernatural light showed up when he used his recuperative abilities. While some injuries, like broken bones, took more time, most of his wounds fully healed quickly when he directed energy into them.

Though he wanted to let his instincts take over, to unleash the metaphorical beast inside him, Kyote kept control. He needed his wits about him. Otherwise, he might kill Jeffries outright.

He blew a dejected breath out through his nose. The world around him snapped back into place as colors and sounds resumed their original vibrancy. His brain rattled as his senses regained their clarity.

While Jeffries was not their main target, his capture would make this endeavor profitable. If they brought him back alive and mostly in one piece, they would get almost double their payout for the job. The big deal—the real reason they'd gone through all this trouble—was the bag of jewels he'd lifted before his disappearing act. Returning that was more important than anything else, and failure to do so would void the contract. Tucked away in Rolde's bags was a manifest of the pilfered items; Jeffries had done them a favor by storing it all in a sack that, until recently, was foolishly stashed in his jacket.

Now, though, the whole bundle was sinking below the river. They'd watched him pull it out and heave it.

It was a surprise that Jeffries pitched the rucksack containing the gemstones into the aqueduct as he fled. Kyote figured Jeffries thought he'd be able to retrieve it after losing the bounty hunters. Perhaps, he counted on it being a distraction. Fortunately, Kyote left Rolde behind to dive in after them.

Rather, Rolde breathlessly volunteered as he waved at Kyote. Rolde often referred to himself as 'not built for long bouts of running,' saying he didn't have the constitution. Even in their time together during the war, he'd never had the stamina for long treks. His skill as a medic kept him out of the field. Because of Rolde's unique gift, O'mas never cared about his level of fitness. Still, their march through the Regenwald had challenged him. Now that he was out of the service, he didn't run long or hard if he could avoid it.

Though a part of him wished Rolde was with him to help trap the fleeing crook, if Rolde recovered the treasure before it floated out of the city, then they wouldn't come away from this empty-handed.

Kyote barged out of the alleyway, looked to his right, and immediately spotted Jeffries. The thief, though winded, was still running with all he had. Kyote's chest heaved, and his legs ached as he took off again.

Get outta the damned way, he thought as he brushed past a pair of onlookers. One screeched in protest at being jostled. Kyote made no effort to look back, much less apologize.

Even as locked in on Jeffries as he was, Kyote glanced at his surroundings. They were on a main roadway that connected to low-income residential wards. Foot traffic included people on their way home from work. Fortunately, there were no motorcrafts parked on the streets. Considering the prohibitive cost of such a possession, it made sense. Jeffries would have to head either into the crowds or one of the many alleyways that ran through the neighborhood.

The glint of afternoon sunlight reflecting off of polished metal caught his eye. Kyote spotted something a few blocks southward that made his heart sink.

At the end of the street, parked diagonally by the sidewalk, was a hovercraft. Marked with the silver shield of Trone Stenan's police force, the flat-bottomed steel craft rested on a matching pair of landing skids. Though he'd only seen a handful of the vehicles fly across the metro skyline, each one propelled by a row of directed thrust jets mounted into the underside, this was the first time he'd seen one left out unattended. Within the open cabin were three rows of bucket seats.

In the half-second it took for Kyote to notice the vehicle, he realized that Jeffries was heading straight for it.

Where are the constables? Kyote frantically wondered, realizing that there was no one to keep the thief from hijacking the craft. His eyes dashed back and forth. No one wore the gray and black of the Trone Stenan law enforcement division. The front door of a nearby townhome was bashed in, as if a raid was underway. *Who the fuck left this out? Someone ought to get fired for this.*

Jeffries leapt over the side of the vehicle and dropped into the passenger cabin. He latched his hands onto the steering controls, frantically searching for the ignition. He loudly swore as he pawed at the dashboard.

Time slowed to a crawl, as Kyote closed the distance. Once the engines were powered, Jeffries would be airborne and out of Kyote's reach.

Kyote's left hand clasped the driver's side panel just as Jeffries cried out in joy. He depressed the starter, and the craft came alive. After a hard yank of the throttle, the hovercraft lurched forwards and upwards. When the vehicle began to gain altitude, Kyote's legs were knocked out from underneath him. He was tossed head over heels as he flipped into the passenger cabin. A string of obscenities flew from his mouth as he crashed headfirst into the second row of bucket seats.

Jeffries clearly wasn't an expert pilot. The vehicle lurched about like a ship on rough waters. Still struggling to get to his feet, Kyote was upright long enough to look over the side of the craft, noticing that they were already a half-dozen meters above ground. Out of the corner of his eye, he saw two constables rush out onto the street, bellowing after the departing craft.

Better hold on best I can. Don't wanna fall out. Can't imagine I'll get as lucky as in Moa'rehnza and crash through a roof to soften the impact.

Somehow, Jeffries managed to level out the hovercraft as sent it southward. The wind screamed past them as they got up to speed. Kyote had just enough time to leap into the front row of seats. Finally acknowledging his unwanted passenger, Jeffries tried to shove him out of the cabin. Kyote batted the open palm away.

Before Jeffries could try again, Kyote balled his fist and swung it in a wide arc. When his knuckles struck the side of Jeffries' head, the impact sounded like a rock falling on hollow wood.

A second blow to the skull knocked Jeffries out. The thief's head flopped to one side, and the muscles in his torso and arms went slack. His hands, still at the controls, swung to the left. The hovercraft followed suit.

"Ho-shit!" Kyote screeched, clutching at the upholstery as the vehicle twisted mid-air.

As he struggled not to be thrown free, Kyote leaned over and took command of the craft's steering. With a twist, he spun it away from the steep descent. The whiplash of the sharp turn flung both Kyote and the unconscious Jeffries to the right. The dead weight of the slumped thief slammed into Kyote, which almost knocked his grasp from the curved, leather-bound wheel.

"Get off me," he snarled. He threw a sharp jab with his elbow at Jeffries' back, trying to move the comatose man out of his way.

When Jeffries' weight shifted again, his shoulder plowed into Kyote's chest. With the breath briefly knocked out of him, Kyote released his grip on the controls and fell backward.

This time, Kyote curled up with an arm draped over his head. They were so close to the ground that he had only seconds to react. With his free arm, he grabbed Jeffries and pulled him close. Maybe he could use the man to soften the impact. If the craft exploded or they were thrown in the collision... well, that would be a more serious problem.

The hovercraft slammed driver's side first into the pavement with a bone-rattling clatter. The chassis creaked and the windshield shattered in a spray that peppered Kyote's face. Steel screeched in protest as it bent into new, impossible angles.

For a second, the world seemingly stood still. Kyote could hear parts crushing under the craft's weight. Something popped with the sound of arcing electricity. The casing for one of the directed thrust jets cracked open, and a small explosion rained metal and ore on the street. The force from the blast rolled the vehicle over onto its top.

Kyote fell out of his seat and landed headfirst on the pavement. He saw stars for a moment as his eyes fluttered. The wreckage settled with a booming crash around him. Though a few of the seats collapsed under the weight, nothing fell on top of him. Kyote blew out a faint sigh of relief at his good fortune.

This feeling was fleeting. When Kyote noticed that everything had gone dark, panic began to set in. *Am I buried under the vehicle? Have I gone blind? Which is the better option?*

He reached forward and immediately struck bone and muscle.

Gods damn it, Jeffries, he thought to himself as he struggled to push the thief's body aside. Once there was just enough room, he crawled out from beneath the hovercraft. Gravel and broken glass dug into his arms and legs. The sleeves of his jacket were a tattered mess.

That could've gone a lot worse. Hovercraft coulda blown up on me. Still could, I guess. This thought caused him to move with a bit more haste.

Just as his head was about to peek out from under the wreckage, a thought occurred to Kyote. *Probably should pull Jeffries out if I can. Can't leave a potential sack of coins just sitting under there, can I? I mean, if he's still alive…*

Though he briefly considered abandoning Jeffries to his fate, Kyote turned back and dragged him out of the overturned passenger cabin. Each yank met resistance from Jeffries's limp weight. Kyote muttered a long string of semi-coherent swears. Once the unconscious man was pulled clear, Kyote scrambled back a few paces and propped him against a dislodged steel panel.

Surprised to come out of the wreck with only a few bruises and a handful of scrapes and cuts, Kyote wiped a bloody hand across his face. His knuckles were raw, and there was a small gash on his forearm that had bled through his jacket. Though none appeared broken, his bones ached something fierce. As he got to his feet, Kyote's head spun for a few moments. He'd taken one too many shots to the skull. The cacophony of interested bystanders roared in his ears. His surroundings, though, were a blurry mess of grays and browns, lit in early evening oranges.

Once his vision began to clear up, Kyote found himself only two meters from the crash. Jeffries remained where he was, unconscious and in need of medical attention. Though bloodied, he appeared to be breathing.

Got to be the luckiest sumbitch ever.

Kyote quickly realized that he was not.

"Freeze! Hold it right there!" a series of voices called out to Kyote. Or it was only one person whose words echoed inside his muddied head? When he turned about, he spied the quartet of security officers, each of whom brandished a nightstick and moved in to corral him.

"Would it make any difference to say that I was trying to bring it back to you?" Kyote asked as he slowly turned around. He glanced back at Jeffries for a second. Despite visible injuries, which included cuts and abrasions to his face and arms, the man was alive. The scalp wound pouring blood probably looked worse than it was. It was certain he would later wake up in a prison hospital.

"Hands up!" one of the constables ordered as he leveled his pistol at Kyote. "I won't say it again."

At this, Kyote grunted. The odds were not in his favor. His legs and chest ached from the chase. Everything else was sore from the crash. Odds were that he might even have a concussion. No manner of smooth-talking was going to get him out of this situation.

After a few seconds, Kyote let out a breath and threw his hands in the air.

"I guess it would be too much to ask if I'm going to get to plead my case, right?" he asked sardonically as the first pair charged in to detain him. "Like give you my si—"

A swift blow across the back of the head took the fire right out of him. A few more made him far too woozy to put up much of a fight.

The building to which they dragged Kyote was like most of

the administrative structures erected across the city. Built from steel and concrete with a faux-marble façade, the detainment station was meant to be imposing. It stood in stark contrast to the blocks of low-income housing which bordered its property. The staff, dressed in stiff gray and black uniforms, tended their wards with open disdain. More than once, Kyote felt an unnecessary strike across his skull before he was tossed into a cell with eight other detainees. No effort was made to interrogate him.

After talking with witnesses of the incident, it became clear to the local law enforcement that Kyote was not the instigator of the hovercraft's theft. Jeffries, who was in a medical ward down the street, was identified as the culprit. Though his actions certainly did not lead to the vehicle's safe return, Kyote was only tracking down the thief. More than one of the spectators referred to Kyote's actions as "daring" and "heroic." Little did they know he was attempting to capture his target.

Despite a lingering desire to charge him with something, the precinct's lead investigator eventually relented to Kyote's release. He was warned to leave Trone Stenan with haste. Without mincing words, it was made clear that his kind was unwelcome inside the metropolis.

Left unmentioned was the superstitious rumor that had spread among the staff. By now, Kyote's injuries had entirely healed, which unnerved some of the junior officers. Rather than deal with him and the disruption he caused, the senior administration wanted him gone.

Once through the station's front doors, Kyote found a friendly face waiting at the bottom of the steps. He snorted as a crooked smile curled his lips.

"I take it you heard the good news."

"I'm surprised they turned you loose," Rolde commented as he met Kyote streetside. "Like, at all. I always heard Trone

Stenan justice was, well, ya know…"

This statement elicited a hollow laugh from Kyote, who glanced over his shoulder. He rubbed at the back of his head with one hand. The lump that once throbbed there was long gone. "I don't think they really cared to, but they didn't have much. 'Public nuisance' is about as much as they could trump up, especially once they started getting witnesses talking about the whole thing. Apparently, I was *courageous* and tried to stop the thief. Or, that's how the story goes. Better than the truth, I think. Still, we should get going."

The pair began to march eastward. As they pushed their way through the late-evening crowds, Kyote snuck occasional glances at the faces around them. Largely oblivious, Rolde merely attempted to keep pace.

Before long, Kyote leaned in and spoke to Rolde.

"Did you get it?"

"The package? Yeah. Got a bit wet, but I grabbed it before we lost it. It's with our gear at the inn. Had to pay to keep our room, but at least we have it."

"We should, uh… we need to grab it and go. Get outta town before trouble finds us again."

"It's kinda late. Don't you want to rest up and—"

"We *really* should get out of Trone Stenan while we can," Kyote cut him off. "Don't go looking around but we've picked up a tail."

For a second, Rolde struggled with the urge to glance behind them. All he saw were drably-dressed people in a rush to be somewhere other than on the streets.

Kyote continued. "I figure it's one of the local constables, sent to keep an eye on me. Make sure I took their *suggestion* to heart. Probably has a pal somewhere else, but I haven't picked him out, yet. I'm an undesirable, and it's only a matter of time before I screw up and they have to re-arrest me. So, rather than stick around, we should get our stuff and get outta town."

Rolde nodded.

"The worst of it, though, is that we're gonna lose the bonus on this job. Ain't no way to recover Jeffries now that he's in custody. Gonna be a while before he's even able to serve time for stealing the hovercraft. If they ever find out why he was in town… well, he might not get outta Trone Stenan for a while."

"Staying in town a few extra days probably ate into our profit all the same," Rolde added sourly. "Don't know how much longer we could afford to stay if we wanted to."

"So, we break even on this job by turning in the package? Ugh." An already lousy night was becoming worse by the second. Kyote wanted to be done with Trone Stenan as fast as he could.

It took almost an hour for the pair to return to their rented room. While the streets weren't all that congested, Kyote intentionally took a circuitous route, hoping to lose whatever tail they'd picked up. When the roar of hovercraft jets neared, both men disappeared into nearby alleyways. Kyote was aware that there was no public air traffic in Trone Stenan; local security forces piloted the only vehicles. The aircraft was not yet something that even the richest of private citizens could afford.

Kyote felt no relief as the front of the dingy hovel, tucked in the back corner of a poorly-lit lane, came into sight. At best, even if they'd arrived without company, he knew they only had an hour to waste. They needed to gather their luggage and disappear before sunup.

Kyote barely acknowledged the man at the desk as the pair charged through the lobby and down the east wing to their quarters. He was part of the night crew, more interested in his reading than who might be coming in at such a late hour. For this very reason, they'd been happy to board here. No one asked questions as long as there was no trouble. The inn's interior was shabby and smelled of mildew. The carpet had once been crimson; now, it was varying shades of red and brown. Glass lampshades hung from wall sconces were layered in grime that discolored the light to a greenish hue.

Kyote flung the door to their room aside and rushed to the pair of unmade beds on the far end. It had been days since he was last here and his sheets were still as he'd left them. At the foot of cot were their packs, both still open with an assortment of unwashed clothing littered around them. He began to scoop up his apparel and cram it back into the rucksack.

"Not to mean this in some kinda insultin' way, but I get the feeling that we may need someone smarter than either of us to make sure these plans work out better," Rolde noted as he joined Kyote in hastily repacking. "Someone to keep track of all the *finer* details."

"A third head for our little enterprise?"

"One who's got a head for logistics."

Kyote chuckled. He knew exactly who Rolde meant.

"Ain't he still with the LIO?" The Logistics and Information Office was a subdivision of the VMF in charge of managing the day-to-day paperwork and coordination of incoming intelligence.

"Last I spoke with him, it seemed that his contract was due to expire soon."

"Spoke?"

"Okay. Not spoke. Read his letter."

"You said soon?" Kyote pulled the cords tight and slung his pack over one shoulder.

"Mid-Ninimond."

"That's not soon. That's like two months away."

"Still…" Rolde frowned for a second before he finished his own packing. "I don't think Flynn'd be against it. The idea of working with us. It'd be steady work coming straight out of the service."

"Just 'cause he listened in while we shot the shit, killing time in that Moa'rehnzan bar, about being mercs doesn't mean he'd be all-in."

"It couldn't hurt to ask."

"You plan on hitting him up the minute he's clocked out with the LIO?" Now that both men were ready, Kyote moved for the still-open door.

"Well, I was thinking we could take him out for drinks and a celebratory meal. I mean we do have reason to throw a small party." Rolde paused for a second to consider something. "I think he's one of the last of the 12th to finally get out of the service."

Kyote nodded solemnly. He knew all too well that if events had played out differently, this would not be true. A lifer like Sergeant Harkwill, had he not died in the assault on Gran'palacio Imperial, would have been still with the VMF. Perhaps he would have received a commendation and subsequent promotion. Same with Corporal Longswit, who was severely injured in the fighting and discharged for medical reasons.

Back down in the lobby, Kyote paused long enough to toss the key onto the front desk before they were on their way. It bounced once, skidded to a halt, and was gathered up by the employee, who only gave the men a cursory glance before he returned to his book.

Once back out on the nearby thoroughfare, they stopped just long enough for Kyote to gain his bearings. As he did, he spotted two men in suits who failed miserably at hiding. While neither looked directly at Kyote, they didn't quite fit in with the crowd of first-shift laborers marching to work and late-night revelers on their way home to sleep off a few too many drinks.

"Where to?" Rolde inquired as he shuffled his feet impatiently.

"South," Kyote noted as he nudged his friend to their right. "We catch the coach station on the other side of the southbound checkpoint and take the first ride to Chancel."

"This late… well, early?" Rolde looked at the sky, where the black-blue of night was beginning to fade. For a moment, he was entranced. Cutting across the sky was the bright tail of a meteorite as it carved a northeastward path across the sky.

"We catch the first one out of town," Kyote noted. "Even if we gotta wait a bit." *I think our friends just want us gone,* he thought to himself. With a glance over his shoulder, he noticed that both were trailing them by almost the length of a full block. *We could lose them if we wanted, but that'll just make things worse. Rile them up enough to have more than just a tail on our ass. I'd rather just two guys be interested in us than half the city's security force.*

"What's up?" Rolde inquired, noticing that Kyote was distracted.

Kyote grunted as he turned his attention forward. "Nothing worth mentioning. Not as long as we get outta town."

Chapter 02

The Sixteenth of Ninimond
Chancel

Paperwork.

It was amazing how much of it the VMF could generate in such a short period of time. Entire acres of forests were razed to satisfy the administration's need for excessive bookkeeping. Fortunately, it would soon cease to be Flynn Earrele's problem. By the time this day was over, he'd be through with this phase of his life. Through the frosted-glass door, marked "The Logistics and Information Office" in gold lettering, was a future devoid of such tedium. Perhaps what waited for him was a different kind of monotony, but it would be one of his choosing.

In truth, Flynn didn't mind poring over documents, but he would prefer more interesting material than the never-ending cavalcade of requisitions and debriefing statements. The level of banality was soul-crushing for any person with aspirations. Some of his cohorts, who were on far-lengthier contracts, sank into the routine. Seeing no better options, they chose a career, and they went through the motions to collect their coin each pay period.

For Flynn, though, there was an end in sight. His time with the VMF was coming to a close, and no amount of persuasion was going to change that. Not even the trio of recruitment officers, who'd regularly stopped by in a vain effort to convince him to re-enlist, could delay his forthcoming liberty.

Freedom was enticing. Unlike some of his fellow soldiers, who'd left the VMF (back when it was still known as the Gendarmery) after their time in Moa'rehnza and partied until they ran out of money, he had more responsible pursuits in mind. At the very least, he wanted to resume the studies he'd earlier abandoned when he reported to Port Hadley in Semmond of the previous year. Once he lost himself in the archives of the Evisran Library at Kit'abana, he might not take a breath of fresh air for days. There were so many subjects he wanted to research that he'd created a mental checklist, one that had grown longer in the months since his transfer to Chancel.

Flynn never had the time to keep up with his personal readings, which made the remainder of his contract feel like a prison sentence. His time with the LIO had him trapped in Chancel without any hope of relocation. Though he had been back in Verenigen for almost a full year, Flynn had not been able to revisit the Library. As a practicing Evisran, it was unheard of for him to miss the semi-annual pilgrimage to the ancient campus.

For a while, he considered studying individuals who were extraordinarily gifted, like himself. It was an interest he'd picked up during his time with the 12th's commanding officer, Marianus O'mas. The lieutenant's focus on the topic, especially during their mission in Moa'rehnza, was something on which he'd often meditated. Ultimately, his interest fell by the wayside; there were more pressing subjects. Flynn's focus would be on learning the ancient Byraelian language and the study of rare imbued ores.

Dressed in the drab olive uniform of his office, Flynn shifted back and forth at his desk. Only a month ago, the laminated hardtop was littered with piles of documentation.

Now, he only had a few sheets splayed out before him, detailing a more personal matter. A single lamp brought sharp contrast to the paragraphs of tedious legalese.

Without a thought, he brushed a few strands of sandy blond hair away from his flat forehead. It was a move he made purely out of habit, to keep his hands busy as his mind focused on more important matters. Cold blue eyes scanned the last few lines of the five-page document before he grabbed a pen and scribbled his signature at the bottom.

Done, he thought to himself. He felt like letting out an out-of-character cheer. Many of his coworkers were slaving away at their workstations, far too engaged in their own tasks to be concerned about his impending release.

Cynically, Flynn wondered if the exit process was such a chore that re-upping became the path of least resistance. Flynn had not realized how much time he would spend affirming his confidentiality agreements on any files rated orange or higher on the LIO's color scale. Fortunately, except for his stint with the 12th, he hadn't been privy to much classified information. Still, his time under Lieutenant O'mas created a daunting pile that he was painfully forced to revisit.

During the entire activity, he kept his mind focused on the future. Once done with his discharge paperwork and an exit interview, he planned to head back to his quarters. With his lease ending in a few days, he'd have no reason to linger. He would put Chancel behind him. Anything of worth to him in the pre-furnished apartment was already packed up in a duffel bag that waited on the domicile's lone cot.

At some point, despite his reluctance, he would eventually go to visit his father. Except for some terse letters, the two hadn't conversed since his assignment to the 12th. He knew of his father's ailing health, and for that reason alone he felt compelled to return to his childhood home. Depending on how the situation played out, he would make plans for an extended visit to the Library at Kit'abana. He wanted to get started as quickly as possible.

Pleased, Flynn stood up and glanced at his desk one last time. Nothing except the standard-issue office supplies remained. He'd removed any personal effects some time ago. It was not as if his supervisors allowed many decorations. Anything more than family pictures or flowers drew the ire of those who demanded uniformity amongst the rank and file.

Before departing for the last time, Flynn made the rounds and said goodbyes to the few coworkers who'd not gone home yet. Two forced hollow promises from him to stay in touch. One, a rather attractive redhead by the name of Nancy Humbold, who had on-again/off-again flirted with him, interrogated Flynn on his plans for the future. Her disappointment was apparent when he made it clear that he was leaving Chancel.

While he regretted never daring to fraternize, he shook her hand and departed on good terms.

Softly, he closed the door behind him as he left the LIO offices.

Less than a year ago, the headquarters of the LIO had been stationed in one of the back corridors of the Government Hall. As a part of postwar arrangements, which included the renaming of the Gendarmery, most of the VMF's personnel were moved to accommodations elsewhere in Gortsa Ward. Anyone not easily duped realized it was merely a public relations move, intended to reassure the populace that there was a division of power and responsibility between the two organizations. Stories of the Moa'rehnzan High Council and the vice grip their military once held on the people made

Verenigen's citizens vocal about the need for transparency in such matters.

Transporting the LIO's catalog three blocks down the street to their current residence had taken months of tedious work. Even then, there were multiple instances where documents were misfiled and had to be uncovered. The only real benefit of the new locale to Flynn was that he didn't have to weave his way through crowds of politicians and lobbyists to leave every day. Also, the trip back to his residence was reduced by fifteen minutes.

Anything to make the drudgery more palatable, he often thought to himself.

As he walked out the side door of the three-story brick building and down the stairs to the adjacent roundabout, he finally felt free. He let out a long-held sigh. He was no longer Warrant Officer Flynn Earrele of the LIO. He could slip away and never see another man in a VMF uniform if he so wanted.

His ecstatic sense of independence swiftly faded.

He'd not even cleared the bottom step when he spotted them. The pair was loitering by a fountain at the center of the nearby junction. Though he'd not seen either since their return to Port Hadley, he recognized them instantly. Rolde had gained weight around the waist that he failed to hide with a thick sweater and oversized coat. Large bright eyes flared wide as he saw Flynn through the thinning crowd. Kyote, on the other hand, looked freshly dragged from the gutter; the sleeves of his jacket were tattered, and Flynn swore there were patches that might be bloodstains.

Once Flynn met Rolde's gaze, he knew he couldn't avoid the reunion.

"Hey, Flynn!" Rolde called out with a wave. Kyote turned to face him with an upwards nod of his head.

"Gentlemen," Flynn replied as he stopped before them. Without a word, he offered his hand purely out of social convention. Though he still felt the kind of comradery that soldiers who'd survived combat together experienced, Flynn wasn't sure he considered them friends. Rolde was genial enough, but it wasn't like they shared any common interests.

While Kyote gave him a few pumps before releasing his grip, Rolde took the opportunity to pull Flynn in close and embrace him.

"We came to take you out to dinner to celebrate your getting out!" Rolde exclaimed as he released Flynn. Kyote merely stood silently behind him. "Or at least drinks. I mean, if you're not hungry. Though, you did just get off of work. You *should* be hungry. I know I would be."

"Really?" Flynn cocked a single brow. "You came all the way out here just for this? I wasn't even aware you were in the area."

When he met Kyote's gaze, he saw something else there. Through the scraggy beard peeked a sly smile.

Flynn was torn. Both men would provide sufficient entertainment, and Flynn certainly didn't dislike their company. On the other hand, he knew there was something else, another matter that would be broached a few drinks into the meal. He almost wanted them to come forth with it right then and there, so it wouldn't hang like an executioner's axe over the proceedings.

Ultimately, he nodded.

"Doesn't sound like the worst way to spend my first night away from the VMF," he noted wryly.

"Good, good," Rolde joyously bellowed as he clapped Flynn on the shoulder. Rolde's effusiveness was contagious.

Flynn let a thin smile show on his face.

"So, you, uh, know any good places to eat nearby?" Rolde asked. "And one that's not too pricey."

At this, Flynn derisively snorted as he rolled his eyes.

Chapter 03

The Sixteenth of Ninimond
Chancel

While Flynn was tempted to lead them straight to the Iron Mug, favored eatery of the VMF stationed in Gortsa Ward, he decided against it. The establishment was conveniently located on the street corner to their west. That the tavern would be full at this time of day wasn't his main objection. He had a fair idea that Kyote and Rolde wanted to discuss something of importance. He'd not seen either man in almost a year, and for them to turn up out of the blue on today of all days was suspicious. They'd want somewhere quiet and away from prying eyes to deliver some sort of pitch.

Though it took the trio a few blocks out of the way, Flynn eventually escorted them to a back-alley joint known locally as Tah'Tharqieneth Saet. Snuggled tightly between two gambling halls, the building itself was unremarkable. A squat, single-story structure featured a flat, blacktopped roof and perpetually-shuttered windows. To his knowledge, the establishment had never displayed any visible signage. Flynn had heard the name bantered about among those in his office who were looking for an exciting evening.

Although there was a streetlamp posted just at the mouth of the stone-laid alley, its bulb had gone dark long ago. The crackle of something damaged inside the casing hinted at the reason. Only with the aura of distant evening light were they able to press on through the winding lane. The pair of inebriates who stumbled from the entrance to one of the nearby betting dens all but confirmed they were in the right area.

Even before they were through the front doors, Flynn guessed what to expect. The locale had a reputation. Poorly-lit, smoke-filled, and propped up by a patronage of local misanthropes, Flynn figured it would be the best place to have a private talk. As long as they kept to themselves, no one would pry. Certainly, no one from the VMF would be there in an official capacity.

Once inside, it was as he anticipated. A garishly-lit bar was bordered by a hodgepodge of tables and booths, none of which appeared to be part of a set. A low murmur amongst those already seated was almost drowned out by the music of a jukebox at the back of the main room. An ensemble of mournful brass played over a casual drumbeat.

Before long, one of the wait staff ushered them to a table. A girl, barely out of school and dressed in a low-cut top, rushed out with a half-hearted smile as she proceeded to take their drink and meal orders. Large eyes, rimmed in long lashes bounced nervously from one patron to the next.

They made idle chatter until the first round of beers was delivered. Flynn sipped at his ale as both Rolde and Kyote took hearty swigs of darker beverages. Their real reason for visiting would ultimately be blurted out. Maybe the evening's meal would delay the inevitable, but the booze would end up getting them to the crux of the situation.

Two-thirds of the way through his first glass, Rolde opened up. His cheeks were already flushed.

"So, Flynn, been anywhere since you got back? You know… uh, worth talking about?"

"I was stationed in Chancel straight after our return to Port Hadley."

"No kidding. Didn't even take a side trip? Kick up your heels and rest after what you went through? I woulda thought *you* of all people would get some form of leave once you got back from Mercarton." While Rolde's inquiry was innocuous enough, this topic seemed to cause Flynn some discomfort. He scowled ever so briefly.

"I wasn't entirely looking forward to making a return home," he eventually admitted. "If that's what you were thinking."

"No victory parade for the favorite son?" Kyote commented dryly as his countenance soured. "Damn shame that so many people on the home front already wanna forget what happened that they blow off those who fought this war." Excluding an argument that ended with a hasty retreat from the hamlet, his own return to Dulton may as well have never happened. Only two people thought twice about his departure, much less his reappearance.

"Eh… Not exactly. In truth, my mother passed away from an illness while we were in Moa'rehnza. I didn't learn of it until after we disembarked in Port Hadley. The Gendarmery wasn't exactly in the business of delivering correspondence to those abroad."

"All the more reason," Rolde interjected. At this, Kyote reached over and nudged him in the arm.

"Look, my written communications with my father on the subject were… *contentious.*"

"What does that even mean?"

Flynn let out a slight snort of dry laughter. He flashed a hand in the air, as if to wave the matter aside. Out of the corner of his eye, Flynn noticed the waitress as she came out with a tray full of food. He felt a moment of relief. He knew Rolde didn't mean to be cruel. Perhaps the meal would distract from the sore subject.

Eventually, he turned to Kyote.

"Whatever happened to your girl?" Flynn inquired. "Didn't you join the Gendarmery to get enough coin to take your female friend away? I'll admit that I'm surprised you're still hanging around Verenigen." From the pained look that crossed Kyote's features, Flynn quickly regretted broaching the topic.

Well, isn't this dinner full of uncomfortable subjects no one exactly wants to talk about.

The conversation came to a halt as their meals were delivered. Another round of drinks was likewise deposited as the trio dug silently into their food.

"Things, well, they didn't quite work out like I expected." Kyote volunteered in between mouthfuls of gravy-coated sausage and potatoes. The awkward silence between the men seemed interminable until he spoke up again. "Seems that I wanted to *go* and she wanted to *stay*."

Despite the desire to extricate himself from the awkward conversation, Flynn asked a follow-up question. "So, was it some other guy, or…"

Kyote laughed dryly. "Nothing so easy. If Celene woulda found someone else to be in her life… that I coulda understood. That woulda made some sense, I guess." Kyote returned his attention to the mug of ale. He didn't put the glass down until the contents were gone. After swiping his hand across his mouth, he motioned to a passing waitress for another round. "Wouldn't a been the first guy to come back to that, I guess."

"Well, I, uh… sorry." It was all Flynn felt he could say.

The trio focused intently on their food and drinks for some time. Once done with his meal, Flynn pushed the dish away and picked up his mug. Unlike Kyote and Rolde, he was still only part of the way through his first beer.

After another modest swig, the alcohol loosened his tongue. Flynn needed to pry some answers from his former squadmates. While it was nice to reconnect, he wanted to get to the true motivations behind their reunion.

"How did you know today was my last day?" Flynn inquired pointedly. "Not like it's a matter of public record. Or that either of you are patient enough for that kind of investigation."

This query caused Rolde to pause. A forkful of beef wavered midair before him.

"True that," Kyote muttered.

"Didn't need to look it up," Rolde noted, washing down a bite with a swallow from his mug. Flynn noticed that, while Rolde had been a relative lightweight during their brief stay at the Royal Hotel de Sēmināre, he now held his own when it came to pounding down brews. "I remember when we talked about you getting out. Back in Gran'rehnza. You were already countin' the days then. It just, well, it just stuck with me, I guess. I mean, I can't remember my folk's wedding anniversary for the life of me, but the Sixteenth of Ninimond got lodged in my head."

Surprised, Flynn leaned back as his brow rose. "And you just happened to be in town, or did you make a special trip?"

"Look," Kyote spoke up. "We get that you're a bit suspicious about this. The boy here—" He motioned to Rolde. "—hasn't shut up for the past two months about making sure we were in town to properly send you off. We passed on a potential job in Eithos Los just to be sure we were here. Left coin on the table, as it were."

"Job?" While trying to prove their innocence, Kyote had tipped his hand.

"Yeah. A job." Kyote slumped back in his seat and crossed

his arms. "Ain't gonna lie, there is another reason we wanted to take you out on the town. Rolde says we Twelves gotta look out for each other, especially those of us… well, you know. Us special ones."

Flynn understood. Early in the mission, he recognized that O'mas had assembled his squad from special members of the Gendarmery and allied militias.

"That said, we wanted to run a *business proposition* by you. That's how they call it, right? The guys in the nice suits who talk about signing contracts and shit? Making agreements on things someone else will be doing the shit work for."

Flynn nodded for a moment. After clearing his throat, he spoke up. "So, what exactly is the work you two are doing? I only ask because this feels like the most awkward recruitment pitch ever."

This elicited embarrassed laughter from Rolde.

"Well, we've been doing a bit of side work as mercs for a few months now. Since, uh…" He glanced at Kyote, who only shrugged his shoulders. "Beginning of the year. Maybe just before. Taking the odd contract. You know, bounty hunting, protection, repo work, and the like."

Flynn snorted as he slumped back into his seat. "I'd heard that there was an upswing in 'for-hire' work. A lot of former militiamen looking to put their skills to use. Become a member of the VMF, local law enforcement, a highwayman, or a merc. So, what exactly are you getting into?"

Kyote leaned in and placed his elbows on the tabletop. "Mostly bounty work. Going after bail jumpers or petty thieves on the lam. Recently had a recovery job where a burglar scarpered off with some jewels. We ended up chasing him into Trone Stenan before we got the goods back. Not without a bit of trouble and a stern 'get out and don't come back' from the local law. If I'm being honest, it probably would've gone without a hitch if we'd planned a bit better."

"And this is where I come in?" Flynn asked as he crossed his arms.

"Of course," Rolde piped up. "We figured with a third head, a lot of this work'd go more smoothly. And, you're the smartest person we know."

"That we'd want to work with," Kyote mumbled.

Rolde shot a glance at Kyote before he returned his attention to Flynn. "Still, with you on board, we figure that we'd avoid any major screw-ups and make a killing."

"In so much as one can make a killing as a for-hire," Kyote once again added under his breath.

"That sounds… well, not exactly enticing, if I'm being frank."

"Ya gotta forgive Rolde," Kyote spoke up as he leaned forward. "Despite his positivity, he's not the best pitchman." He chuckled briefly. "I probably ain't much better."

Sheepishly, Rolde shrugged his shoulders.

"Let me try this another way," Kyote said as he collected his drink and drew it in close. "Do you have any work lined up, now that you're out? Any long-term ventures to make some good coin?"

"Not entirely. My plans, as they existed in the back of my head, were to eventually take me to Kit'abana, back to the Library so I could return to my research. I've been away from my fellow Evisrans for far too long, and I would like to get back to it."

"And to pay for this excursion?"

"I have a sizable chunk of my LIO pay socked away."

"Figures. You was always the practical one. How long that last, you figure? Before you're out of coin and havin' to look for new employment?"

Flynn's eyes rolled upwards as he performed some mental calculations. He flicked a pair of fingers in the air and muttered incoherently for a few seconds. Once he had a number in his head, he nodded. His jaw set as his brow furrowed.

"Not as much as you thought it would be, right?" Kyote asked before Flynn could reply.

"Maybe a year. Year and a half. Two if I'm frugal."

"Gendarmery don't pay nearly so well as we figured when we joined, eh?" Kyote cracked a smile that was mostly a sneer. "Look, we ain't looking to get into this business forever. I don't know about Rolde, but me? I wanted to get in, make as much as possible and get out. So, we take a few *legally-questionable* contracts, a few dangerous jobs and we bring in twice the expected coin. And a year or two down the line, we have enough to invest in something. Like this place." He motioned to the established around them. "Well, maybe better than this place. Somewhere nice that doesn't stink of desperation and fried foods. Flip it for an investment with returns. A little shop or tavern to manage. Or maybe you pay someone else to do it while you go off to do whatever you like. Buy up a farm or ranch and live the rustic life."

"He's right," Rolde agreed. "So, instead of going to Kit'abana right away, where you only get to stay for a few months to a year before you gotta go back out into the workforce, you could make enough to allow you to never have to leave the Library. Ever."

"Well, I don't think *ever* is gonna happen, but we could make enough that you don't have to worry about being a day-laborer. You won't have to be some other man's bitch if you don't want." Kyote paused for a moment. Since Flynn's face gave nothing away, Kyote continued. "Look, we had to pass up more than one job that came with a hefty price. Not enough manpower to pull it off. Which was a shame as the payday was more than you could earn in a year."

"More than a year?" This interested Flynn more than he wanted to let on.

"Yep. For what was probably ten, fifteen days-worth of travel and work. At best. Just not enough bodies and certainly not enough heads to make sure it went off without a hitch." Kyote nodded and then took a long draught from his glass. "There's stupid coin to be earned from private citizens who don't want to involve the VMF in their business. Callin' the Gendarmery something different doesn't exactly fool everyone."

"It's a really great opportunity," Rolde added. "A little hard work for more pay than I would have ever expected. Don't know how my folks could stay on the farm if they knew what they could make—"

Kyote stopped Rolde, raising a hand in the air. From the tense look painted on Flynn's face, it was clear he was conflicted. "Ya know, Rolde, maybe Flynn just ain't looking to get into this line of work. It's just as easy as that."

Before Rolde could protest, Flynn spoke up.

"You don't seem too interested in my participation," he addressed his comment to Kyote.

"Just being the pragmatic one here," Kyote noted as he met Flynn's gaze. "Not everyone can be an optimist like Rolde. Thinking that people are just waiting around to head into trouble for a bit of coin. You just got out and fighting wasn't really your thing, as I recall. When we shot the shit about this kinda thing, I just figured it was the booze and the boredom talkin' for ya."

"To a degree, you would be correct. We were spit-balling ventures to kill the time." Flynn let out a deep sigh. "If I'm being truthful, I am a bit ambivalent about the whole thing.

Just glad to be out from under my contract. There is something enticing about it, but I also badly want to rekindle my relationships with the Library staff."

Both Kyote and Rolde nodded. After a few seconds of silence, Rolde spoke up again. "You didn't really consider what you was gonna do once you got out? Employment-wise, I mean."

"I knew I wasn't interested in re-upping. The VMF, and the LIO in particular, weren't for me. It was a paycheck and nothing more. That I survived… well, you know… At the time, I was certain none of us would come back."

"Gotcha."

Flynn didn't exactly have a set future laid out before him. Something was enticing about their proposal, even if bounty hunting wasn't a career he wanted to pursue for too long.

Still, Flynn held back. His military service wasn't even finished for an entire night. He wanted time to weigh the pros and cons with a clear head.

"Well," Flynn said with a sigh as he pushed away from the table. "I know it's not exactly what you're wanting, but I'll have to consider the offer for a bit before I can give you an answer."

"Understood," Kyote said with a nod. "Would expect you'd want to sleep on it. Check out what other options you have. We'll be in town for a few days. I'm sure we can catch up with you later, if that works for ya."

"Perhaps," Flynn noted as he stood up and began to dig around in his pockets.

Rolde quickly flicked a hand in the air. "No, no, no. We got this. We got the check on this. Our treat."

At this, Flynn's face softened.

"My gratitude, then." He patted the table once with an

open palm, bowed slightly, and stepped away. "I will speak with you two at a later date. Give you my answer as soon as I can."

In his own way, each man wished him well and watched him depart. As Flynn disappeared through the exit, Rolde leaned in.

"He didn't turn us down."

"It ain't a yes."

"It *ain't* a no, as well."

Chapter 04

The Twenty-second of Oadimond, Year 2062 BAE
Eithos Los

Despite some reservations, Flynn eventually decided to join the pair in their venture. Though he was looking forward to his freedom, they had made a good point; he would eventually need to return to the workforce. Even if he lived frugally, his funds were not limitless. Flynn convinced himself that at least a career as a for-hire muscle would allow him to see and experience new locales and people. He wouldn't be lashed to a desk, toiling in a never-ending cycle of drudgery.

Although they came to a verbal agreement, the trio did not leave Chancel together. While Rolde and Kyote departed for Eithos Los to secure future work, Flynn left for a brief stay in Kit'abana. It had been some time since his last visit, and he wanted to rekindle old relationships with both the staff and his abandoned research. After losing himself for a few days inside the Library's dusty halls, Flynn headed on to meet up with his new partners.

A half day's travel north along the coastline, the trip by stagecoach was short. Still, it left Flynn enough time to contemplate. He calculated how much coin he would have to earn to be a free man once again. None of the estimates were favorable. Without an aggressive pace, it would take years, if not a full decade, before he could return to the Library for good.

The largest seaport in all of Verenigen, Eithos Los sat along the northwestern coast. The free-trade township was the home to multiple naval and trade guilds, many of which dealt in commerce with Tir, Moa'rehnza, and the various city-states of Verenigen. It was because of these business concerns that Eithos Los was a prime location to find contracted work. Many entrepreneurs were looking for muscle to complete tasks of varying complexity and somewhat dubious legality. Almost all wanted to avoid involvement with the VMF.

Despite his previous trips to Kit'abana and his time in Moa'rehnza during the war, Flynn had never been to Eithos Los. Though he'd spent almost a year in the densely-populated metropolis of Chancel, he immediately found the port city wholly unique.

Through eavesdropping on a conversation held by two salesmen, Flynn discovered that, from the western harbor, one could take a day's boat ride across the Dwyr Sea to the island nation of Tir. In the future, he might travel to the capital city of Issuhn on Tir, even if only for a short stay to visit the ancient Byraelian site in the south.

As he waltzed through the city streets on his way to meet Kyote and Rolde, Flynn assessed the citizenry. While Chancel had a sizable population of minorities, many of who lived in the southern wards, Eithos Los had a more diverse and integrated populace. Though unfazed by the number of Tireans who called the area home, Flynn was more surprised by the presence of so many Moa'rehnzans. Most were refugees, forced to flee their home country during the war. He assumed that Eithos Los' stance on immigration was far more liberal than other cities in the region.

The longer he spent in the port, the more he understood why so many chose to stay there. The VMF had little to no presence. By and large, it seemed to Flynn that the citizenry was far more interested in their day-to-day lives than the goings-on of the world beyond the city limits.

If he had nowhere particular to go, Eithos Los wasn't the worst place in Verenigen to be.

Three months later, the trio returned to Eithos Los fresh off of a successful protection detail. A trader's caravan, flush with a haul from Bruskmark in the southeast, had requested some extra muscle for the trip back to the seaport. Some of their wares were bound for sale in Tir. There were stories of highwaymen robbing carriages along the trade routes that connected Chancel to Eithos Los. Not one to pass up an opportunity for quick coin, they took the contract. To their good fortune, the only problem they ran into was a crew of rowdy drunks during their overnight stay in Terenton.

Once the job was over, Kyote and Rolde wanted to kick up their heels and rest for the night. Flynn, on the other hand, pushed for them to secure a new contract as soon as possible. This had become the usual refrain: Flynn insisted on keeping them almost perpetually busy. He wanted as little downtime as possible. If their jobs ended abroad, he would network with the locals to see if there was anything available for the mercenaries. On occasion, they were tasked by tavern owners with the collection of unpaid debts or the retrieval of purloined property. Sometimes, they would discover that there were disagreements over what was considered "stolen." Flynn hated being dragged into such petty situations, but as long as it paid coin, he suffered through them.

It was after sunset when they passed through the southwestern checkpoint into town. They moved through the adjacent marketplace, now emptying as the last of the customers trickled homeward. A few stalls not yet picked clean were in the process of closing up for the night.

While they pushed past a crowd of older ladies gossiping in a nearby intersection, Rolde spoke up. Ever since their arrival at the stagecoach station, he'd been chomping at the bit to speak his mind.

"You know, guys, I've been reading—"

Before Rolde could finish the thought, Kyote shot him a look. Rolde stopped mid-sentence and turned to him.

"I read, damn you. Pick up the local papers when I can, 'specially when you're sleeping off a good drunk. Been seeing some write-ups about Eithos Los in particular." He then glanced back at Flynn. "Well, I've been seeing articles about... uh, well they call it an 'upswing' in refugees coming in from Moa'rehnza. Says its people that were displaced by the hostilities, forced out of their homes."

At this, Kyote spoke up. "I guess the Twelfth and the NDP didn't end the war nearly fast enough."

Flynn popped a hand up. "Not entirely. What was accomplished was the shortening of a conflict that could have gone on for years without a real end. Still, between the NDP, the Moa'rehnzan military, and the Gendarmery, there was more than enough fighting to be had. More than enough people forced to flee their homes rather than be caught in the crossfire." A recollection of the refugee camp north of Gran'rehnza briefly flashed into his mind.

"And some of them made their way to Verenigen, 'cause despite all its problems, at least we're *only* killing each other in the streets over drink or petty theft," Kyote added.

Undaunted, Rolde continued. "From what I read, there are a lot of different opinions on the matter. Politicians saying how we have to keep the refugees away from the rest of us. That they're just criminals, the worst of Moa'rehnza's undesirables shuttled off to be someone else's problems. That the good people stayed home to try and rebuild, while the crooks moved on to find new grifts elsewhere. On the other side, I read some opinion pieces going on about Byraelian charity and how Verenigen should open its streets to anyone in need of a home."

"Byraelian charity," Kyote said with a sarcastic grunt.

Though he noticed the comment, Flynn refused to take the intended bait.

"Yeah, that the writings of Copeland and Lekwyth should be applied to our daily lives," Rolde noted. "That this is the greatest opportunity for practicing Byraelians to do the most good."

"One would think," Kyote quickly stated. "If people truly want to get why people would flee their home country, they should spend a month in Gran'rehnza. Right now, even with Ceosan and the High Council removed."

"It's debatable that the situation is better now than it was three years ago," Flynn said under his breath. This seemed to bring the discussion to a close.

The trio continued deeper into the heart of the city. The further west they trekked, the more congested the streets became. Long walkways gave way to crooked lanes that splintered off in multiple directions. The older sections of Eithos Los were a jigsaw puzzle of alleys and intersections.

They took a right at a familiar crossing, where a blue banner hung from a lamppost, and headed north. The gold-stitched fabric, demarked in a mixture of Tirean and Common script, was a sign that they were close to their destination. There was a sudden upswing of foot traffic that only increased as the night grew.

"Hey, you know, I hear Agilis is doing this legit," Rolde noted as he pushed his way through the throng.

Kyote shot him a sideways glance. "Legit?"

At this, Flynn spoke up. "Went through the proper channels. There's a whole series of permits, licenses, and whatnot to allow people, such as Agilis, to be recognized as licensed gun-for-hires in Verenigen. Saves a lot of hassle from the local magistrates as long as, on arrival, she identifies herself to the proper authorities. It means she doesn't have to leg it when things don't go as planned."

It's something we should have done, he thought to himself.

If he was being truthful, Flynn disliked that, because they were technically considered freelance, they took on some of the more unsavory contracts. Their semi-lawless state excluded them from a whole tier of jobs that licensed mercenaries could perform for legitimate employers. This included security details for the Evisran Library and local law enforcement in the smaller hamlets not immediately under the protection of the VMF. Even in Eithos Los, they were excluded from a stratum of work.

At one point in time, he'd broached the subject with Kyote. He quickly discovered that the man steadfastly refused to submit himself to such a process. Flynn wondered if he didn't want to be publicly documented in any manner. If this was the truth, Flynn felt he should remind Kyote that he earned a paycheck from the Gendarmery during the war. They already had his information on file.

"Agilis and I never really saw eye to eye, ya know," Kyote noted, entirely out of the blue.

"I think that was true for a lot of people," Flynn said with a dry chuckle. The Azzotian woman had not been the most genial of team members during their time in Moa'rehnza. She was one of a handful of women in the service and had to fight twice as hard to get an ounce of respect.

"Well, no skin off my nose," Kyote sneered.

Lagging back a few paces, Flynn turned to Rolde. "You in regular contact with Agilis?"

"Hunh? Oh, no… uh, not really," Rolde admitted sheepishly. "It's one of those 'know a guy who knows a guy who did a job with her' kinda thing. We *sorta* run in the same circles, though she's doing it on the up-and-up."

And probably had access to a better tier of work, Flynn thought wryly. He quickly shook his head. It would only sour his mood to consider it for long.

Flynn could tell by the growing aroma of the day's unsold catch that they were getting close. The deeper into the city they traveled, the more convoluted the back alleys grew. Instead of making a direct path to the harbor along the main thoroughfare, they cut northward into the more shadowy wards.

The gambling house was a seedy establishment, one in dire need of a good cleaning. It did not have a formal name; instead, it was referred to by a number. Flynn never quite understood how Kyote had stumbled across Den Six, but now that he knew where to go, it was only a matter of pushing past the regulars who choked the alleyways.

The lighting struggled against a cloud of smoke above the tables. The surfaces looked like they hadn't seen a washrag in years. If it wasn't for the job posting board in the backroom, this was a place that even Kyote might consider avoiding. Hearing the chorus of male and female groans that rang out across the alley, Flynn assumed thriving brothels flanked it.

After forcing their way past the entrance, Flynn snaked a path across the main floor. He headed for a doorway in the northwest corner, behind a row of chest-high slot machines. It took nimble footwork, but Flynn was able to avoid most of the rabble. Some aimlessly wandered with drinks in hand. Others moved from one table to another, as if that would change their luck. As always, they knew the odds favored the house. Few would leave richer than they arrived.

Flynn let out a sigh, as if he'd held his breath since entering the den. He turned right and marched down the wood-paneled hall, past a pair of restrooms, neither of which was barred by a door. A pungent odor of urine caused his nostrils to curl. From behind him, Kyote grumbled.

"Place could use an open window. Or six."

The comment caused Flynn to chuckle.

"Ew," Rolde exclaimed as he trailed behind the pair. "Every time. Every single time." He placed the back of one hand across his nose.

At the other end of the corridor was a storeroom that also acted as an unofficial clearinghouse for bounty work. Amongst the stacks of crates and metal shelves was an oaken display, atop which was mounted a cork posting board. Though it lacked any style, the display served its purpose.

When a haze of various alcohols quickly replaced the bathroom smells, Flynn sighed in relief. He scanned the nearby shelves to find boxes marked with the branding of regional distilleries. Most were familiar to him. One was a rice wine from somewhere in western Tir.

As Flynn stood before the board, he wondered how such work made its way to Eithos Los. He was never sure which of the local guilds was in charge of keeping it maintained. Every time he came here, a man in the backroom kept track of work coming in and out. Today was no different.

On a makeshift seat of wooden crates to the right was their so-called liaison. Balding and dressed in a button-down shirt and vest that both looked past due for a washing, the employee barely gave the trio a second glance before returning to his reading.

At the end of the day, the nameless operative would report to an office on the second floor where his boss Hammerfeuer waited at his desk. From the short time he had spent in the man's company, Flynn suspected it was a nickname. He was Tirean and Flynn had never heard of anyone from Tir with such a surname. Any curiosity he had about Hammerfeuer's real identity quickly died; a few brief conversations with the chain-smoker left him chilled. The first time he sat down in Hammerfeuer's office, the man knew his first name, last name, his unit during the war, and his hometown. Flynn wouldn't be surprised if he knew his shoe size.

Hammerfeuer was in the business of managing "off-the-books" work. Even though he paid well, Flynn was under no illusion about the contracts' legality.

Flynn and Kyote approached the board in radically different ways. Whereas Flynn took the time to read each and every posting line by line, Kyote briskly glanced over the selections, only pausing when something grabbed his attention. Specific words always caught his eye. Despite their differences, both men were often drawn to the same jobs.

Rolde lingered a few paces away. He knew not to ask Flynn's opinion before he had processed it all. Once his limited patience was at its end, he made a beeline for Kyote.

"Anything?" Rolde inquired as he came up beside him. Scowling as his shoulders slumped, Kyote flicked at a few pinned notes.

"Nothing worth the cost of travel." He reached out a tugged at the corner of one page. "This one *here* would put coin in our pockets just to stand around for a few days. It'd put us in Port Hadley, though."

"Which means we'd spend a third of the take on stagecoaches."

"Yup."

Rolde turned to Flynn just as the introspective man placed a hand on his chin. Flynn let out a soft sigh and then met Rolde's gaze.

"May have to keep that one in mind if nothing better turns up," Flynn eventually noted. "Any coin is better than none."

"And if we wait around—"

Flynn interrupted Rolde before he could finish the thought. "Something better could be posted. Yes, yes. The odds are just as great that this is what we have for the meantime."

"You wanna take it?" Kyote proposed.

Flynn ruminated for a few seconds before he shook his head. "Let's find room and board for the night. If nothing more interesting is posted by midday tomorrow, then we'll reconsider it."

Kyote nodded in agreement.

Slowly, the trio turned from the posting board. As they did, Rolde spoke up.

"So, Flynn, you still wanna check out that seafood place in the wharf district?" he queried as he rubbed his stomach.

Before Flynn could even respond, an unexpected voice called out to them. It was coarse with a thick local accent.

"Hey," the usually-silent employee spoke up from his seat. "Hey!"

This caused Flynn to halt mid-stride and look back over his shoulder.

"You Earrele?" the man asked as he nodded to Flynn.

"Pardon?" Flynn was stunned that anyone in the building knew his name. The contracted work was paid in coin, and they had very few interactions with those who managed it.

"Flynn Earrele? You him?"

"Uh, yes… yes, I am."

"Good." The man reached back and dug out an envelope from a nearby stack of paperwork. "Hammerfeuer wants you should have dis. Said it was right up your alley."

Flynn scowled at the offered missive. He was uneasy that Hammerfeuer knew anything about him. He'd only shared passing conversations with the man, when Flynn returned bounties directly to the second-floor office. How might Hammerfeuer have any inkling about Flynn's interests? Maybe the minions staffing the job board were not his only eyes and ears.

"Thanks for keeping us in mind," Rolde said effusively as he stepped in and retrieved the letter. He then turned to Flynn and pressed it into his hands. "If the man upstairs wants us to take this on, that means we must be doing good work. Right?"

Flynn looked over Rolde's shoulder to the employee and spoke up. "This came straight from Hammerfeuer?"

"From his desk, it was handed straight to me. Says to me that it's about collectives or collectors or some such drivel. Nones of my business, really. Says that if I sees you three to make sure it lands in your hands and your hands alone. No one else to gets it. Would'a said something earlier, but I didn't realize it was you until he spokes your name."

"And we appreciate it," Rolde noted with a smile as he pushed Flynn to the open doorway. "Tell Hammerfeuer we're grateful for him keeping us in mind. We'll get to this posthaste."

"But…" Flynn muttered at the unopened envelope. Before he could offer any objections, Rolde and Kyote dragged him from the room.

It wasn't until they were outside, under the moonlight

of a clear night sky, that Flynn opened the letter. He stopped beneath a street lamp, tore the envelope and withdrew the folded sheet. He scanned the contents once, scowled, and reread it.

"Well?" Rolde inquired. His lips pursed tightly, Flynn handed him the sheet.

"Looks like we have us some work," Flynn announced. His flat tone made it clear that he wasn't particularly happy about the opportunity.

"You seem awfully squirrelly about this," Kyote noted, which didn't exactly improve Flynn's mood. "Something—well, besides your usual gripes—seems to have got you in a twist. More than getting work straight from the head honcho, I think." He glanced at Rolde, who'd finished reading the letter before he returned it to Flynn.

"I'm of the opinion that Hammerfeuer didn't hand us this job because of our track record or the types of work we prefer. I *think* he held it back for us because of where it'll send us. And who the requestor is." Flynn offered the sheet to Kyote, who quickly scanned it for the highlights.

"Norte'wald? That's… well shit, that's out there, right? North edge of the Hinterlands, right on the North Sea, right? Gonna be a bit of a haul. Outside of being stranded, I don't see any real issues. Well, *yet*. Maybe give me some of that context you always like to hand out."

"And?" Rolde wondered aloud. Flynn's reluctance was far more enticing than the request, which was a simple invitation for an audience. There were no concrete details revealed in the three-paragraph missive.

"I grew up in Norte'wald."

"And the client?"

"Friend of the family."

"And your father?"

"Still lives there."

Flynn refolded the letter and returned it to the envelope. He crammed the papers into his jacket pocket and began to walk off.

"Well, ain't this gonna be all kinds of awkward," Kyote grunted with a half-smile. "For you, I mean."

Chapter 05

The Twenty-ninth of Oadimond
Norte'wald

The journey from Eithos Los to Norte'wald took a tedious six days by stagecoach, with stops in Scae'hale, Chancel, and Lakewise. While Flynn was happy to occupy himself with his readings, his partners struggled to find entertainment during the lengthy trip. By day two, Kyote began to nap off and on to pass the hours. When not busy with a deck of cards, Rolde merely watched as the world passed them by through the coach's open windows. From time to time, he would offer a simple observation, to which Flynn would nod politely.

On the twenty-eighth, they stopped for the night in Allhbienmark, a small hamlet anchored to the southern edge of the Hinterland Forest. It was a simple town with few distractions, but considering the toll travel was taking on them, the trio was relieved to be free from confinement. Having been there many times before, Flynn arranged their room and board.

In truth, he knew Allhbienmark all too well. The familiar clock tower stood tall above the roofline. Acres of woodlands swallowed up the city's northern borders. To the east, he could spy the Wyreiniol Mountains. Every time he traveled home, he witnessed these landmarks.

As such, he understood what the following day held for them. There was a winding trade route that led northeastward out of town. The road itself was bumpy, and the path was clogged with dense overgrowth. The horse-drawn carriage would trudge slowly through acres of untamed flora for hours until they eventually arrived at Norte'wald. There wouldn't even be a slow approach to the village proper during which he could mentally prepare himself. They would come around a sharp corner in the rise and the city limits would be right there, waiting for them. Swaths of dark-hued, wood-paneled structures would be laid out before them. A stiff, cold breeze from the nearby sea would whistle, sometimes loudly, through the streets. On the far side of town, they could walk up to the cliffs and stare down at the roiling surf as it crashed impotently against Verenigen's northern face.

While Kyote and Rolde were relieved to reach their destination the following day, Flynn remained apprehensive. Despite his fervent desire for emotional self-preservation, he could not avoid meeting with his father. It was something that had to be done, if only for the fact that he might not be back to see the man alive again.

Flynn indulged in uncharitable fantasies, creating scenarios that would delay his return. Perhaps a sudden quake, violent enough to shear a portion of the town's sea cliff border directly into the dark waters of the North Sea, would be enough to end the village. They couldn't meet with their contractor, Hayden Wallowrich, if the way was impassable. If that were to happen, there would be no reason to continue their trip.

Once the fancy passed, Flynn felt guilty about such daydreams. Norte'wald was filled with people who had done him no wrong and to wish disaster on them was beneath him. He would have to endure a short stay with his father and brave the emotional landmines.

The next morning unfolded just as Flynn imagined it would. Childlike, Rolde was excited by the new sights as they rode through acres of forest. By mid-afternoon, the coach arrived at the south side station and they disembarked. There was no one there to greet them. Not even a representative of Wallowrich's waited to escort them to the estate on the other end of town.

For a second, Flynn paused just outside the coach station and looked to the east. There was a steep rise just beyond town that leveled out a few dozen yards above the village's skyline. Though layered in dense vegetation, glimpses of the Wallowrich property peeked out between the patches of leafy canopy. Unless things had changed since his last time in town, there would be a walking path that hugged the sea cliff as it weaved upwards.

After pointing out local landmarks to his allies, Flynn led them into the heart of town. Familiar faces stopped the trio to welcome Flynn home. One was his grade-school teacher, and another worked at the local general store. They were effusive in their greetings. Word of Flynn's arrival quickly spread like wildfire.

As they continued through the village, more and more people approached the group. They flocked in crowds of eight and ten at a time. Women and men alike called out to Flynn by name. Children gathered roadside with their elders to cheer for the former soldier. A few came forward, shook his hand, and offered their gratitude before returning to their daily lives.

At first, Rolde gave the crowd strange glances. When he looked at Kyote and Flynn, neither of whom seemed fazed, he shrugged his shoulders.

"Well, ain't you popular," Kyote noted as the last of the locals dispersed. The joyous celebration lasted just long enough for them to arrive at the town's center. "All but a ticker-tape parade for you."

"Didn't you come home earlier?" Rolde asked. "The locals

act like it's the first time they've seen you since… well, uh, I guess since you left for the service. You'd've thought you rose from the dead the way they were going on."

"Not really," Flynn replied tersely.

"Man, if I had such a warm homecoming waiting for me," Kyote began. "I'd a turned up in Dulton as fast as I could. I didn't get so much as a 'thank you kindly.' In fact…" He fell quiet as his thoughts returned to the contentious exchange he had shared with Celene. Before long, he let out a sigh and shook his head, as if that would purge the painful memory.

Flynn quickly motioned to the inn on the other side of the main square. It was a two-story edifice that swallowed up a good quarter of the plaza's frontage.

"Why don't you two book us a room, get a bite to eat?" Flynn suggested. There was a tension in his voice. "I'll catch up with you in a bit."

"Aren't we going to meet with Wallowrich?" Rolde asked. He glanced back and forth between Kyote and Flynn. Kyote shrugged his shoulders as he shook his head.

"It's too late to properly call on the man," Flynn was quick to explain. "I doubt he'd be seeing guests after sunset. Better to go first thing in the morning. It's in our best interest to get a good night's rest before we show up. I imagine we'll be there for a good part of the day."

"So, no get in and get out, eh?" Kyote asked with a disappointed look on his face. A quick examination of the surrounding blocks did not promise much in the way of entertainment.

"Wallowrich isn't one to be rushed," Flynn replied. "And the next coach out of town won't be for two days, so we might as well make the best of it." He paused as he rubbed his scalp. Blond locks flipped about as he nervously tousled his own hair.

"You should be able to get us rooms without trouble. I've never seen the place full. Norte'wald is not a *destination.* If you have any trouble… drop my name." With a sigh, he dismissively flicked his hand to the building's front porch.

"You're not coming with us?"

"I have personal business that should be tended to sooner rather than later."

Kyote reached out and tugged on Rolde's sleeve. "Let's handle this. Least we could do. We'll meet up with him later."

Without another word, Flynn continued. After watching the man stride off, his shoulders slumped, Rolde turned to Kyote. Before he could ask, Kyote spoke up.

"Best to leave him to meet with his father on his lonesome. They got some kinda unsettled business between the two of them, and it'd be for the best if we kept our noses out of it." He paused for a second before adding, "Plus, I kinda don't wanna be around if it gets awkward. And it's certain to get awkward."

"Okay," Rolde eventually agreed with a disappointed grunt.

Flynn hesitated at the front door of the aging cottage for what felt like an hour. No matter how long he held his breath in anticipation, he refused to move from his spot. He raised a balled fist and let it linger midair. The condition of his family's home did not instill him with confidence. Two door-side planters that once were lush with flowers now only contained dried dirt. Compared to the neighboring homes, the Earrele homestead looked like a dusty, untended relic, a month of bad storms away from being condemned.

"Damn it," Flynn swore under his breath as he eventually rapped at the door frame.

When he heard the muttering of a male voice and the

scraping of furniture on wood flooring from within, he knew he couldn't avoid the reunion any longer.

"Who is it? It's late, and you should know better than to call on a man at this hour!" From within, Stellan Earrele bellowed, though his voice was weaker than Flynn remembered.

"It's your son, Father," Flynn responded dryly. *Open up and you might see this.* He drew in a deep breath and forced his face to contort into a smile.

The door swung wide to reveal a father who was smaller than he recalled. Instead of the towering, broad man with shoulders like iron beams, Flynn saw a hunched-over elder whose limbs shuddered uncontrollably. In one hand was a walking stick that did its best to keep him upright. The black hair that had always been brushed away from his flat brow was now gray and frayed. Sallow skin sagged from his skull, and once-brown eyes looked sickeningly ochre. A thick, unkempt beard rimmed his round jawline.

Flynn's heavy fear of his father scattered to the wind. Now, he only felt a surge of pity at the man's rapid decline. The Stellan of Flynn's childhood could have done pushups all day long. This ragged puppet could barely keep himself upright.

Before age and illness had robbed him of his mobility, Stellan Earrele enforced the law in Norte'wald for decades. Later on, he functioned as sergeant-at-arms for the village's governing council. He was a stable element in the community, an overbearing presence who kept the peace for as long as Flynn could recall. Flynn wondered if this decline was due in part to his mother's passing. Without her constant presence, Stellan seemed to be spiraling down toward his own death.

For a second, the two men stared at each other. Eventually, Stellan wiped his lips with the back of his hand.

"Get in here," Stellan ordered. "Don't act a stranger to your own home." He backed away with a slow, unsteady shuffle. The end of a cane tapped noisily at the tiled floor of his foyer.

Flynn followed his father into the deepest part of the house, past rooms that appeared unchanged since his last visit, years ago. Furnishings and décor were all just as he recalled. A dense layer of dust coated everything.

Stellan came to a stop in the cottage's den, where, placed around a small table, was a quartet of upholstered chairs. Unwashed dishes and a stack of books were piled up on the flat tabletop. A small fire flickered in the nearby fireplace. The room had two windows, both of which were covered by floral-patterned curtains that had yellowed some time ago.

"How are you doing, father?" Flynn eventually asked as he watched Stellan slump into a dusty, overstuffed chair.

"I'll live," Stellan replied as he stared off into the distance. Stellan never met Flynn's eyes, but this was his usual way.

Flynn moved on. Stellan wasn't one to be forthcoming about his health. In his mind, Flynn ran through a short list of safe topics. His father sat sullenly in his chair; his labored breathing was the only sound.

Flynn felt a mixture of sorrow and anger; he accepted that this visit was more for himself than his father. Flynn needed to see the remnants of his family before it was completely gone. As such, he had answers he wanted. If his time with Stellan was limited, then it was best to ask directly for what he wanted.

"Can you tell me about Mother?" Flynn inquired with a wince.

"Cremated. No need to take up space with a gravestone or urn. Cast what was left of her into the North Sea." After a few seconds of tense silence, he added. "If there's anything of hers you can find in the house, take it for yourself. Grab up as much as you like, if only to get some of this clutter out." While the words were sharp, they didn't hurt Flynn nearly as badly as he thought they should.

They sat in silence for a few minutes. When Flynn thought he might raise some other questions, his father spoke up again.

"Surprised you bothered to come out here. Figured you would be ass-deep in your Evisran readings by now." Stellan finally glanced at his son for a second.

Yeah, well, so did I, Flynn thought to himself.

As a devout Byraelian, Stellan had made it clear early on how he felt about Flynn's religious choices. That there was little to separate the two philosophically was irrelevant. In his father's eyes, Flynn was a traitor to the Byraelian Assembly and a heretic who no longer believed in the pantheon of deities. The gods would someday strike him down for his crimes. So indoctrinated by his beliefs, Stellan could only see the differences rather than the similarities.

"Well, duty calls," was how Flynn chose to respond. He offered a thin smile that caused his father's brow to crease. Bringing up his military service would hopefully keep Stellan from ranting as he retread the same old diatribe.

"Gods only know, the only thing you ever did that I was proud of was you joining the Gendarmery, and you even did that as a paper-pusher. But when they sent you to the front, I couldn't a been more proud. Someone thought you was good enough to give you a gun and send you to the front. You were there to fight the good fight, to show those 'rehnzans that they can't start a beef with the big boys." Stellan's face grew flushed.

"That wasn't how it was, Father. Things weren't nearly that simple."

Stellan leveled a finger at Flynn. "Damned if it wasn't. They thought to invade—t-to try and take our land—and we… we went in and bloodied their noses for the trouble. Gave them what for."

"It was nothing like that. We were sent in to effect regime…"

Flynn trailed off. For a moment, he struggled with the urge to tell his father everything, to lay out the gritty details of why they fought in the war. He considered explaining why the 12th VRF trudged their way into the capital city and worked with the NDP to usurp Ceosan and his High Council.

The words caught in his throat. At this point in their lives, would the explanation even have an impact? Whether Stellan was too senile, too infirmed, or just too hateful to change his mind, anything Flynn said would likely get lost inside his head or add fuel to his righteous fire.

"You know what, Father, forget it," Flynn stated as turned away.

"It's what I thought…" Stellan muttered as his gaze fell to the fireplace.

Flynn spent the rest of his time there rummaging through the house. He pocketed a pearl brooch that he remembered Nance Earrele wearing often. From time to time, his father would yell out from the den. Flynn was never sure whether Stellan was barking at him, some imagined visitors, or the world at large.

Rolde and Kyote made an early retreat to their lodgings after a meal and drinks at a nearby diner. The food, a dense platter of slow-cooked beef and potatoes smothered in brown gravy, had sunk like a stone in both of their guts. After the second round of beers—a local stout that was richer than either expected—they paid their bill and departed.

They paused in the courtyard for a moment to watch as the sun finally fell behind the western tree line.

"Didn't expect to be hanging it up before sunset," Rolde noted with a soft chuckle. When he rubbed at his belly, a pained look crossed his face.

"Gotta get up too damn early for tomorrow's meet to tie one on too hard," Kyote noted as he scratched at the brisling hair along his jawline.

Once back in their room, the men passed the time with idle chatter. While Rolde had brought some reading material, it sat untouched on the nearby nightstand.

On the other side of the chamber, Kyote paced back and forth. As he did, Rolde noticed his peculiar stride. There was clear supination in the way his feet rolled from the heel forward. After a few moments spent in observation, Rolde eventually spoke up.

"So, you doing some kind of exercise?"

At the mention of this, Kyote came to a stop. "Ah, oh, no. Nothing like that. Back when we were in Moa'rehnza, I noticed that the Lieutenant had an odd way of walking. He could traipse across just about any surface and make almost no noise at all. Like he was walking on air. In the jungle, it was harder for him to pull off, what with the downed limbs and leaves. Uneven surfaces and all. Things that crunch no matter what you do. So, I ended up hitting him up over it, and he told me it was a skill he'd learned a long time ago."

"Really? I hadn't noticed."

This revelation didn't exactly surprise Kyote. Unless he focused intently on a task, Rolde was prone to distractions.

"Yeah, he said he picked it up from some Evisran he knew in Ierija'roca. Same place he picked up his meditation techniques. Tells me that he learned how to walk without making a whole lot of noise. I figured it was a good enough trick to have, so, what with all the time we had to kill after the mission and before we returned back to Verenigen, I asked him to teach me." He dropped to one knee and began to rub at the muscles along his calf. "First couple times I did it, my legs hurt like no man's business. Like I got into the wrong end of a pipe-beating. Even now, it takes a bit of effort and a whole lot of concentration. I figure, in time, I'll get it right enough that I can do it without thinking too hard about it."

"So, you do it now to…"

"You never know when we need to sneak our way in somewhere." Kyote was struck with a thought. A strange, tangential memory popped into his head. He smirked ever so slightly. "That reminds me of something. You know, the word 'stealth' ain't a verb? Or, you shouldn't use it that way. Like, for a second there I was gonna say 'to stealth our way in' but that isn't right. Stealth is a noun."

Rolde cocked one brow. "Okay…? And what brought this up?"

"Oh, nothing really. I was just reminded of a conversation with O'mas. He corrected me once while he was training me, and I guess it just stuck. Not that it really matters, I guess."

Left unsaid was that neither man was well-educated. Kyote had left Dulton before his compulsory education was complete. Before going off to war, Rolde's courses in Scae'hale schools had been focused on agriculture.

Kyote shrugged his shoulders. "I figure it never hurts to learn something new."

It was late in the evening when Flynn rejoined his compatriots. By the darkness of his expression and the unusually strong aroma of alcohol on his breath, it was clear how his meeting had gone. After sulking silently for some time, he chose to turn in for the night.

In the morning, he would need a stiff cup of coffee to dull the throbbing behind his eyes.

Chapter 06

The Thirtieth of Oadimond
Norte'wald

Almost a half kilometer of winding stone-laid path ran along the forest's northern edge leading up to Wallowrich's estate. From time to time, it weaved to the left and abutted precariously against the earthen shelf which overlooked the North Sea.

Having paid little attention to where he stepped, Rolde stopped short as they approached the cliff to keep from slipping over the crumbling ledge. As his eyes bulged and his heart halted for a second, he could feel the cold, briny breeze buffet his face. Rolde swore that the paver beneath his heel shifted slightly.

"They should consider putting in some railing along here," Rolde mentioned as he leaned out over the edge of the cliff face. His eyes narrowed as he watched the dark waters smash violently against the rocks below. He wondered if anyone had ever survived the fall. "T'aint what I consider safe."

"I'll be sure to mention it," Flynn noted dryly.

As his partners pushed on, Kyote paused briefly and looked out at the horizon. Anchored some hundreds of meters in the distance were boats of varying sizes and makes. Their presence immediately struck him as curious. Despite its proximity to the sea, Norte'wald had neither a harbor nor any semblance of a fishing industry. As such, the ships had to hail from other ports. That they lingered off the coast struck him as odd.

He hurried to catch up with Rolde and Flynn, who were already a few dozen meters away.

Within fifteen minutes, they arrived at the mansion's front gates. A wrought iron fence that was strangled by untended topiaries encircled a three-story manor which was likewise dwarfed by the surrounding forest. Even without the creeping vines that wrapped around the first floor's exterior, the aging edifice would have looked a half-century old. The front yard was overgrown, and many of the windows were darkened. A lit door-side lantern was the only sign that the place hadn't been abandoned.

As they climbed the steps to the front porch, the main entrance opened. Backlit by amber lamps was a manservant whose lanky frame towered over all three. A gangly man with ashen-colored skin was dressed in a well-tailored black three-piece suit. Thinning hair was slicked back away from his stern features. His slow, deliberate movement hinted at an economy of effort. Cold, blue eyes jumped from one man to the next, sizing up the new arrivals.

"I… I think we were expected," Rolde commented, as he shrank away from the man's gaze.

"Ain't that a bit creepy," Kyote muttered.

"It's just as likely notification of our arrival reached Wallowrich," Flynn suggested to Kyote. "Norte'wald is a small town, and as you saw yesterday, word travels quickly."

Before any of them could announce the reason for their arrival, the servant spoke up.

"You are here for an appointment with Mr. Wallowrich, are you not?" Though his voice was raspy, his tone was flat and without inflection. Long, talon-like fingers flicked in the air as he motioned with a wave.

Though hesitant, they marched into the foyer. Once inside, the servant closed the doors with a dull thud that resonated around the empty room.

The interior of the home was decorated in dark blues and greens, with accents of bronze and ivory. A series of marble columns lined the main hall that led to a wide set of stairs. Wavering slightly from its mount in the vaulted ceiling, a crystal chandelier radiated cold yellow light.

As they crossed the room, an older gentleman dressed in a blue velvet suit jacket, matching slacks, and a white button-down shirt, began his descent from the second floor. He was a stout man with thick features and a ring of silver hair at the top of his head. Beady blue eyes peered down on his guests from behind oval-shaped specs wedged into the tight space between brow and cheeks.

"Well, if it isn't the youngest Earrele," he boomed across the hall. Flynn immediately recognized his jolly voice. Except for the additional weight on his frame, the man was just as Flynn recalled.

"Mr. Wallowrich," Flynn hailed as he moved to meet him at the foot of the steps.

Kyote held back for a moment. He reached over and tapped Rolde, who was still entranced by the interior's opulence, on the shoulder.

"Hunh?" he muttered.

In reply, Kyote motioned to the head of the house. "Wallowrich."

After a handshake and a brief hug, Flynn and Wallowrich separated.

"So, good to see you well." Wallowrich's face lit up. "It's been some time since you went off to war. I was elated to hear of your arrival."

"But not surprised," Flynn replied with a soft chuckle. "Since you arranged for this to occur."

"Oh, pish posh." Wallowrich flipped a hand in the air. He coyly winked before he turned away for a second. "Just the indulgence of an old man who wanted to mix business with pleasure. And, as you well know, my brand of pleasure is to fill the estate with baubles older than myself. With my wife gone and my daughters married off and living abroad, I don't have much else to pass the time."

Flynn let out a laugh.

From behind him, Kyote watched as the pair talked. Kyote could tell that Flynn was working Wallowrich. Wallowrich likely even knew this and played along. Kyote hated this part of the job; this form of jockeying was posturing for talkers. He merely wanted to be told what to do so they could be on their way.

In truth, this was precisely why adding Flynn to their venture had been vital. Flynn understood all the moves for dancing in business relationships.

"It saddened me to learn of your father's condition," Wallowrich eventually noted as he placed a hand on Flynn's arm. His cheeks sagged in an exaggerated mask of sorrow. "Far too late, I understand, for the doctors to do their best. I thought to provide assistance in paying for his medical treatments, but—"

"Father's far too proud for that," Flynn stated with a dour laugh. Wallowrich nodded knowingly. Stellan Earrele was not one for handouts, especially from those who might be deemed friends. "Borrowing from comrades turns them from friends to creditors," he had once announced.

Wallowrich joined him in sardonic laughter. "There's a

surplus of truth in that. Never have I met a man so proud and hardworking. To a fault, I think."

After a short, uncomfortable pause, Flynn waved his allies over and made polite introductions. Both Kyote and Rolde accepted handshakes. Wallowrich's beefy paws swallowed up their hands, one at a time, crushing their fingers with his grip. *Extra pressure really is unneeded. The man holds the purse strings on whatever venture he has planned. No need to make himself bigger than he already is,* Kyote thought.

"Now that formalities and reunions are out of the way, let me guide you upstairs to my collection. As Flynn can surely attest, it's grown some in the past few years. Without much else to occupy my time, I continue to collect trinkets and artifacts, as if they were side dishes at the grandest of meals. Still, there are only so many opportunities to add to the collection, and one must take them as they come."

Flynn's eyes narrowed at the last statement.

Without waiting for a response, he led the trio upstairs. Though he waddled back and forth, he took the steps spryly. Once on the second-story landing, Wallowrich marched directly for a pair of ivory-hued doors, one of which he brushed aside with his forearm.

Beyond was another sizeable room, this one filled exclusively with display cases and exhibits. Brass plaques were mounted beside wood-and-glass cabinets. A series of oil paintings, both portraits and landscapes, were hung on the damask-patterned wallpaper. The north wall was composed entirely of floor-to-ceiling windows, presenting an impressive view of the North Sea. Blue velvet curtains were pulled aside, allowing the midmorning sun to cast long shadows across the parquet flooring.

"Man, I ain't seen museums that looked half this nice," Rolde blurted out as he entered. This comment caused

Wallowrich to beam with pride.

"Very few, barring the Library and the Byraelian Assembly in Gold Flats, could compare," he stated as he placed a hand on his chest. "In earlier years, I had many a guest come just to gawk. Nowadays, not so many." He paused for a second.

"More than once did I catch this one—" He motioned to Flynn. "—perusing my collection with such curiosity. He would randomly turn up on any given day and stare longingly at the aged curios for uncountable hours. When I learned of his more… *intellectual* pursuits with the Library at Kit'abana, I found myself wholly unsurprised."

Despite himself, Flynn blushed for a second.

"Please, feel free to look around," Wallowrich suggested. "Bit of a self-guided tour. And since the Evisrans haven't seen fit to catalog my collection in some time, it's not often I have guests. One might think *location* is my issue." Wallowrich chortled, a hand on his belly.

At this, Kyote and Rolde began to move through the room, stopping only to examine one exhibit or another. There were several aged documents under glass, including a few maps that showed a centuries-old version of Verenigen. One case exclusively displayed ancient mariner's tools. As they explored, Flynn moved in close to Wallowrich and spoke up.

"If you don't mind me asking, whatever happened to Cuddy?" Flynn inquired. He knew the question was personal, but this was the opportunity to inquire.

In response, Wallowrich's brow rose. "Oh, good old Cuddy. Never could ask for a better, more dedicated manservant. He retired a few months back. The years finally caught up with him and the physical toll of his duties proved too much, I fear. Resigned from his position and went to live with his children in Gold Flats. I think the drier, warmer air will be better for him in the long run. As much as I love Norte'wald, its late season weather is particularly unkind. Hard on the joints for us old people." He tapped at one of his elbows.

Flynn nodded quietly. He couldn't recall a time when Cuddy wasn't gray-haired and wrinkled. It made sense that he would leave the service to tend to his own health. After a few seconds, another query came to mind.

"And his replacement? We met him on the way in."

"Mr. Artis Gohn? Yes, yes, came with many written references. Highly recommended by many people who I'm told are well-to-do. Time spent in Tir, Moa'rehnza, and even Ierija'roca, as I understand it. Plus, if I'm being particularly honest on the matter, he came bearing presents. I won't lie that a little 'greasing of the wheel' made an impression." Wallowrich chuckled. "An old man, such as myself, is not immune to a little tribute."

"Oh? You don't say."

Wallowrich motioned to the display cabinet on the far side of the room. Within was an ancient mask of blue stone, carved into the image of a man's face.

"The Cerulean Visage, or in the original Byraelian, the *Masq oph'Aserhe*. Said to be a ceremonial artifact for those who wanted to commune with the gods. Was said to be Moa'rehnzan in origin—pre-BAE—but the lack of distinct markings, the lack of tooling in general, doesn't quite match that. At some point, I might have one of your fellows at the Library give it a proper examination, to determine its era and place of creation properly."

So many questions presented themselves. How did simple manservant like Gohn come by the object in the first place? Why did he feel the need to offer it up to Wallowrich? *Let's not kid ourselves here. I think that one's pretty obvious,* Flynn thought as he admonished himself. *Gohn wanted to ingratiate himself with Wallowrich and what better way than to offer the man a new item for his collection.*

Flynn let the subject drop; they were also there seeking employment. Plus, speculation about other people's ulterior motives never ended well.

As his gaze lingered on the mask, Flynn found himself curiously drawn to the display. A magnetic pull threatened to drag him forward. The object was speaking to him, whispering in the back of his head. The voice—if it was even that—uttered nothing but faint noise which breathed something to him, like the promises of future glory. He could feel his heart rate accelerating at the incomprehensible murmuring.

"Would you like to take a closer look?" Wallowrich offered as noticed Flynn's interest. This broke the hold the mask had on Flynn. The chatter quickly faded away, and he was left with a pang of inexplicable disappointment.

Flynn turned to Wallowrich and nodded sheepishly.

While Kyote and Rolde aimlessly rambled on the other side of the chamber, the pair moved in beside the glass-encased display. Wallowrich remained quiet as Flynn leaned in and examined the carven visage.

"I've never heard of this object before," Flynn commented. "I mean, mind you, I've not pored over everything in the Library's collection, so there's likely a fair bit I don't know, yet, but even this strikes me as particularly obscure. One would think that the… Masq oph'Aserhe, was it? One would think that this would have garnered a mention or two in other ancient writings."

"I know! That's what makes it all the more alluring," Wallowrich noted as his face lit up. He tented his fingers beneath his chin. "As I understand it, there are a few references to be uncovered in some of the older tomes on the second and third floor, but the more detailed entries, of course, reside within the private collection. I guess it shouldn't come as a surprise that Ra'khavale wishes to keep some of the more enticing elements hidden from the public."

Flynn knew the name. Agava Ra'khavale was the Library's Chief Custodian. Though Flynn had met him a few years back, he had not met with the man since. Most of his interactions with the staff included the lower-ranking librarians and researchers. At best, he could consider that he was cultivating relationships that would pay off in years to come.

Flynn reached out with one hand and let it hover just centimeters from the display's glass front. From where his fingers bobbed innocently, he could feel something radiate from the blue relic. There was an aura that pulsed with life. It exuded a sensation of undulation, like waves lapping at the coastline.

It's actually an imbued ore, Flynn reflected as he nodded softly. *The original stone must have been huge, for the artisans to carve this from it. Doubt Wallowrich is fully aware of this. Only those who are gifted could even feel this… force. It's not so strong that Kyote or Rolde noticed it, yet, but it's there. I'd be curious to corner Wallowrich's man and find out where he came across it.*

Before he became lost in his musings, Flynn felt a tug at his sleeve. He turned to face his host, who was smiling smugly.

"I would love for you to spend all the time in the world giving the collection your attention, but we have business to hash out. Shall we adjourn to discuss the matter of your employment in my office?" Wallowrich suggested. "Your allies appear to be entertained."

Flynn glanced to where Kyote and Rolde peered into a display of what looked like gemstones. Kyote reached out, as if warming his hands at a fire.

"Kyote, Rolde," he called out. He beckoned for them to join as he headed for the doorway at the back of the chamber. "It's time to go over the details of the job."

Both men hustled after Flynn as Wallowrich led them into his study. The space was part office, part personal library, with rows of bookcases tightly crammed into the crowded area. Perhaps, at one time, there was more room to move about, but Wallowrich's interests had taken a turn towards the obsessive. Dusty tomes were arranged in precarious stacks that swallowed up all but the northeast corner.

As he settled into the high-backed chair behind his desk, Wallowrich let out a relieved groan. He wiggled a bit and took a glance through the single window at the back of the room. Vivid sunlight and blue skies caused him to smile warmly.

Once settled in, he returned his attention to the trio on the opposite side of the heavily-littered tabletop and cleared his throat.

"I will go ahead and lay out what you already know. It is true that I arranged for you, Flynn, to be offered this contract. To have what they call the 'right of first refusal.' To have a crack at it before it's offered to the public, in so much as such mercenary business is publicized. Be it a personal familiarity, a family favor to reward long-time relationships, or merely a shared interest between the two of us, I could not resist indulging my old man's whims. I get so few opportunities. I mean, you've met Mr. Gohn only recently. I doubt you'd be surprised to know that he's the most humorless of fellows. But, I digress…." He rubbed a pair of fingers across his lips. For a moment, he considered a nearby mug full of a cold brown liquid.

"What I want… *would like* for you to procure is a rare imbued own known as the World's Eye," Wallowrich started, nudging a small stack of books across the cluttered surface to Flynn. Flynn reached out and took the topmost one. Along the spine was imprinted *Years Spent Abroad: The Northern Wastes.*

Wallowrich continued. "The item of interest has recently

turned up in the hands of a private collector in Port Nym by the name of Jon Arques Pourrie. I personally have never met the man, but he's known in certain circles. Not so much for the means by which he procures his curios, but because of how stingy he is in response to requests for viewings, be they private or public."

This caused the trio to give Wallowrich strange glances.

"I, uh…" Rolde sputtered as he timidly raised a hand.

Wallowrich began his explanation. "There are certain unspoken arrangements held amongst the more prominent antiquarians of Verenigen that their collections are made available, on request, to those from the Evisran Library or the Byraelian Assembly. It's a polite courtesy that allows for a certain degree of shared knowledge while permitting people such as myself to continue to foster our own interests. I can't imagine either organization wishes to get into a protracted legal battle over the ownership of curios and historical baubles. If certain legal decisions arose which were unfavorable, the whole proverbial house of cards might fall apart."

"And Mr. Pourrie isn't exactly playing nice?" Kyote hoping to keep Wallowrich on topic. The man seemed primed to follow a tangent that would take them further away from the conversation's end. He'd witnessed similar tendencies in Flynn, which led him to wonder if the more educated a person grew, the more prone to digressions and over-explanation they became.

"To put it in the layman's terms: yes."

"And you want to make it *more available*?" Kyote added. "If we're to get to the heart of the matter, you want to hire us to—"

"Any means possible," Wallowrich said grave tones as his countenance suddenly darkened. Gone was the jolly elder, replaced by a grim man fueled by the strength of his desire. The façade of playful host fell away, if only for a second. He then punctuated the comment with a sharp grin that caused his cheeks to bulge.

Kyote opened his mouth for a second before he bit his tongue. No matter how Wallowrich wanted to spin this, they were moving the object from one private collection to another. Even if Wallowrich was more willing to allow others to view the stone, it was still theft, plain and simple.

Kyote turned to Flynn, who appeared unaffected. He fully expected Flynn to voice some objection. Of the three of them, he was most likely to oppose the contracts that put them on the wrong side of the law.

"If there is any issue about the nature of this arrangement," Wallowrich began after a moment of uncomfortable silence. "Then please let me know now. I would have this matter handled sooner rather than later. Since I hear there's not much else there, I do not expect Mr. Pourrie will keep the Eye at his Port Nym estate forever."

Kyote quickly glanced at Flynn, who seemed introspective.

"None at all," Kyote eventually announced as he met Wallowrich's gaze. When Wallowrich's eyes moved down the line, he received polite headshakes from Flynn and Rolde. The older man nodded slowly for a second. He reached into a desk drawer for a series of documents that were bound by a staple.

"As you will see by the terms of the contract." Wallowrich pushed the stack of sheets across. Flynn gave the first page a quick reading. "The payout upon success is a fairly lucrative. I pay well for good work. Doubly so for discretion and timeliness."

Kyote leaned over and looked for a total. Flynn pointed to a line near the bottom of the fourth page, at which he hummed aloud with a half-smile.

"You're none too stingy with those zeros," he noted.

"I *really* wish to add the Eye to my collection."

A copper-coated pen was produced and Kyote hastily signed the bottom of the last sheet. Rolde followed suit. Once done with their part, the two slipped away to admire the view through the office's window.

As they did, Flynn gave the agreement one last quick read. He found nothing objectionable about the arrangement. In fact, the payment schedule was surprisingly favorable for them. Flynn wondered how much trouble Pourrie would prove to be. The excessive payout suggested that there would be unexpected challenges in completing the work. Until they were in Port Nym and had time to survey their target and his property, Flynn wouldn't know for sure.

He scrawled his signature beside his allies' names and returned both the pen and contract to Wallowrich. The older man gathered them up and stuffed everything back into his desk. Just as he was about to say something directly to Flynn, he was interrupted.

"So, uh, what's up with all the boats?" Kyote inquired as he turned away from the window. "Got yourself a regular old fleet parked out there. Considering what went down south of the Vale a few years ago, one might be a bit antsy with the sight."

"Hmm?" Wallowrich's brows rose curiously. He started to join Kyote and Rolde when it occurred to him Kyote's meaning. "Oh, the… uh, *scavengers*, for lack of a better term. Or salvagers, as I hear they wish to be called, though there's no wrecked ship out there."

Flynn glanced back and forth between Wallowrich and his friends for a moment. "Pardon?"

"My apologies. I forget you might not be up on the latest in town gossip. Word of a meteorite landing has made the rounds. Or *splash down*, rather, since it struck water instead of land. From what I'm told, it came out of the sky, slammed into the

North Sea, no more than a couple hundred meters from shore. Made a mess of the shoreline afterward. Fortunately, most of Norte'wald was founded up along the cliffs. No damaged beachside docks to fret over." Slowly, Wallowrich made his way to Kyote.

As he did, the older gentleman continued his explanation. "Word got around to some of the more *zealous* religious types that the meteor was 'brighter than any seen before,' which immediately put the word 'Byrael' on people's lips. That another Byrael had come to Tah'afajien."

"Really?" Rolde asked, craning his neck upwards. His back straightened as he peered intently at the distant grouping of boats.

"Hardly," Wallowrich dismissively flicked the air. "If it was, I'm certain there would have been a chorus of horns blaring across the sky to announce the advent of a sixth Byrael. Those fools are merely scouring the ocean with the hopes of digging up a fresh new chunk of imbued ore. I gather that anything of decent size will probably go for a fair bit of coin on the open market. You're more likely to see a hefty chunk of rock sold in Eithos Los than you are to see another Byrael added to the Assembly's literature."

At this, Rolde sighed dejectedly.

"Now that the business has been settled, let us finish our tour of my collection before I see you on your way," Wallowrich suggested as he motioned to the exit. "Can't be wasting too much time in town. There are travel arrangements to be made, things to be collected. Contracts to be fulfilled."

Chapter 07

The Thirty-first of Oadimond
Norte'wald

By mid-morning the following day, the trio boarded the outbound transport. There was no fanfare at their departure. It appeared that Flynn's return to Norte'wald was already forgotten. Considering that both Rolde and Kyote had indulged in a few too many drinks the night before, this came as a welcome turn. Neither man was up for the cheers of locals who might wish to see Flynn off. Even the rustling of the trees as a gust blew out of the north seemed like an excruciating symphony to them.

For Flynn, there was only a sullen sorrow. The visit with his father had not brought him any resolution. If anything, it only confirmed that he was right to stay away. The pearl brooch tucked into his rucksack would serve as the lone pleasant reminder from his homecoming.

By the time the carriage was a hundred meters into the Hinterlands, both of his partners had begun to sleep off the remainder of their hangovers. Flynn empathized with the desire to pass the time in rest. They had a daunting trip ahead of them. As far as he knew, few cross-continent routes were longer. Barring complications in their connections, their transit to Port Nym in the southwest would take seven days.

As his allies proceeded to snore in a polyrhythmic tempo,

Flynn dug into his pack and produced a bundle of hardbacks that were tied together with twine. The aroma of Wallowrich's office, one of coffee and musty paper, wafted from the package. Flynn knew his time would be best spent diving into the old reference material. He was glad to be left undisturbed to do the research that he greatly enjoyed. Kyote and Rolde could sleep for as long as they wanted if it meant he had the opportunity to read uninterrupted.

Hours passed by as he flipped through the first book. When he paused to let his eyes rest, he gazed out of the window on his right. The only thing visible was a seemingly-endless backdrop of verdure. There were no landmarks to pick out, no way to tell how much distance they'd covered. By the color and intensity of the light, Flynn guessed it was nearing noon.

Another four or five hours—depending on how well the driver knows this route—before we reach Allhbienmark, Flynn thought to himself before he returned to his work.

Lost in his reading, Flynn didn't notice that Kyote had woken until the man spoke up.

"So, I've got a question for you," Kyote said as he cleared his throat and shifted in his seat. He stretched to work some of the kinks from his neck and shoulders. With the back of his hand, he brushed a few stray locks from his face.

At first, Flynn didn't even look up. A few seconds later, he shook his head and sat upright.

"Pardon? Was a bit into *this*." He tapped a finger at the open spread. "What were you saying?"

"Just wanted to have you spell something out for me. Still a little fuzzy on how no one balked on this. Hit me with the reason why you didn't tell Wallowrich that we weren't right for this caper." Kyote tilted forward and peered closely into Flynn's face. While still a bit flushed, there was enough life in his deep brown eyes to show that he was sober.

Flynn scowled.

"I figured if anyone was gonna have issues with the deal, it'd be you." Kyote leveled a finger at Flynn. "Dress it up like some kind of noble cause all he wanted, but Wallowrich wants us to rob a man. At best. Depending on the kinda security he employs, we may have to get a little bloody. Maybe your morality's loosened up a bit because you know the man…"

This accusation caused Flynn to set down his reading as his brow creased. Whether Kyote meant it as an insult or not, Flynn was irritated. "Or maybe, just maybe, I saw the eventual payout and thought it was too good to pass up. Wasn't getting paid part of the reason we're doing this venture? Eventually, I would like to not have to do *this*." He motioned to the carriage around them. "I'm not in this line of business for the long haul. One day, I plan on taking my share and going my way. If signing up for contracts like this one moves that end date up a little, then so be it."

Before Kyote could say anything else, Flynn leaned in.

"I won't lie that a prior relationship with Wallowrich did make me more inclined to take it. I do know him personally. I knew his wife and his daughters. They had a relationship with my parents. We are what one might call *intertwined*. The family money comes from a lucrative, regional freight business and he's seen fit to reinvest some of his wealth into Norte'wald. I know his reputation as a collector and if he's asked us to liberate an item from someone for the so-called greater good of the community, then I'll keep my reservations to myself."

"And if we're being told false? And Pourrie's being set up? 'cause Wallowrich was flashing an awful lot of coin for what's being proposed as a simple breaking-and-entering theft. This strikes me as something run-of-the-mill street thugs could've been paid to do."

"I'm not inflexible. If the time comes and the situation is

not as originally communicated, then… then, I'll be sad to lose out on this very lucrative deal." Flynn glanced over to where Rolde was still soundly asleep. He snorted as a half-smile split his lips. "If we have to walk away, we walk away." There was a hint of regret in his words.

Flynn knew that, on some level, his personal interests were as much to blame for his willingness to take this job as anything. This rare ore was the kind of artifact that was underrepresented in the Library's catalog. At first glance, even Wallowrich's own research seemed inadequate. If Flynn's studying the Eye could benefit him, it was an opportunity on which he seemingly couldn't pass.

In the end, Flynn was thinking of his future plans. Certain situations could lead him to potential opportunities. If he wanted to join the Evisran Library as a part of the staff, he had to bring something of value to the table. Tenured members were experts in one field or another, be it Tirean Archaeology or the study of Naturalism in Vale Grans'tsarren. If he could produce a comprehensive assessment of the World's Eye, it might aid in his future employment.

Eventually, he turned back to Kyote and raised a point that just came to mind.

"And, I'm not entirely certain why *you*, of all people, have suddenly become worried about the work being on the up-and-up. In light of the fact that we've never gone through the proper channels, maybe we *have* to sign on for *these* types of contracts. Before long, we were certain to run out of legit work."

"Yeah, you keep harping on that," Kyote noted with an accusatory bob of his finger. "Too much time as an LIO got you thinking being all up on our paperwork is a good thing. The rest of the world don't need a permission slip to take a piss."

"You know what 'being all up on our paperwork' is good for? It puts us in line for real work, not these side jobs that skip past legal, waving as they go. And then we wouldn't be having this exchange about whether or not Wallowrich is being honest with us."

"Yeah, but these *fringe jobs* pay better."

"Well, when you factor in hush money, yes, they do." Flynn rolled his eyes as he turned away.

The Thirty-second of Oadimond
Lakewise

Any heated emotions from the conversation had cooled by the time their coach arrived at Allhbienmark. Both men knew there was nothing to be done until they had more information. The argument was tabled for the time being and they carried on. Rolde had slept through the exchange, so he noticed nothing different.

After a single night's stay in the quaint village, they rode westward for the next stop on the trek. The township of Lakewise was a few hours east of Chancel. Unlike the smaller hamlets, the more industrialized community showed the kind of modernization usually featured in Verenigen's larger metropolises. With the presence of Bellwise's Auto Shop and a few manufacturing plants on the outskirts of town, there were enough contemporary elements to make the trio feel they were finally out of the boonies.

The presence of a half-dozen motorcrafts parked streetside in the downtown area indicated the affluence of the populace. Even now, as the post-war economy picked up, the vehicles were considered a luxury. More than a few locals were getting along well here.

After eating a meal and downing a single drink, Flynn

excused himself and retreated to their room in the nearby inn. Though the accommodations in the single-story establishment weren't exactly luxurious, the lodgings were well within their budget. As he walked back from the restaurant, Flynn fretted over the cost of transit, room, and board that was eating into his nest egg. If they decided that Wallowrich wasn't entirely on the level with them and balked on this contract, he'd be out a fair bit of coin.

Now despondent, Flynn chose to throw himself into Wallowrich's literature. By now, he'd flipped through the three books; currently, he was rereading for the sake of cross-referencing the data. Since two of the tomes had only passing mentions of the Eye, he left makeshift bookmarks formed from torn pieces of paper in place.

Far sooner than he expected, Rolde and Kyote returned to the room with a raucous clatter. Both men barged through the door and slumped down on their respective cots. Their giddy laughter slowly petered off. Somehow, Kyote had brought a half-empty mug of ale with him from the tavern.

"Apparently, Lakewise is NOT a party town," Rolde noted with a belch. He then waved the fumes away from his nose. Though there was a ruddiness in his cheeks, he seemed just sober enough to carry on a conversation.

"Wear out your welcome?" Flynn inquired as he looked up from the open book in his lap. A lack of bloodied knuckles or facial bruises suggested that they'd at least avoided getting into a fight.

"It seems that I was *rude* to someone," Kyote announced with a sly grin. "And the staff was having none of that. Cut us off and sent us on our way. Shouldn't've had to pay if they were going to kick us out, I say."

"And you kept a memento, I see."

"I wasn't done with it." He downed the last of the drink.

He wiped at his lips as he set the mug on the nearby bedside table. After a relieved sigh, he slumped into the mattress and turned back to Flynn, who had already returned to his studies. "So, I see Wallowrich gave you some homework," Kyote noted with a nod to the two books in Flynn's lap.

At this, Flynn offered a wry smile.

"Some supporting documentation about the Eye," he announced as he lifted one of the tomes into the air. "One appears to be a collection of excerpts from the journals of Edward Wake. Part of a series, reprinted in the '40s, that chronicled his travels across the known world."

"Edward Wake?" Rolde piped up. Having already flopped onto his bed, he turned on his side to face Flynn.

"Was one of Mastrius' aides."

This caused Kyote to nod. From his limited schooling, he remembered Mastrius' name. Starting circa 1035, a trio of explorers, Hadley, Mastrius, and Nymoroff, traveled the known world to map as much of it as possible. The three men were credited with charting the main continents of Tir, Verenigen, Moa'rehnza, and most of the surrounding islands. After they went their separate ways, their paths took distinctly different turns. It was reported that Nymoroff eventually perished during an attempt to chart the Great Sea. Mastrius continued his own work by leading an expedition to the Northern Wastes, a largely uninhabitable arctic wilderness to the north of Verenigen. Unlike his compatriots, Hadley retired to a quiet life where he died surrounded by his family.

"This one in particular—" Flynn continued. "—appears to detail their attempts to chart the Northern Wastes. Wake mentions that he was injured early on, so he was forced to remain behind at their base camp. As such, he had an excess of time to write, so he tended to converse *at length* with anyone who arrived with supplies and wares sent back by the main party. A fair amount of what he authored was second- or third-hand accounts framed as interviews. Doesn't explain what ultimately happened to Mastrius, but he does go into great detail over the artifacts that others in the expedition recovered."

"And the Eye? Did he talk… uh, write much about it?" Kyote inquired.

"There's a small passage, near the back, on it." He quickly flipped to the first page of the entry. "Apparently, it was brought back to the base camp with some procured cargo. Wake writes that the exploration team came across a village a few dozen kilometers to the north. They proceeded to trade with the locals, and through some serious negotiation, they were able to get the Eye. He's of two minds on the matter as to why the locals gave up such a seemingly-valuable ore. One was that they didn't understand its inherent value, that to them it was merely a pretty bauble, something to collect dust, and that what Mastrius' team had to offer struck them as more precious."

"And the other theory?" Rolde, who sat up on the edge of his cot, inquired.

"That it was stolen." Flynn let out a dry, uncomfortable laugh.

This caused Rolde's eyes to widen.

Kyote, on the other hand, muttered, "Starting to sound like a familiar theme."

Flynn ignored him and continued.

"That the story about bartering for it was a lie. It was tucked away in a crate filled with blankets, as if hidden from view. Though he made some inquiries about its acquisition, he didn't want to press the matter too much. That he wrote down such damning speculation was probably enough. Perhaps he never considered that his journals would be reprinted. Wake spent a few passages telling about his investigation among those who came back with the cargo. None claimed to have seen the ore before their return. One, a man by the name of Rafferts, avowed he was with Mastrius during most of the negotiations and never once heard anything about the object. As far as he was concerned, the stone just turned up in their crates, like some kind of free prize."

Kyote scowled. "Uh, that's nice and all, but I was more thinking about what the thing looks like. So we could identify it when we come across it. I wanna know that we can spot it when we see it. Did Wake describe it?"

"Oh. Oh, let me…" He trailed off and he began to flip through the pages. Eventually, he stopped at a segment that was accented with some of Wallowrich's own handwritten notes and began to read aloud. "Says here '…*a block of polished imbued ore roughly 28 centimeters in length and half as much in diameter along its widest point. Oblong in shape and displaying various pink and orange hues that seem fluid in the light of day. There is a distinct warmth to the stone, as if rich with energies. Along the central axis of the exterior are a series of indentations, as if smaller ores could be inset into the larger piece…*' There are some more detailed passages later on—"

"I think I got it just fine," Kyote said as he waved off the suggestion. "All I care to know is can we just pocket the damn thing and walk out?"

"Did he say why it was called the World's Eye?" Rolde inquired. "I mean, I ain't no expert on this stuff, but most ores don't have such normal, *catchy* names, ya know. They're usually stuff like *aeustes* or *iolide*."

"True. Usually, the more rare ores are named after some old Byraelian term that pertains to their properties. The name 'World's Eye' apparently is an amateur translation of something the natives mentioned about it. Something along the lines of 'Ocellar oph Tah'afajien,' though there's no clear indication where the reference exactly came from. Like the stone itself, it merely showed up."

"Ugh," Kyote groaned. "This is starting to give me a headache. Does everything like this got to be so complicated? Why don't we just go back to protection details?" He rubbed at his forehead as he flopped back onto his cot.

This caused Rolde to bray loudly. As Flynn closed his reading materials with a snap, he offered a thin smile.

With the subject dropped, Rolde wanted Flynn's input.

"Oh, hey, we was talking earlier, right after you left, about—"

"About Wallowrich's butler," Kyote interrupted as he stared at the ceiling.

"What about him?"

"Well, isn't he—"

"Gotta say, I don't care for the man," Kyote again cut off Rolde. "I mean, first and foremost is how he's up his own ass, looking at us like we're beneath him. Just 'cause he's got a nice suit doesn't make him better than us."

"Yeah, he does come across as kinda snooty," Rolde added.

"And what kinda butler wears that kinda suit and carries around a priceless artifact like that? Why not sell it on the black market and take his pasty ass to a beach for the rest of his life?" Kyote queried.

Flynn held his tongue. He didn't know Gohn; to make a snap judgment seemed unfair. Still, with his cold, aloof nature and the way he seemed to curl his nose at the trio, he did not exactly endear himself. *Reality is that we'll likely never see him again after we're done with this. He can be whatever he wants once this job is done.*

Ultimately, he attempted to end the discussion by stating,

"He came across as largely harmless."

"Still, not the kinda person you wanna have drinks with," Kyote muttered as he turned over and closed his eyes.

94

Chapter 08

The Thirty-second of Oadimond
Dulton

Exhausted and with her hands full, Celene Kaize shouldered her way through the entrance into her single-room apartment. A cold night wind tried to chase after her. With a kick of her heel, she nudged the door shut and looked at the kitchenette on the other side. Above the sink, a lone bulb cast a sallow glow across the countertop. Though she knew the layout of the main room, she paused to let her green eyes adjust to the poor light.

While she owned very little, her apartment always seemed so cramped. The upholstered chair on her left was flanked by a side table, lamp, and a stack of newspapers. To the right waited her bed and a dresser that had seen better days. There were few decorative touches; most of her wages went toward paying the bills or putting food on the table.

Celene dropped both grocery-filled bags and paused long enough to shake the soreness from her hands. It wasn't so much the weight that wore on her during the long walk from the marketplace. It was that she only had time to shop right after her evening shift let off. Her fingers weren't the only thing that ached; everything from head to toe throbbed with pervasive fatigue.

As she moved the provisions into the cabinets, she removed

the ribbon that bound her long hair. Straight and black as coal, her locks tended to get in the way if not gathered up properly. As a swath fell and swept past her tan cheeks, she smelled the odor of fried foods trapped in her mane. This stench caused her nose to wrinkle in distaste as the pangs of hunger briefly subsided.

Once done with the restocking of her limited stores, she sighed as she propped herself up with both hands. The linoleum countertop felt cold against her palms. Though exhausted, she knew she had to eat and wash up before she even considered crashing for the night. Only by sticking to her routine could she keep up with the day-to-day life she had chosen.

Quitting her compulsory education two years early had left her few options, especially in the dusty mining village of Dulton. When she wasn't working at the orphanage, she picked up shifts at Olhweddy's Wine & Dine, a local diner that, curiously, did not sell wine. While it provided a decent wage, the waitressing was a temporary gig. Because there was a slight ochre tint to her skin, due to what she believed was a mixed Tirean heritage, she found it harder to earn the same tips as the other girls. Once she came of age, she'd likely be forced to work in the local ore mines like nearly everyone else in town did. It was the only way she could afford to continue living there.

As it was, she always came home tired, and with the feeling that no bath would make her clean. Between the grime and the haze of oil that hung inside the diner, she was surprised that her skin hadn't permanently changed hue.

For Celene, being weary was better than the alternative. Once done with her nightly regimen, she often crashed onto the tiny cot and slept until the morning alarm went off. Beneath her hand-me-down covers, she didn't have to mull over choices not made. Or worse, decisions that she regretted.

On bad nights, her subconscious would deliver reminders,

wrapped in the shape of memories that had been warped by her current feelings. Everything came down to that moment when Kyote had arrived home. He had walked into the orphanage and told her that they could leave together. It had been a lifelong dream of hers to head for Tir and find her family. What little knowledge she had of them was second-hand; Miss Halliweil had told her that she was left in the Home's care by a Tirean mother who promised tearfully to one day return for her child. Ultimately scared to leave the only home she knew, she had told him that that his efforts were in vain. Even if he wanted to go, she was staying in Dulton.

At the time, it made sense to refuse Kyote. She at least had a job of sorts. Miss Halliweil had provided an opportunity for a young woman whose only other prospects involved working in the mines or worse. Miss Halliweil had made such a convincing case that only now, months later, did Celene begin to question her decision.

When she and Kyote had talked about leaving for Tir to find her family, that was the kind of youthful dreaming you could do when you did not have adult responsibilities. If she had known then that her so-called future would be such a grind, she might have fled with Kyote.

In truth, when Kyote showed up, ready to take her away, a primal fear sunk in. The Dulton Home for Wayward Children was safe and familiar. The nearby village was small, and she knew every meter of its sooty lanes. It was a hard choice to make. They'd been so incredibly close as children. He was the only person she truly loved. He was more like family to her than anyone ever would be. Still, she'd refused him and the pain of that regret lingered.

Kyote stormed out after their exchange and never came back, and that was something she hadn't expected. A part of her thought he would linger in town, maybe settle into a day job as well.

Seeing him again after so long had been a surprise. He'd gone off to fight in the war. After not receiving a single letter from him, she'd had to assume he was not coming back.

Celene took a few deep breaths and compelled herself to move. She had to stay on schedule if she was to make it through the following day. Eight hours of working at the orphanage, followed by four at the diner, was going to take everything she had.

Celene stripped out of her work clothes, balled them up, and pitched them into the hamper. She ignored the wooden bin, which briefly wobbled as she walked past it and into the bathroom. The overhead lights hummed to life as she drew a bath. Even though she wasn't a tall girl, standing only 160 cm barefoot, the porcelain tub was barely big enough for her. She allowed herself a few seconds for the hard lukewarm water to soak her skin before giving herself a vigorous scrub.

After drying off, she picked at a quick meal while she read a newspaper by lamplight. The bowl and fork were washed, and the paper was added to the towering pile of others.

She paused for a moment to gaze out her lone window at the adjacent street corner. For a second, she wished to see a familiar face, under the halo of the nearby streetlight. When no one looked back at her, she sighed and closed the blinds.

Eventually, she crawled under the woolen cover and closed her eyes tightly. She struggled against the tears that welled beneath her eyelids.

Tomorrow the cycle would repeat. Celene wondered how many days in a row she could endure before the grind would be too much.

Chapter 09

The Second of Shumond
Port Nym

Even though none of the trio had visited Port Nym previously, they had a fair idea of what to expect. All of them had been to Eithos Los and Port Hadley enough times to be familiar with the bustle of a seaport.

The city of Port Nym was founded where the Marecale Valley descended into the southwestern delta. Initially settled as a trading post for merchandise and produce imported and exported from Moa'rehnzan markets, the township expanded quickly over the span of a few decades. Much like Port Hadley on the eastern coast, the city showed all the influences—both architecturally and culturally—of its lengthy history. Older residential wards featured rows of cottages and townhomes, all topped with steeply-pitched roofs, and fashioned from wood and brick plastered in tinted stucco. In the poorer districts, multi-story shacks were lined up in tightly-bundled blocks.

Despite the entrenched VMF presence at Fort Marligate to the west, Port Nym maintained a degree of independence. While it didn't flirt with the semi-lawlessness of Eithos Los, the local administration maintained some distance between Verenigen's law enforcement branch and those whose businesses flourished within the city limits. A lack of strong governmental oversight kept the coin from other regions flowing into the metropolis.

It wasn't until their coach arrived at the northernmost station that the three men discovered an unexpected complication. Upon spying the banners of green, purple, and gold fabrics and painted with seasonal iconography hanging from the nearby lampposts, Flynn swore to himself about the timing of their visit. It merely hadn't occurred to him to check the calendar before their arrival.

For the first ten days of Shumond, Port Nym celebrated Tah'Rhicah Aarhbiest, an annual festival which hailed back to the city's founding days. Back then, it was a time for offering up a portion of the year's crop and livestock to the Byrael in thanks for their continued blessings. Now, it served as an extended binge, with tenuous ties to Port Nym's history and culture. Daily parades and musical performances on almost every street corner caused the downtown streets to be impassible to all but pedestrians. On top of that, the ornate and lewd costumes worn by many of the attendees often caused bottlenecks as gawkers took in the display. Visitors from throughout the world came to join in one of the more indulgent celebrations in all of Verenigen.

"Our timing could not be worse," Flynn said to the others as he collected his bag and slung it over one shoulder.

"Eh," Kyote replied with a shrug. "We might be able to use the crowds to our favor. Or, at least, the chaos that this kinda party causes will make for a nice distraction."

Though he was loath to admit it, Flynn knew Kyote was right. This type of gathering was a treasure trove for those who made a less-than-honest living. Pickpockets could earn enough to last them for months, if not the entire year. Anyone who wanted to flee could disappear at will. Their mission might benefit from the same madness. At the very least, it could help disguise their surveillance of Pourrie's property.

Because of the revelry that was in full swing despite the

early hour, they were forced to seek lodgings to the north, a dozen blocks from the town center. As they collected their room keys, they ran across a party of academy-aged boys who stumbled their way through the lobby as they lurched towards their quarters. The shouts that rang out from all corners meant a poor night's rest was in store.

Once thoroughly checked into their accommodations, they went into town to canvas the locals for information. As they pushed their way through the surging crowd while it gawked at a procession of dancers and musicians, Flynn slipped off into a small dive bar. A handwritten sign on the door stated "OPEN - DON'T EXPECT QUICK SERVICE." Though lit by neon lamps, the interior was surprisingly devoid of life. A lone employee attempted to entice Flynn with a rundown of the day's menu. While the smell of fried seafood in the air was initially tempting, Flynn made it clear he was only there for some direction. After the drop of a handful of coins, the bartender became more loquacious and directed them blocks to the south.

After some time, they met up with Port Nym natives who, after a liberal application of financial tribute, directed them to Pourrie's estate. Well known to some of the locals, including a streetside performer who talked after a bribe fell into his tip cup, Pourrie lived in the East Grove. A good fifteen blocks outside of the downtown and garden districts, this ward was where the richest of Port Nym's citizens resided. These estates were arranged on large plots thick with well-manicured copses of local flora. While they shared design elements with the city's more demure domiciles, these mansions were taller and far more ornate, with multiple attached balconies that rested on rows of square columns.

Unwilling to make their presence known, the trio lingered a block down the street as they examined the property. Though he only used it briefly, Flynn produced a spyglass from his pack and trained it on the estate. In the distance, the clatter of a trolley drew his attention for a moment.

As expected, the sizeable mansion was bordered by a brick wall that was covered by a creeping vine. Blooming flowers, many with pink and white petals, softened the appearance of the unwelcoming abode. Above the barrier, Flynn spied the second and third floors with ornately-fashioned metal bars mounted to the windows. A single sentry made the rounds along the south-facing terrace.

For some time, they watched the flow of traffic in and around the neighborhood. Except for pedestrians, most of whom were heading downtown to the celebration, there was no one of note. A lone motorcraft swerved as it rumbled past the trio.

"So, what exactly is the plan here?" Rolde eventually asked as he propped himself against a wrought iron fence. With a finger, he played with one of the floral embellishments.

"Place looks to be locked down pretty tight," Kyote noted. He motioned to some of the surrounding structures. "None of his neighbors got even so much as a lock on their front grates, and Pourrie's hired himself some armed muscle. He really don't want people getting inside. Whether they want to look at his shit or not. Bet he doesn't even invite family over for dinner."

"Realistically, we need to get a sense of his security detail," Flynn commented as he slipped the monocular into a pocket. "Two at the door and one making the rounds on the third floor only hints at what he may be employing. We can't exactly tell how much muscle he has on the payroll from our view streetside."

He turned to Kyote, whose focus was on a neighboring house, it's windows dark. Kyote spoke up as he motioned to the structure.

"Why don't you two see if you can get to a vantage point,

check out the compound from above?" He pointed to a circular stairwell on the side of the home. Attached with a series of wall-mounted bolts, the curling set of rusted steps only led to a small flat spot on the house's western-facing roof.

"And you?" Flynn knew he didn't have to ask. Kyote was about to create an opportunity.

"I'mma stir things up for a second. See how quickly they respond to trouble. See if they really want to keep getting paid." Kyote brushed his hands on his pants and marched directly for the front gate.

As he did, Flynn and Rolde scurried across the open yard to their right and quickly climbed to their position. Though he didn't see anyone through the darkened windows, Flynn was hopeful that the owners would not come home any time soon. Constables investigating a trespassing call would make Pourrie's men a less immediate concern.

Once at the top, both men crouched down and watched as Kyote walked up and pounded on the gate. Flynn held his breath as he waited.

Kyote offered a cockeyed smile to a pair of guards as the gate opened. Both were dressed in button-down shirts and ties and had hands on their hip holsters. Neither looked like they were in the mood for casual conversation. One had a deep scar along his right cheek.

"What—" The other began only to be interrupted by Kyote, who attempted to barge inside.

"Thanks, man, I thought I was gonna be late for the party," Kyote blurted loudly as he pushed between them. Even from where they waited, Flynn and Rolde could hear him. "I got the invite way too late and hauled ass to get here—"

The taller of the two, a balding man with a ratty mustache, reached out and grabbed him by the arm. Rather than resist,

Kyote paused as he turned and met the gaze of the man's beady eyes.

"Hey! What are you doing here?" he barked as his grip tightened.

"I dunno, what are *you* doing here?" Kyote wiggled his arm, as if to shrug off the hold. It did nothing more than heighten the man's anger.

"What, me? The fuck, man, I'm on guard duty. You're the one who shouldn't be here." Though his free hand went back to his pistol, the guard did not pull it.

"Well, I was gonna make it to the shindig on time, but that don't look like it's gonna happen, now. I mean if you're gonna make some trouble over this, I'mma have to tell my friends not to hire you no more. You keeping guests from the bash like some kinda party cock-blocker." Kyote's head bobbed back and forth as he quickly scanned the property. He could already see another grouping of guards moving in to support their teammates. Each looked like a carbon copy of the pair that manned the front gate. "Look, man, if this is gonna be a problem, just let me pop in and let Terry know I showed up. Dude would get bent out of shape if he thought I didn't show. Give me five minutes, and I'll be out of your hair." He shot a glance at the man's thinning pate.

Flynn and Rolde watched as the guard struck Kyote across the head. Flynn produced the brass eyeglass from his back pocket and trained it on the fracas just as the second sentry came around and threw a few shots into Kyote's ribs. After delivering a series of blows, the men dragged him out and pitched him onto the street. After a stern warning, both returned inside and closed the gate.

After the show was over, Flynn and Rolde rejoined Kyote as he walked away from the property. There was a hitch in his step that improved as he rubbed at his lower torso. As he wiped the blood from his lips, Kyote let out a dry laugh.

"Well, it's better than the security details in Gran'rehnza, at least. They didn't shoot first and then ask questions never."

For Flynn, this comment brought back memories of their time in the Moa'rehnzan capital during the war. Well-armed, private security details staffed many of the estates that flanked Gran'palacio Imperial. At the time, moving through the city's more affluent wards was an exercise in conflict avoidance. After Ceosan's very theatrical demise, many were just trying to protect what was theirs.

Rolde moved in to check on his friend. "You gonna be okay?"

"They roughed me up a little, but I figured that would happen. Guys paid to keep folks out don't take kindly to people trying to get in. Just kinda how it works." Kyote rubbed at a tender spot along his jaw. "Definitely not hired to take names. No effort made to check to see if I was a guest, so I doubt Pourrie's looking to entertain. I saw five; two at the gate and three who were patrolling the yard. They came to gawk when I started making a mess of it, so they're easily distracted."

"There was a sixth on the third floor," Flynn revealed. "Likewise entertained by your distraction. Beyond that, I didn't notice any more. No one came out of the mansion, especially when you barged in."

"Couple possibilities," Kyote noted as he started counting off with the digits of one hand. "Firstly, it could mean that all the muscle is outside. That the master of the house doesn't want the hired help anywhere near him. Outta sight, outta mind. Two, it could mean that the men are told not to leave their posts unless necessary, especially the guys on the inside."

"Not until they hear gunshots," Rolde added.

"Or something like that. People always have stuff planned

out just the way they want it until shit goes sideways." Kyote tapped at his ring finger. "Thirdly… well, I don't exactly have a third scenario. They either have additional muscle inside or not. Best to plan for more than less."

After a second spent thinking, Flynn posed another question. "So, what're we looking at, weapon-wise? You had a good look at what they're carrying, right?"

"Riot sticks and small-caliber firearms," Kyote noted. "Mostly semi-automatic pistols from what I could tell. And the guy on the third floor?"

"Assault rifle with a scope and shoulder stock. He brought it out for a moment until he saw that you were detained. Probably would have popped you a few times if you made a break for it."

"Then it's best I just let them beat on me." Kyote briefly touched at a bruise on his cheek that was beginning to swell. "Anything else you notice?"

"There's a delivery entrance at the back," Flynn noted with a nod. "One of the guys who came up to see you *escorted out* was posted there. Would make sense that it's locked most—if not all—of the time."

"Odds that we could waltz in pretending to be delivery boys?"

"Slim. I doubt they let anyone on the property. I haven't seen anything delivered as of yet, but it wouldn't surprise me if it's left just inside the fence, and someone from the house staff brings it in. Still, it's *currently* our best option to get inside without having to fight *all* of the exterior security."

"House staff," Kyote said with a sour grunt. "Another wrinkle to deal with. Getting to be a lot of eyes to sneak past."

Flynn nodded. "Realistically, we'll need to arrange some form of surveillance. See if we can catch them mid-shift or when they handle deliveries. There has to be a hole in the security that we can exploit."

"And if there ain't?"

"Then I fear we'll need to get out of Port Nym in a bit of a rush."

Flynn knew that, while the job promised to be profitable, they certainly had several roadblocks ahead of them. If they stumbled over any of them, they could end up being wanted by the local law. The best-case scenario, it things went wrong, they'd be on the road before someone knew to look for them. The idea that Port Nym might potentially become off-limits to them was only now sinking in. The longer he thought on it, the more Flynn wondered if Pourrie would consider reporting the theft to the VMF. If the Eye was valuable enough to him, Pourrie could turn to an organization with a much broader reach. No matter how well the heist went, they might have to keep a low profile for some time. Wallowrich's payment might have to cover for lost time while they stayed out of the VMF's gaze.

After a lull in the conversation, Kyote spoke up again. "So, like you said, we're gonna need someone to watch the place. See who's coming and going. Just to get an idea of what the schedule is around here. So, who's going to take the first shift?"

"I nominate Rolde," Flynn hastily suggested.

"Seconded," Kyote was quick to add. Rolde's mouth dropped open as he failed to protest fast enough.

"Motion is carried. We'll be back sometime in the morning," Flynn said as he placed the eyeglass into Rolde's hands and began to back away.

"Thanks, you assholes," Rolde grunted as he watched his partners depart.

As they left the yard, both men could hear Rolde bark

something about bringing him a bite to eat when they returned. They swung left and continued down the sidewalk.

"How you feel about this?" Flynn inquired after they were a few dozen meters away from the mansion.

Kyote was quiet for a second as he considered his response. "I feel that we ain't thieves and that stealing this Eye ain't gonna be a tale for the ages. Unless someone wants to write about one of the worst robberies of all time."

Flynn snorted as his lips pursed tightly. Kyote's blunt assessment wasn't exactly unwarranted.

"It'll probably go down like 'Three dudes busted into some guy's house, beat up his men, stole some crap and then ran out of town as fast as they could.' As long as we don't add anything about us getting shot and killed, we'll be okay, I guess."

Flynn was up early and on his way by the time the sun broke over the Horans to the east. Even after a long night of rowdy partying, people still filled the streets. Flynn could tell some were looking to soothe hangovers with the local cuisines. Others appeared to be still drunk; it was possible they hadn't gone to bed yet.

He popped into a local diner that specialized in fried pastries and coffee and picked up an order for two. With this in hand, he headed for the Pourrie estate.

From on the sidewalk, Flynn saw that Rolde no longer hid on the neighboring rooftop. A cobalt blue motorcraft was now parked in the driveway. He stood and watched as multiple people inside moved past the open windows.

Well, shit. Where did Rolde…

Before long, he heard a call from the other side of the stone-laid lane. It was there, between two overgrown bushes, that he uncovered Rolde, who looked in dire need of rest. His eyes were red and his face was paler than usual.

Flynn crossed to him and quickly offered the breakfast. Though it was now lukewarm, Rolde consumed the food and drink greedily. His mouth and chin quickly became dusted with powdered sugar.

"How did it go?" Flynn asked, sipping at his beverage. There was a smoky flavor of chicory in the milky drink.

As he polished off his own serving, Rolde motioned for Flynn to follow him. After the pair hastily slipped behind a row of hedges, Flynn continued. "Anything of interest happen? I noticed that you moved. Looks like the neighbors came home. Did any of them spot you?"

"Yeah, just a little," Rolde replied as he scowled. "Place wasn't nearly so abandoned as we'd hoped. I guess nothing stays empty for long out in the East Grove. They came home and saw me sitting out up there. Was none too happy about it. And pretty vocal about me getting lost. Pretty uppity over the whole thing, like I crapped on their doorstop or something."

"Oh."

"Yeah… 'oh.' I handled it just fine, though." He rolled his eyes. "Pretended I was drunk and crashed out up there to get some peace and quiet. They still wasn't too happy about it, but they just ran me off instead of calling for the constables. Though, I have to think that Port Nym's patrolmen are a bit tied up, what with all the partying going on downtown."

"That's some quick thinking on your part. What gave you the idea?"

"Since we showed up in town, I've seen all sorts of drunks just passed out wherever they fell. And no one gives them a second glance, like it's just how people are supposed to act during the fest. Ya drink and drink and party until ya can't stand anymore and then you wake up the next day and do it all over again. I ain't never seen this kind of… well…"

"Rampant debauchery?"

"I guess, if that's what it's called." He stopped and let out a long, tired sigh.

"So, since you no longer have that vantage point…"

"Oh, down the street. Corner of the intersection at the end of the block." Rolde pointed to a home with a row of recently-planted shrubs struggling in vain to cover the north face. From where they stood, Flynn noticed a stack of raw lumber and a tarp tacked to the back end of the home. "From the pile of mail left by the front door, I'd say the owners haven't been around for a bit. Looks like they hired some guys to add on a room to the back of the third floor. Also, some renovations to the first and second. There's a big ole opening where there should be a door. I just walked right in, all how you please."

"And the carpenters?"

"Haven't seen a sign of them yet. Figure they're enjoying the festival, ya know. Can't imagine too much work actually gets done in town until it's all said and done."

Flynn nodded silently. He'd come to the same conclusion.

"From the third floor, you can look into Pourrie's property. Don't see everything—there are some blind spots—but it works well enough to keep them from noticing that I'm watching them. Plus, I got to raid the kitchen when I was hungry. Nothing fresh, but a few crackers was enough to tide me over." After a few seconds to rub at his weary eyes, he continued. "Truth is, my having to move was all the excitement I had. Didn't see much happening around the compound. A shift change of the guard at sunup was the highlight. Outside of that, no one in or out. Pourrie isn't exactly what I'd call a social person."

"So, have you spotted the master of the house?"

"I haven't even seen anything like an open window. For all we know, he ain't even in there."

Flynn patted him on the shoulder. "Not to worry, he is. Last night, I made some inquiries, and it seems that Pourrie has a bit of a reputation with the locals. What little I've been able to gather, Pourrie is somewhat of a hermit. A very rich one, which means he gets to be called eccentric rather than antisocial. Some of the delivery boys from the nearby market say he rarely makes public appearances and almost never leaves town. They were a bit spiteful as the man's a poor tipper. There's supposedly a regular schedule of shipments of local fruits and vegetables that's brought to the back entrance."

"Well, I guess that's promising…" Rolde trailed off as his gaze turned back to the street. Though the caffeine had brightened his eyes, Rolde still appeared weary.

"Is everything alright?" Rolde's distraction could be just a side-effect of his exhaustion.

"Just, uh… just recalled something I thought was odd at the time. Could'a swore I saw some other guys hanging around on the other end of the block. At first, I thought they were just more security, but they hung out for a while like they was casing the place themselves. I lost sight of them during the shift change and they were gone. Didn't go in. Didn't meet up with anyone on the inside. Just… gone."

"Okay, I'll keep that in mind. What did they look like?"

"Like Pourrie's dudes. Big, burly, and dressed nice. I seriously thought they were replacements until the actual day shift came a knocking at the back door. By then, they was gone. It was dark when I noticed them, and they were a good bit away, so I didn't get a great look at them, ya know. I don't know if they were up to something, but keep an eye out all the same."

"You think they might be watching Pourrie's compound as well?"

"I don't even know, man. Could just be they were out late and carrying on a conversation before going home, ya know. Not even sure why I brought it up."

"That's fine." Flynn gave him an assuring. "I'll be on the watch. Head on back to the room and sleep this off. Get yourself a nice shower and a meal while you're at it."

"Don't have to tell me twice." Rolde downed the last of his drink and strode off.

Kyote was surprised at how easy it was to track down a single man. Even in a city this large, and so engorged by visitors for the festival, it only took him a short while to uncover his first lead. In a few hours, after some pointed inquiries, he was able to narrow down his potential search area. Fortunately for him, his target was not trying to hide.

The Green Lily District was a lower-income neighborhood just outside the local VMF base, Fort Marligate, which rested within the lowlands on the western edge of town. After canvassing the nearby greengrocers, he was directed to a cul-de-sac shadowed by a dense thicket of nearby willows and oak trees.

Kyote was pleasantly surprised that no one responded to his queries with suspicion. Many were happy to help him to his final destination. The closer he got, the more willing people became. They spoke glowingly of the man he sought; he was someone whose sacrifice was for the people of Verenigen. To send a visitor his way seemed like the least they could do.

By mid-afternoon, Kyote stopped outside the small single-story abode at 1123 Wencess Lane. Peeling pale green paint and a waist-high wooden fence of rotted boards made the house look like it might collapse under the abuse of a bad storm. Kyote thought it odd that a man so esteemed among the locals was relegated to an aging shack in what appeared to be one of the poorer wards.

Kyote shook his head and pushed the gate aside. Rusty hinges squealed as he walked past. A few strides along the stone path took him to the front door. He paused for a moment to consider whether he should even bother to continue. It had been some time since he'd last seen him, and it wasn't like the two were the best of friends.

Still, he'd gone through this much effort. Even if he only stopped long enough to say hello before he was on his way, Kyote wanted to see this to its end.

Raps on the wood thudded sharply as the door rattled in its frame.

"…a moment…" A muffled voice blurted.

Kyote let out a long sigh. He felt a twinge of nervousness.

Before he could act, the door swung inwards. Standing on the other side of the doorway was Pahl Longswit, former corporal and member of the 12th VRF. It took Kyote a second to recognize his former squadmate.

Even beyond the apparent injuries, Longswit looked like a man defeated by life. His eyes were dull and tired, and his dark skin had an ashy sheen to it. With the help of a walking stick, Longswit unsteadily stood in place.

"Can I…" Longswit began before narrowing his eyes. "Kurttsen? Kyote, is that you?"

"Who else?" Kyote replied with a half-smile. "Look at this mug. Ain't no one else gonna want to look like this." At this, Longswit's face brightened as he reached out with his free hand. Kyote took it and gave him a few shakes before releasing it.

"Well, at least you finally grew into your beard. Doesn't

look nearly so scraggly any more. Someone might mistake you for an adult now." He motioned to the untended whiskers that hung from Kyote's jawline. "So, uh, what brings you out this way? Oh, wait, you have a moment to talk, right?" Longswit asked as he motioned for Kyote to come inside.

"Yeah, just in Port Nym for work and had a break in my schedule," Kyote replied as he stepped inside. A mixture of floral scents and cooking smells still failed to mask the underlying aroma of mustiness in the air.

As his eyes adjusted to the interior's darkness, he was surprised to find it so warmly decorated. Toys in one of the adjacent rooms hinted at the presence of children. He shrugged his shoulders and followed the man into the den.

"Wanted to check up on a former 12th, to see how you're managing," Kyote added. He then motioned to Longswit's hip. "The leg seems to be doing better. Or at least better than when we left Mercarton." Longswit had been confined to a wheelchair when they'd sailed from the port city.

"I make do," Longswit noted as his face tightened. "Kinda depends on the weather. Some days I can make the rounds. Others, not so much. Can tell when the next big storm is rolling in, so there's that. Never gonna run a race, but I survive. If it's the worst thing I have to deal with… well, that and my vision, especially on this side of my head—" He tapped his right temple. "—isn't what it used to be. I mean, I can see and all, but some days it's a bit blurrier than usual."

Kyote grimaced. He could feel his chest tighten. "They— uh, the VMF—they takin' care you, at least?"

"Beyond a thank you and some pain meds before patting me on the back and sending me on my way? Not really," Longswit scoffed. "Got better things to do, I guess. Now that the war's over, they're kinda done with me. Politicians already moved on to other matters. Don't wanna think about those who came back from the war. Certainly, don't want to spend any more than they have to on wounded veterans. So, even with the hazard pay and the bulk payout of my future wages after being discharged, I'm not exactly what you might call 'rolling in the coin.' And, as you can tell, my injuries kinda limit my ability to make a living. Fortunately for me, my sister and her family was kind enough to put me up until I can get back on my feet." He paused for a moment as his cheeks sagged. "I hate to tell her that I don't know when that's ever gonna be."

Kyote held his tongue. He didn't know what else to say. Anything beyond "I'm sorry" felt like an empty platitude.

"So, what has you in town?" Longswit slumped into the well-worn chair. His eyes flickered off to the side. "Oh, wait, forget that. You're here for the festival, aren't you? One way or another, *everyone's* here for the party. Tourism usually is booming this time of year."

"Actually, I'm not. Like I said before—and it's not like I wouldn't want to throw down with the best of them—but I'm in town on business. The kind that keeps me sober. Shame I gotta miss out on the fun, but bigger things are afoot. Me, Flynn, and Rolde are working a job that brought us here."

"Oh?" He sat up and leaned forward in his seat. "So, uh, they're around?"

"Yeah, Rolde's sleeping off a long night and Flynn's, well, being Flynn. Probably won't pull his nose out of the books unless he has to." Kyote fudged a little. He didn't want to tell Longswit more. If the situation went poorly and law enforcement came looking for answers, he wanted to allow Longswit some degree of plausible deniability.

Longswit frowned. Seeing this, Kyote spoke up.

"I'll be sure to let them know I saw you. Tell them to catch up with you when they have the time."

Longswit nodded softly at this.

Over the next hour, the two men chatted. Though Kyote tried his best to keep the conversation light, he could see that Longswit had anger roiling within him. Before the afternoon skies darkened, Longswit's nieces and nephews returned to their home. As they did, Kyote said his goodbyes and left before he overstayed his welcome. As it was, he felt as though he'd stirred up something unpleasant in the former soldier with his presence.

As Kyote strode away, he glanced over his shoulder to see Longswit in one of the windows. His hands tightly clutched the blinds as he stared out intently over the surrounding subdivision.

Chapter 10

The Fifth of Shumond
Port Nym

After three days of nonstop observation, Flynn knew that they weren't going to be handed the key to the Pourrie compound. The round-the-clock security was seemingly airtight and left no opportunities for easy access. As he'd expected, all deliveries were dropped off by the back gate. When guards carried bundles inside, Flynn wondered if Pourrie had any household staff at all. He had yet to see the arrival of anyone likely to be a manservant. It seemed that Pourrie lived alone. The only people who turned up daily were the similarly-dressed musclemen.

When his watch was over, Flynn went back to the inn and crashed for the night. The constant vigilance exhausted him, proving tedious and mentally-taxing at the same time. This was made worse by the neverending revelry in the streets. He hadn't spent an unbroken night of rest since their arrival.

By midday of the fifth, he rolled out of his bed and rubbed at his dry eyes. Not even seven hours in the rented bed was enough. Though he wanted to slip back under the sheets, he hastily brushed the urge aside. He needed to get something to eat. It might be the day for a well-needed break. He doubted that more interviews would provide intel above and beyond what he already knew.

"Morning," Rolde called out from the other side of the room. He was flipping through a newspaper as he finished off his lunch. The aroma of his deli sandwich with olive relish triggered a gnawing sensation in Flynn's stomach. "Or, afternoon, I guess," he added.

"Morning," Flynn's reply was more of a grunt. He scratched at the top of his head. Before he could lift himself up, Flynn heard the rattle of the doorknob. His neck craned upward.

"Who the…" Rolde muttered as he set down the paper and glanced over his shoulder.

We're paid up, aren't we? Flynn thought. Though still befuddled by sleep, he retraced their activities. The hotel staff had no reason to complain. Perhaps some drunk was trying to enter the wrong room.

Surprisingly, the door swung open. In bounded Kyote, bouncing on the balls of his feet.

"We got ourselves a lead," Kyote boasted as he stopped beside Rolde, who shifted in his seat. "Or something that comes close to one."

Flynn slipped out of his bed and faced him. He wanted to know why Kyote'd abandoned his post, but stopped himself from asking.

"Do tell," Rolde mumbled and rose from his seat.

"Saw this guy, looked like a real nimrod with his reflective sunglasses and slicked-back hair. Kinda guy you just wanna punch because of the choices he's made about how he wants to look. He's dressed like all the others, except he shows up during the middle of the day, not at shift change. And alone. No bodyguards with him. At first, I figured he was late or maybe he's called in to replace someone who ain't feeling so good. Someone who went out and drank a little too much last night. Tied one on but good and is feeling it. Except, he goes to the back entrance and lets himself in. Doesn't ring up the guys on the clock to let him in like they usually do. May as well be master of the house the way he strutted around."

"Was it Pourrie?" Rolde inquired.

"At first, I wasn't sure. He seemed pretty chummy with the muscle. A lot of handshakes and fist bumps. I figured he might be one of them. Plus, he wasn't exactly dressed like someone who owns a mansion. Or a collection worth stealing. I mean, unless you want to grab a set of beers or sunglasses."

His interest now piqued, Flynn spoke up. "He had a set of keys? On him?" In all his time on watch, he'd never seen anyone let themselves inside the property.

"That's what it looked like. Unlocked the back door, went in, spoke to a couple of the guys, and headed inside the house. Ten minutes later, he's done with whatever he needs to do and leaves the same way." Kyote paused for a moment. "So, I followed him. Trailed him back to this apartment, which was a bitch-and-a-half because he made two other stops for groceries and some smokes. That and it was on the north side of downtown, so there's a sizable crowd to deal with. Good to hide in, bad to trail someone. It looks like he might live there, so I figure it can't be Pourrie. A real dump, you know."

"Okay, since we know where this guy lives," Rolde started as he brushed a few crumbs from his shirt. "Do we need to start staking out his place? 'cause that sounds like *even more* work."

"Naw, we don't watch this guy," Kyote responded. "We grab him. Take his keys and get him to talk."

"Oh?"

At this, Flynn spoke up. "Once we do, though, we'd better be ready to hit the property. There's only so long a keyholder can go missing before someone comes looking for him."

"I guess we may get an extra day or two what with the

festival going on," Kyote noted. "So, do we pick him up?"

Flynn mulled over the inquiry for a few seconds. There were still so many unanswered questions, and he'd yet to devise a plan for breaching the compound without violence. Even with the keys to the back door, there was a plethora of hired muscle to avoid. Preferring discretion, he shook his head.

"Not yet, at least. I'd like to continue the surveillance a day or two more before we do something so drastic."

Rolde nodded in agreement.

"Okay," Kyote grunted as his countenance sagged. His crossed his arms showed that he didn't agree with Flynn, but he did not contest the decision. "Guess I'll get back to it, then. Gonna stop and get a bite on my way back through. Watching nothing all day's hungry work."

After another day spent watching the house, no new information came to light. The one time a delivery boy from the local grocer stopped by, it was just long enough to drop his package off before he scurried away.

With this in mind, Flynn wasn't exactly in a hurry to return for his shift. He stopped off at a small diner for a local delicacy: a fried seafood sandwich coated liberally in regional spices. The heat brought a light sweat to his brow. He washed it down with some iced tea and was out the door with a few minutes to spare.

Flynn arrived at the tarp-covered back door of the neighboring home, expecting no news from Kyote's shift. Maybe Kyote would share a story about stumbling partygoers. Eventually, he would be on his way and Flynn would spend hours trying to fend off boredom.

When he reached the second story, he was surprised to hear Kyote engaged in a heated conversation. He paused at the landing and cocked his head to one side.

"What the fuck do you want from me? Turn me *loose*, asshole!"

Though Flynn couldn't see, he had a pretty good idea of what was happening.

"Now, now, did your momma not tell you how important it is to say 'please' once in a while?" Kyote responded. "She certainly didn't wash your mouth out enough."

Flynn rushed along the hall and barged into the back bedroom. There he found Kyote standing over a man who was lashed tightly to a chair. His button-down shirt was partly open, and a blue tie hung loosely around his neck. A pair of sunglasses had been flung on the floor. The captive's face was red from yelling, but he wasn't bleeding or bruised, Flynn noted with relief.

"Oh," Kyote said as he turned to greet Flynn. "It looks like we have company." He raised a single finger and waved it back and forth. "No names, though."

Flynn understood what he meant. Again, Flynn felt a little better since Kyote did not intend to kill his detainee. At this point, anyway.

"So, we're just going ahead with this," Flynn commented as he moved in close to Kyote, who only grunted in response. Flynn glanced over his shoulder at the bound man, who furiously thrashed in his seat.

From out of one pocket, Kyote produced a palm-size leather case and flipped it open.

"Our friend here, one Kelvin Hallows of 204 Branch Lane, Suite D…" Kyote paused as he peered closely at Kelvin's ID. "Well, Kelvin here does *not* photograph well. Or maybe that's why he decided to trim his hair, because this—this right *here*—this is not a good look for you." He folded the wallet and pitched it to Flynn, who gave it a quick scan.

"What the fuck am I doing here? What do ya want from me?" Kelvin barked as he continued to struggle against his restraints.

"A little info and the use of your keys for about one night will do," Kyote noted. "I don't think we'll need much else. Right?" He glanced at Flynn, who shrugged his shoulders. He set the leather case back with the rest of Kelvin's possessions, on a stack of unfinished lumber. Besides a pistol, still in its holster, were some loose change, a handkerchief, and a pack of chewing gum.

"What makes you think I'm gonna tell you anything? You can go spin for all I care, you shit." Kelvin was now apoplectic.

"Well, I can always start whaling on you until you do. Real talk, though, I don't care if you give up the info or not." After cracking his knuckles, Kyote picked up a thick board of pine.

"I, on the other hand, do," Flynn spoke up as he placed a hand on Kyote's shoulder. He wanted to offer the man an opportunity before things went too far. He slipped past Kyote and moved in close. "All we're asking is for is a few—"

"Go. Fuck. Yourselves!" Kelvin seethed as he spat at Flynn.

That's nice, Flynn thought to himself. Flynn seriously doubted Kelvin was going to be forthcoming. At least, not without an incentive of one kind or another.

"How rude," Kyote said under his breath as he watched Flynn back away. He wasn't certain whether the scowl on Flynn's face was for him or Kelvin. "Want me to loosen him up a bit? Pop him in the chops a couple times for good measure."

Flynn knew he had to relent. They had limited time and Kelvin was curiously confrontational for a man bound to a chair.

"Just keep him conscious and don't bust up the mouth too

much," Flynn coldly stated as he marched to the other side of the room. "He *does* need it to talk."

"I can manage that." Kyote hefted the lumber in his hand as he skipped forward. He spoke in a lower, more menacing tone. "My friend, this is gonna go one of two ways. You can either be cooperative, and in a day or two, you'll wake up on the other side of town with some serious chafing around your wrists and ankles. If you don't wanna work with us... well, I'll get to beat on you until I get tired. And I got a good night's rest."

"You ain't—"

Kyote interrupted him with a jab to the chest. "Yeah, yeah, I ain't gonna get you to talk. Every tough guy in the world starts out like that, and then a couple broken bones, two swollen eyes, and a threat of chopping off their dong gets them blubbering. At some point, I won't be able to get you ta shut up. Can we, for once, just get right to the end? I can't imagine Pourrie isn't paying that much for your loyalty."

"He pays me good enough."

"Keeps you in booze and ladies, right? Or maybe being head security guard is what gets your rocks off." Kyote leaned in as he pressed the 2x4 against Kelvin's groin. "You the kinda dude to wake up every morning with a raging semi at the thought of strapping on your holster? You take your cup of coffee with the hope that today's the day someone makes the mistake of getting in your way. Maybe you'll get to flex all those muscles that you spent years pumping iron for to make you look impressive. I bet you oil up and stare at yourself in the mirror while making kissing noises just for shits and giggles."

"Are you gonna talk me to death or what?"

Kyote glanced over his shoulder to Flynn, who only shrugged.

Without another word, he hefted the lumber in the air and drove it down on Kelvin's left kneecap. The man screeched as pain instantly seized his body. Spittle flew from his open mouth.

"Not so sassy now, are we? A shot to the knee takes the fire right outta your loins, eh?" Kyote asked with a cockeyed grin. He turned back to Flynn and spoke. "You might wanna go for a walk, maybe get us a bite to eat. I got a feeling it's gonna take some time to soften our boy up. All that muscle needs some tenderizing."

Flynn groaned.

"Just watch for the mouth," Flynn eventually replied before slipping away.

Flynn went back to their room. No matter how much encouragement was applied, he doubted that Kelvin would spill his guts anytime soon.

Once through the door, he found Rolde with his face in the same morning newspaper as before.

"Uh, I guess you're back," Rolde said as he looked up from his reading, scowling at Flynn's early return. "Where's Kyote? Are we not watching the mansion anymore?"

"Apparently, we don't need to," Flynn replied as he went to his gear. "Kyote grabbed the head of security—or at least I hope he's the head—and is in the process of interrogating him."

Rolde came out of his seat. "That's, uh… that's a good thing, right? Or maybe not? I'm confused."

"Whichever it is, our timeline has been moved up. We'll have to hit the place before too long. If not tonight, then tomorrow. At some point, someone's going to report him missing. Maybe he gets called in to settle something at the estate, and when he doesn't, his coworkers start asking why." Flynn motioned to an olive canvas pack on the other side of the room. "Grab yours and Kyote's stuff. Let's get everything packed up. Hopefully, we can at least get one more night here before we have to bail."

"Are we leaving?"

"Not yet. I assume that Kyote will need a couple hours to loosen up his hostage. Get him willing to talk. After that, we may have to move pretty quickly. Once we decide its 'go time,' I don't know if we'll have time to come back for our luggage if we don't bring it with us."

Rolde gathered up both packs and tossed them onto the nearby cot. As he began to repack their clothes, he looked at Flynn.

"Don't you think you're being a bit too paranoid?"

"Isn't that why you asked me to come along?"

It was late afternoon when Flynn returned to check on Kyote and Kelvin. In one hand was a brown paper bag from a deli a few blocks to the north. Written in grease pencil on the front was "#22 HOAG x2."

He was surprised to discover Kyote lounging by himself in the second-story bedroom. Seated in the chair where earlier he'd bound his hostage, he was staring out the window at the view of the Pourrie estate. When he heard the door open, Kyote rose and faced Flynn, smiling.

"What's with the bagged lunch?" Kyote nodded towards Flynn's hands. He quickly crossed to meet Flynn, who hovered in the open entryway.

"I figured that both you and Mr. Hallows could use something to eat. We're kidnappers, not murderers. Or, at least…" he trailed off. A faint scowl creased his forehead. There were spatters of blood on the plywood floor and a pool of liquid that smelled like urine.

"Don't worry your pretty face. I locked him up in the closet." He motioned to the other end of the hall, where a wooden chair was wedged beneath the doorknob. "Only room without a window. Well, I guess I could'a dumped him in the bathroom, but that would'a involved me emptying out all the drawers so he didn't have access to razors or scissors."

"Is he alright?"

Kyote scoffed. "He's a hostage who got worked over pretty good before he talked. Tough as beef jerky, that one. So, no, he ain't alright. He'll live and he's been pissing and moaning for a while now, but he don't need to be taken to a hospital. You feeding him will take care of one problem. The other… well, he's just gonna have to shit in the corner and deal with the smell."

A sour look crossed Flynn's face. He latched onto one of Kyote's statements.

"You finally got him to talk?"

"Yeah," Kyote said with a nod as he rubbed his hand. The skin was broken in places, and dried blood had congealed along the knuckles. His jacket sleeve was soiled with brown spots. "He was a tough one, but he eventually blabbed once it became clear I might rip off his dick. I guess that was more important than his big paycheck. If I'd known that, I might have started with jamming a knife into his family jewels and saved myself the workout."

"And?" Flynn spun his hand to move the conversation along.

"Security's just as we saw it. Two at the front, one at the back, two more roaming with one posted on the upper floor balconies with a scope. Eight-hour shifts. About a twenty-man crew in total. Armed with pistols and batons, except for the guy up top. Both gates are locked, and he and Pourrie are the only ones with keys."

"That's a lot of people employed to keep unwanted visitors away."

"I said the same thing. Our good friend didn't really think anything of it. I guess as long as he got paid, he didn't care why the man wanted so many guards around. Seems like it was a cushy job, and no one wanted to rock the boat. Don't ask no questions if you want to keep the coin flowing, right?"

For a moment, both men fell silent. When something else occurred to Kyote, he spoke up.

"Oh, apparently our friend here doesn't usually show up to work guard duty because he's too good for that. His words, exactly. Real piece of work, he is. He's the boss man who runs the crew. Collects the coin and dishes out the pay. Sets the schedules. Only comes around when asked for by Pourrie."

"So, we can assume…"

"That unless Pourrie sends for him, ain't no one gonna be missing him for a few days. Maybe around payday or when someone needs a day off."

"Well, that gives us a little more time," Flynn noted with some relief. Truth be told, the best plan they had devised involved a distraction at the front gate paired with a grocery drop-off around back. With the keys, their options opened up some.

"He has anything else of value to say?"

"Uh…" Kyote trailed off as his eyes rolled upwards. "Oh, no inside staff."

"Really?"

"Yeah. Surprised me as well. Pourrie isn't one for having people inside his place. Apparently, one of the housekeepers was pocketing curios, and he found out about it. Fired the lot and doubled the security. Considering he doesn't have guests, it's not like he's got to do the table service himself. He *really* doesn't want people getting into his stuff."

"Well, that's good news, then."

Kyote grabbed the takeout order from Flynn and opened it up. He pulled out a sandwich and set it on top of a stack of lumber. A second hoagie rested in the bag like a lead weight.

"Let's get this to Kelvin 'fore he gets all pissy about something else besides how much he's bleeding on his work clothes."

Deciding not to linger, Flynn left Kyote to his guard duty. Since they would likely hit the mansion the following day, he wanted to get a decent night's rest. They would be checking out in the morning. If Rolde felt up for it, Flynn might have him relieve Kyote. Either way, he and Rolde would eventually join Kyote the next day until nightfall, when they would finally make their move. What their strategy exactly entailed, though, was still up in the air. All Flynn knew was that by dawn the following day, they would need to exit the city.

On his way back, he took a short detour to the local newsstand for a copy of the afternoon paper. As he scanned the shelves, Flynn felt as if someone was watching him. He glanced up to the shop owner. With a cap pulled over his brow and an unlit stogie between his lips, the older man was so enthralled by an open magazine that he failed to notice Flynn. The handful of people moving along the adjacent sidewalk appeared more concerned about their own destinations or conversations.

He tossed a few coins on the counter, collected the evening

edition, and tucked it under his armpit. The vendor growled in response as Flynn slipped away. Though the feeling of being watched persisted, Flynn brushed it aside. The cloak-and-dagger game they had been playing must be getting to him, he thought.

This is the sort of thing that O'mas would enjoy. I imagine that the Intelligence Division does this day in, day out. If so, I'm relieved that my career path didn't take me there. It's exhausting to be always looking over your shoulder. Once you start watching people, you begin to wonder who's watching you.

When he turned the sharp corner at the next intersection, Flynn saw them. He'd convinced himself his suspicions were all in his mind. Yet, two guys hovered a few meters behind him as they tried in vain to hide among the crowd of pedestrians.

Now that he was aware of his tail, he began to take a circuitous route through the streets. At first, this was to allow him furtive glances at the pair. Though both were well-dressed, they were distinctly different than Pourrie's men. These weren't overly-muscled thugs forced into shirts and ties. Their suits were well-tailored, so much so that he struggled to tell if they were armed. Of more interest was that one of the men, with his ochre-hued skin, was clearly Tirean. None of Pourrie's crew was anything but native Verenigen in appearance.

If it's not Pourrie, then who? Someone else? If so, what do they want from me? If I was Kyote, I'd just accost them right now. Pick a fight to see what they know.

His thoughts went back to a comment Rolde had made a few days back. *Wait a minute... Didn't Rolde say he saw someone else casing the mansion? Are these the same guys?*

Though numerous questions jockeyed for his attention, he put all extraneous thoughts aside and headed downtown. He needed to lose them before he turned back towards their lodgings. The last thing the trio needed was people tracking their every move. It was bad enough that they might have trailed him from the mansion.

In the midst of a crowd of parade spectators, complete with barely-dressed women who cast flowers into the throng, Flynn moved quickly. He noticed that his pursuers were struggling to keep up with him. He scurried from one choke point to another, often ducking down as he shifted direction.

It took Flynn a few tries, but he shook his tail in the dense crowd of partygoers. Once he was alone, he rushed back to the inn.

Chapter 11

The Sixth of Shumond
Port Nym

Any other time or place, Flynn might have enjoyed the view with his feet up on the windowsill. Flowers were coming into bloom. There was a gentle breeze from the southern harbor, rich with the aromas of local restaurants. It was just warm enough. A part of him wanted to settle in with a rich cup of coffee and some light reading.

Unfortunately, this brief fantasy was broken by the muffled swearing of their prisoner, Kelvin, who was still locked up in the closet at the other end of the hall. The head of security occasionally banged against the door. After thrashing fruitlessly in his makeshift cell, he eventually settled down. Flynn wanted nothing more than to set the man free, if only to be done with him, but he had no choice in the matter. Kelvin's temper wasn't even the worst problem his constant presence produced. A foul odor leaked out from beneath the barred door.

From the window overlooking the Pourrie mansion, Flynn waited patiently as the sun sank beneath the city's skyline. There was little going on below. Flynn was merely waiting. Once it was dark, they would make their move.

By now, they'd transferred their luggage into the house. While Kyote had maintained his watch, Flynn and Rolde settled up with the inn, collected their gear, and migrated. On their way across town, Flynn kept an eye out for anyone who might be tailing them. He was nervous at the thought that someone was aware of their presence.

Though the crowd often became a formless mass that shifted by the second, he failed to notice anything suspicious. Even so, he remained careful; the pair took a roundabout way that eventually brought them to the house through a back alley.

As Flynn lingered upstairs, observing, Rolde and Kyote went out to procure the evening's meal. Thoughts of a fried seafood sandwich made Flynn's stomach growl hungrily.

Just as the sky began to darken from yellow and orange into colder hues, Rolde and Kyote entered the half-finished addition, food in hand.

With the return of his partners, Flynn rose from his seat and turned to address them. After strapping on a shoulder holster and securing his pistol in place, Flynn spoke up.

"Shouldn't be too long before we can proceed," he noted, beginning the mission briefing. Kyote handed him a still-warm sandwich. Despite his hunger, he set it aside for the moment.

Taking a cue from Flynn, Rolde slipped his firearm into the back of his pants. Kyote carelessly tucked his gun into the interior pocket of his canvas jacket.

"Good," Kyote spoke. "I was beginning to get tired of our friend back there. Don't know which is fouler, his mouth or his ass." He motioned over his shoulder.

"Well, let's go over the plan, in so much as we have one," Flynn announced as he clasped his hands together. "With Mr. Hallows' keys, we can enter in through the back. At best, we'll have one guard to deal with. That is, if we don't find some way to pull the staff to the front gate, like you did before." He pointed to Kyote, who nodded once before speaking up.

"Have you thought about what kind of distraction—"

"I got it," Rolde interrupted as he moved to the open window. There was a sly grin on his lips, and his cheeks glowed with mischief. "I've been thinking about it for some time now, really."

"Is that so?" Flynn watched as Rolde pointed at the house to the right of Pourrie's. It was where they had initially begun their surveillance.

"Yeah, I've been eyeing the neighbor's motorcraft for a few days now. They were such dicks when they ran me off that I think that taking their vehicle for a joyride into the front gate should be enough payback."

"Ain't that a little devious," Kyote said with a grin. When Rolde turned to him, he nodded in approval.

Flynn paused. After a few seconds, he offered a thin half-smile.

"Do it and get out of there the first chance you get. We don't need them detaining you."

Emboldened by Flynn's support, Rolde smiled warmly.

"And the rest of the plan?" Kyote prodded.

"If Rolde can pull the security to the front lawn, we'll slip in through the back, deal with anyone who's still lingering about and enter the house before anyone's the wiser. And by 'deal with,' I mean knock them out." He looked directly at Kyote. "If Mr. Hallows can be believed, once we're inside, we won't have to deal with security patrols."

"Just Pourrie himself."

Flynn clenched his jaw for a second. If possible, he wanted to avoid the master of the house. Getting identified by Pourrie was not high on his list of goals for this mission. Killing Pourrie to keep him silent was likewise not a desirable outcome.

"Once inside, Kyote and I will make a sweep—trying to keep as low a profile as possible—and grab the Eye. Kelvin didn't know what or where the Eye was, but he begrudgingly revealed that Pourrie's office would be upstairs and that we might find it there. When it's in our possession, we'll proceed to retreat the way we came. Worst case scenario, we run into the guy who mans the back gate and have to take him out. *Knock* him out."

"And our meet-up point?" Rolde inquired.

"Right here. Downstairs back porch if everything goes without a hitch." Flynn looked at each man and waited for confirmation of their understanding. "Only approach from the back alley to make sure no one streetside can see you."

"And if shit goes sideways?" Kyote asked as the trio began to break up.

Flynn paused with the open bag in his hands. The food's aroma caused his mouth to water. "We do our best to get lost in the city. Mix in with the crowds. By daybreak, we'll need to meet up at the northeast coach station. The one we arrived at a couple of days ago. We'll need to be out of Port Nym on the first carriage, if possible."

While no one cared for the answer, they all knew it to be the right one. If events did not play out their way, they'd have to disappear into the metropolis for the night to avoid both Pourrie's men and any local law enforcement investigating the theft. The only positive in the scenario was that they'd be on the road before Pourrie could file a complaint with the VMF's peacekeeping force.

"Here," Kyote said as he approached Flynn, who'd peeled the paper from his sandwich and was considering the best angle of approach. Flynn glanced up to see the tangle of keys in Kyote's hand. "Better you have them. If Rolde's distraction don't pay off, one of us'll need to run interference. Considering my *condition*, we both know it'd be best if it was me."

"Makes sense."

Flynn took the keyring and tucked it into his pants pocket. He didn't have to say anything else; Kyote was right. If they ran into trouble, Kyote could withstand the initial salvo of gunfire before the rest of the security force was alerted to their presence. If the situation became genuinely hairy, things would get bloody, and fast. Flynn was reminded of the battle at the ruins of Yehtnze and how Kyote had let himself go. Even when wounded by automatic rifle fire, he tore through a pack of soldiers like they were ragdolls.

He hoped that it wouldn't come to that.

Night had fallen.

Outside, Rolde split off from the others. He slipped through a barrier of hedges and disappeared beyond the back corner of the neighboring home. Rolde's circuitous route would eventually take him to the parked motorcraft in the driveway at the far end of the block. If Flynn and Kyote kept on the move, they'd have just enough time to get into place before Rolde attempted his distraction.

As they crossed the street, both men were caught off guard by a series of loud blasts behind them. For a moment, Flynn ducked down. Instinctively, he raised an arm over his head. He was back in Gran'rehnza, and the cannons of Fort Biaa were trying to sink him. His heart leapt into his throat as his brain tried to make sense of the startling noise.

Kyote pointed to the sky. His profile was backlit by orange and green light.

"Fireworks," he said before he continued on his path.

This caused Flynn to spin about, just as more pyrotechnics lit up the night sky with red and yellow flares. Even after seeing the colored flames fan out in starburst patterns and feeling the boom in his ears, Flynn still flinched.

Talk about your happy accidents. Might need to clean my pants out when we're done, though. Wasn't expecting that to happen. Couldn't have asked for a better diversion. Might not even need Rolde to smash the neighbor's vehicle into the front gate.

He glanced down the street for a second. *Too late to call that off, though.*

The pair moved quickly to the backside of the lot, where they found an alley littered with trash cans and refuse. A few discarded crates had seen too much time out in the elements. The dirt path cut a line between the adjoining properties. Even in the gloom, the barrier wall made it was easy for them to pick out Pourrie's estate.

Flynn and Kyote waited. In the shadows of the hedges, they could see the back entrance. Though there were signs of movement on the other side of the wall, neither could hear anything. There were no audible conversations, and certainly nothing sounded amiss.

Flynn cocked his head to the side and patiently listened for any clue that Rolde's plan was underway. He heard the rumble of tires on distant streets, but they passed on.

Before long, their patience was rewarded. A screech of vulcanized rubber on pavement hailed from somewhere to their left. This was immediately followed by the roar of an engine as the motorcraft closed in on the property. Someone was pushing the automobile to its limit. From the whine of the engine, Flynn could tell that the driver was approaching with wild abandon.

His shoulders tightened as his jaw clenched, anticipating a crash. Soon the racket of a steel frame slamming against a stone barrier cut through the night air. Shattering glass produced a cringe-inducing peal. Flynn guessed that the vehicle had successfully breached the wall. Soon, he heard the clatter of broken masonry raining down on the smashed chassis.

A chorus of angry men called out as Pourrie's security force rushed to the front lawn.

Flynn moved to the delivery entrance with haste. Without a word, Kyote followed. While both men were concerned for Rolde's well-being, they knew that this was their only opportunity.

With a twist of his wrist, Flynn unlocked the back gate. He placed a hand gingerly against the wrought-iron barrier and slowly nudged it forward. When one of the hinges creaked ever so slightly, Flynn's chest tightened up. Fortunately, no one was there to investigate.

After pocketing the keyring, he slipped into the backyard and found it entirely abandoned. Still, Flynn knew it wouldn't be long before someone returned to their post.

"We clear?" Kyote asked as he slipped up beside Flynn. His eyes scanned the topiary-adorned lawn. The house's long shadow swallowed up much of the panorama. Only in the bursts of light were they given brief glimpses as random sparkles of color outlined the leafy landscape.

"For now."

Flynn quickly spotted a servant's entrance on the backside of the building. He pointed at the closed doorway, which was temporarily illuminated by a particularly furious staccato of red and yellow starbursts.

Both men were on the move before the light entirely faded. The sounds of raised voices from elsewhere meant that the security detail was still engaged. He could only hope that they weren't giving Rolde too much trouble.

Kyote clutched impatiently at the brass handle. He wiggled it and groaned when he discovered that it was locked.

"Of course," he grunted as he stepped aside. As he pulled the ring from his pocket, Flynn moved in and began to try the keys. With each one, his movements grew more frantic. Fingers fumbled with the knob as he tried to find the keyhole in the dark.

Eventually, he had the entrance unlocked. A heavy scent of soap and wet fabric struck them as they snuck into the mansion's laundry room. A stack of grocery crates by the entryway smelled of days-old produce.

The interior of Pourrie's mansion was surprisingly modest, especially compared to Wallowrich's abode. This was the kind of place someone with a large family might call home. There were no opulent touches displaying the man's riches, no formal arrangement of assorted curios. The only thing worth noting was the apparent lack of upkeep; a fine layer of dust covered the furnishings, and the carpet was worn and dirty in places.

A quick tour of the first floor proved informative. Though Pourrie was a procurer of ancient artifacts, the man made no effort to display any objects of value or interest. Most of his contemporaries had a dedicated space for their collections. A few items on bookcases looked more like mementos of past travels than anything else. Flynn began to wonder if he kept his treasured keepsakes in a vault, perhaps on the second or third floor.

Flynn swore under his breath. He knew he didn't have hours for an extended search—Rolde's distraction was only going to buy them so much time. He hoped that Kelvin had been right and that Pourrie's upstairs office would hold their prize.

Just as he reached the end of the corridor, Flynn came to a stop. He heard a clatter from the front of the property. For a second, he assumed it was the sound of fireworks, but when the staccato came quickly and failed to taper off, he recognized the sounds for what they were.

"Gunfire?" Flynn's head shot up. His eyes widened as he

turned back to Kyote, who was entranced by a gaudy piece of gold-plated bric-a-brac.

"Rolde," Kyote grumbled as he dropped the curio back onto the shelf.

They couldn't… Flynn thought that there was no way Pourrie's men would use deadly force for what should be viewed as an accident. He knew that Rolde wouldn't resist if caught. The worst that he should expect was the kind of rough handling that Kyote had received days before.

"Shit," Flynn swore as he realized that any plan had now flown out the window. As he shifted his stance, he felt a hand grasp him by the shoulder.

"Go," Kyote ordered as he nudged Flynn forward. "Find the Eye. I'm gonna go make sure Rolde ain't hurt. And if they *are* shooting at him… well, things are gonna get messy. Best we be done with this job right here, right now. Once you get the Eye, get outta here, and we'll meet up later."

"I, uh…" Flynn stammered. Kyote was right. He also knew that if the guards were taking shots at Rolde, there were going to be muscled bodies littered across the estate before sunup. "Yeah, let's do this," he eventually said as he waved on Kyote.

Flynn spun on one heel and headed for the stairs. He had even less time to waste now.

Kyote was always prepared for the worst, and Kelvin's interrogation had confirmed that gung-ho assholes were hired for Pourrie's security. If the guards were even half the self-important meatheads that their boss was, there would be no talking them down.

As he scurried back through the house, he could feel his heart rate accelerating. His body was anticipating violence. His breathing became shallow, his senses dulled. It wouldn't take much to let go and let the fury have control.

When the back door swung open, Kyote went for his gun and had it half out of its holster before he recognized the pasty features of his friend.

"Whoa," Rolde called out as he skidded to a stop. His eyes bulged as he stumbled backward into the doorframe. Shock caused him to pause as his breath caught.

Kyote let out a relieved sigh as he holstered his weapon. The gray blur on the edges of his vision quickly snapped back into focus.

"What the shit is going on?" Kyote asked of Rolde, who had a hand over his chest as he hyperventilated for a moment. "We heard gunfire and—"

Another round of shots punctured the night air. Both men flinched. Kyote scowled as his gaze returned to Rolde.

"Not me. They're not after me," Rolde announced breathlessly. "I couldn't even get the motorcraft started. Like a dumbass, I thought I could just jump in and get it going. Vroom, vroom. No key for the ignition, and apparently all those crime novels I've been reading lied to me about how to hotwire one. Worst thing I did was short out his steering column and burn my hand." He held out his fingers.

"So that means what? Someone else..." Kyote trailed off.

"Yeah, a bunch of guys—the same ones that, I think, tailed Flynn the other day—were already shooting up the place when I came around to see what the fuss was about. Apparently, they had the same idea. Drove this late-model Holder & Dash into the front gate and then started mixing it up with Pourrie's men. I hauled ass back here, quick as I could, to warn you guys. Last I saw, Pourrie's guys were still having a regular old gun battle with whoever this new group is. Ain't seen this kinda fighting since Gran'rehnza. Don't know who's winning. Don't care."

Kyote swore. "That's great. Well, we were worried about this shit going sideways, and here we are."

As Rolde's heart rate returned to normal, another thought occurred to him. "Hey, have you guys seen Pourrie, yet?"

"Naw. Probably went into hiding as soon as the bullets started flying." *Which means they got standing orders to shoot anyone if they feel like it,* Kyote thought to himself. *Nice. I guess that's why he hired someone like Kelvin to run this crew. Shoot first, shoot later kinda guys.*

After a few seconds, he motioned over his shoulder with a hooked thumb. "Look, man, I'mma go back in and find Flynn. Help him grab the Eye before one side or the other finishes the fight and starts to make their way back here. Whatever timeline we had for this caper is useless now. We gotta be done and soon." He reached over and patted Rolde on the chest.

"Yeah, I got ya," Rolde said with a nod. He let out a shallow laugh and slumped against the nearby wall. "I need a little time to get my heartbeat back down. 'specially if we're gonna be on the run again."

"Sure, just, uh… just make sure no one comes back this way." Kyote pointed to the door. "Secure the back entrance. I gotta feeling we're gonna need to exit fast."

Rolde flicked a half-hearted salute.

At the top of the stairs, the second-story landing led directly to a hallway with four identical doors. On the other end of the corridor was another staircase that wound upward to the third floor. Flynn decided that, since they didn't know the floorplan, a room-by-room sweep of the premises was the only option he had.

The first two chambers were similarly-decorated guest accommodations that had been unused for some time, judging by the thin layer of dust on the furniture. If Pourrie had a family, each room would have been littered with something, children's toys, or unwashed clothing. Except for a few framed paintings, the walls were bare.

Just as he clutched the third door's handle, an unpleasant thought occurred to Flynn. Still raging outside, the gunfight sounded like an exchange between two distinct groups. Of course, one set of weapons belonged to Pourrie's men. There were salvos from small-caliber pistols and the occasional clatter of a rifle from the third-floor balcony, weapons he noticed during their surveillance. In response, submachinegun fire originated from somewhere near the adjacent street.

A third party… Someone trying to enter the property. Don't even care about who knows. Who could… Oh, shit. The guys who wanted to follow me back to the inn the other day. Could it be? Or, the same ones that Rolde thought might be casing the place. Maybe he was right to think something was up with them. How awful is our timing? Or, maybe… maybe it's not our timing that's the problem.

Flynn shook his head and attempted to force the door open. He nudged his shoulder into it and found it locked. Beyond the dense wooden barrier, Flynn swore that he heard a whimper. He figured someone had barricaded themselves inside.

Pourrie? Has to be. I haven't seen anything that would hint at him being a family man. Well, I hope… I mean, it could be someone else. Still, I hate the idea of him seeing my face, but if I'm going to find the Eye quickly, he's going to know where it is. Best to do this and get out of here before the battle works its way inside. Maybe he'll be too distracted or scared to put up much of a fight.

He whipped out the keyring and began to try each on

the lock. When the fourth key released the deadbolt with a satisfying clack of metal pins falling into place, Flynn attempted the door again. It took Flynn a second to recover as he stumbled forward into the room.

Flynn's gaze fell on Pourrie, still seated in his second-floor office. Though he sank as deep into the plush desk chair as he could, he met Flynn's stare. Pourrie was a thin man, small in stature, who appeared as though he hadn't been outside in years. Pale and frail, he struck Flynn as incapable of much physical exertion. Bulging blue eyes grew wide as he watched Flynn barge into the room. His pasty forehead was dotted with enough sweat that his thinning grayish-blond hair stuck to it in places.

Before Flynn could come to a complete stop, Pourrie's hands nervously scrambled to the top of his desk, where they retrieved a pistol. Clumsily, he whipped the firearm up and leveled it at Flynn, whose first response was to raise his arms defensively.

"Y-y-you aren't going to g-get me so easily," he stammered. Flynn wondered who the man was expecting. He doubted Pourrie was waiting for him in particular.

"Whoa, there." Flynn motioned with an open hand. "No need to shoot, just… just yet. Well, *at all* would be fine enough for me, if we're being honest."

This comment did nothing to ease the tension in the room.

"Wh-h-who are you with?" Pourrie sputtered as he jabbed the gun in Flynn's direction. "I-I knew someone'd be coming. You c-c-came for the Eye, didn't you?"

Of course, I did, but explaining that I'm not part of whatever's going down outside is going to be a harder sell. I doubt you're in the mood to believe anything except what you already think is transpiring.

"Now, if you'd put down the gun," Flynn began. "We can..."

As the sound of movement came from the adjacent hall, Flynn trailed off. Someone had just cleared the steps in a hurry and was making a beeline for the office. Flynn hoped that it wasn't one of Pourrie's men, or worse, a member of the mysterious third party. The stand-off was tense enough.

"Hey!" Kyote blurted as he charged into the room. He didn't notice as Pourrie whipped his aim from Flynn to the new arrival. "Did you find the Eye—oh, shit."

Kyote skidded to a stop and shifted into a defensive posture. He made a move, a slight wiggle of his hips, weighing his options on whether to dodge to his left or backward.

"H-h-how many more?" Pourrie barked as the weapon bounced nervously in his hand. He swung the pistol back and forth for a moment. The muscles in his hand tensed. "How many of your people are down there?"

"This Pourrie?" Kyote asked out of the side of his mouth.

"I think," Flynn said with a shrug of his shoulders.

"So, I take it you've not been formally introduced?"

"Didn't have the opportunity. We went straight into the 'having a gun pointed at my head' portion of the conversation."

"How rude."

"STOP TALKING TO EACH OTHER!" Pourrie screeched. His twitchy rage did not bode well. Flynn assumed someone was about to be shot. "Tell me what I want to know! Who are you, and how many men did you bring? Who sent you?"

Already tired of the exchange and growing increasingly impatient by the second, Kyote grunted as he reached for his own gun. "Look, we're on a short schedule here, and I'm already worn out just standing around while you point your pistol at us."

His eyes bulging, Pourrie aimed the firearm back at Kyote and gripped it tightly.

"Don't you—"

Before he could finish, Kyote leveled his gun at Pourrie. When their gazes met, Kyote winked causing Pourrie to flinch.

"Look, one of two things are gonna happen here. You're either gonna shoot and miss and that's gonna tick me off. Or, you're gonna shoot and hit me, and that's gonna *really* piss me off. Either way, I'm gonna come across your desk and beat on you for a couple minutes, just for the inconvenience. Now, if you shoot me, I might rip something of value off and cram it in your throat for good measure."

He took a stride forward as he continued. Kyote was growling with each syllable. It rattled Pourrie, whose hands shook noticeably as the seconds passed.

"You're probably thinkin' that I'm bluffin'. And I might be. But there's a good chance that I ain't. And if I ain't, this is gonna go badly for you. Broken and bleeding *badly*."

For a second, Pourrie's eyes tightened. Eventually, his grip on the firearm loosened, and he slowly placed it on the desktop. Defeated, he lowered his gaze.

"Good enough for me," Kyote said as he stowed his weapon and crossed the room quickly. He collected Pourrie's gun and hastily tucked it into a jacket pocket. Pourrie slumped back into his seat and stared off to his right. His bottom lip stuck out as he scowled childishly.

While Kyote lingered desk-side, Flynn began to explore the man's office.

Before long, Kyote realized something was amiss. The noise of both the fireworks display and the heated firefight had gone silent. He came around the side of the mahogany desk and took

Pourrie by the collar of his button-down shirt.

"Where's the damned Eye at?" Kyote growled as he lifted Pourrie up. The orange light that rimmed his irises flared as his jaw clenched.

"I, uh…" Pourrie sputtered as his limbs flailed. He pointed at a cabinet in the back corner of the room. "I-i-in there."

Though he set Pourrie back down into his seat, Kyote refused to loosen his grasp. He looked over his shoulder at Flynn, who moved to the wooden cupboard. He pulled the top drawer and peered inside.

"Th-the b-b-b-bottom one," Pourrie noted as he stammered.

Flynn found a sizable wooden crate crammed inside. As it barely fit in the space, Flynn had to wiggle it a little to pull it clear. With a flick of his fingers, he opened it to reveal an oversized stone packed in straw. The object, which was much larger than any imbued ore he'd seen before, had a crystalline exterior that glinted with pink and orange sparks when the light hit it just right. As he'd read, there was a noticeable indentation on the upwards-facing side of the oversized ore.

For a moment, he felt a strange warmth and a giddiness that made his nerve endings tingle. He found himself wanting to stare at it for as long as possible.

When Kyote spoke up, the pleasant trance ended, and he returned to his senses.

"And?"

"I think we have what we came for," Flynn noted as he closed the box and tucked it under one arm. Even through the dense wood, he could feel the Eye's soothing aura. His fingers itched to touch it again.

"Then, we should…" Kyote stopped at the sound of footsteps on the nearby stairs. They were clumsy and hurried.

With his free hand, he went for his gun.

"Guys!" Rolde bellowed from just outside the door. "We have company."

Chapter 12

The Sixth of Shumond
Port Nym

Kyote wouldn't admit it to anyone but himself, but he'd been itching for a piece of the action since the first bullet was fired. After the beating he took at the front gates, he was ready to mix it up with Pourrie's men. Only Flynn's desire for discretion kept him on a short leash. Now that the fight was moving indoors, he was primed for the scrap. Hearing Rolde warn that trouble was coming sent him out the door in a rush. He stopped short as he ran into his friend in the hallway.

"What—"

In a panic, Rolde cut him off. "The fighting! Outside! It's over and the bad guys… well, I guess I don't exactly know which ones are *really* the bad guys—"

"Focus, man!" Kyote barked as he planted a firm hand on Rolde's shoulder. While this caused Rolde to flinch, it did settle him down, even if for only a second. He let out a long exhale as his face sagged.

"Pourrie's men are all dead. Last I saw, the other group was heading for the front door."

Kyote momentarily regretted the missed opportunity.

As the words left Rolde's mouth, the sounds of pounding fists against the main entrance could be heard from below.

At least two people were attempting to bash their way into the home. Steel-toed boots caused a staccato of cracks as the door splintered under the assault.

Kyote took Rolde by the collar and forced him to meet his gaze. "How many? What're they packin'? Any sign of the local law?"

The rapid-fire questioning caused Rolde to sputter nervously for a moment.

"Uh… that I could see, two dead and another five, all armed with submachine guns. Actually, uh, make that three dead. The guy who drove the motorcraft into the front gate died in the crash." At this, Rolde's gaze fell downcast to his right. Kyote didn't have to ask what his friend was thinking. Rolde might have ended up the same way if he'd successfully hotwired the neighbor's vehicle.

"And the—"

"No one but us and them. Port Nym's finest ain't made a peep. Maybe they're waiting for the fighting to be over before they stick their nose into it."

Kyote grunted. *Maybe they've been paid to look the other way.*

Flynn barged out of Pourrie's office and pulled the door shut with a quick tug of his free hand. Tucked under the other arm was the recently-acquired crate. Without comment, he forced it into Rolde's hands. Just as he was about to speak, a crash of broken glass rang out from one of the downstairs rooms. This noise was followed by yelling as the men entered through the damaged window.

"They've given up on bashing in the front door, I see," Kyote dryly noted before he turned to Flynn. "So, you got anything in mind? Running from a fight doesn't seem possible at this point. Stairs dump us into the foyer and right into their laps. Unless you want to try and jump from a second-story window. It's survivable. Trust me on this." A memory of being ejected from the tower of Gran'palacio Imperial as it exploded around him flashed in Kyote's mind. "Worst case, maybe you roll an ankle or break your leg."

Flynn shook his head. He'd already settled on a plan. "We defend the top of the steps. There's just enough room that you and I can create a choke point. Backs to the wall or the furniture." He pointed to a mahogany cabinet on the other side of the landing. "Use it to our advantage."

Kyote shrugged. While not complex, it was the best strategy they could produce. While they wouldn't have the benefit of numbers, they held the higher ground.

"And me?" Rolde inquired as he looked down at the wooden box. He was curious about the radiant warmth that throbbed from within.

"Stay here and watch our backs. Hold onto the Eye." There was only enough room for Kyote and himself on the second story landing. The banister and nearby furnishings provided barely enough cover for two. A third body would cause problems. While Flynn wasn't the best with a gun, Rolde was an even worse marksman. During the war, his skills as a medic had offset any deficiencies that might have made him a liability.

"Okay." After a pause, Rolde looked at the recently-closed door. "And Pourrie?"

"He isn't going to give you any trouble," Flynn noted as he withdrew his pistol. "Last I saw, he was cowering under his desk, hoping that either us or our new friends would leave him alive. Might have even locked the door behind us."

"He better hope *we* win this fight, then," Kyote added.

Without further comment, Flynn moved into position and gazed down to the first-floor landing. After a silent exchange with Rolde, Kyote did likewise.

Flynn pressed against the nearby wall and waited pensively. On the opposite side of the stairs, Kyote paused to take a few deep breaths against a waist-high cabinet. He'd drawn two pistols and held one in each hand. Flynn looked at the second gun.

Pourrie. It's Pourrie's. He snorted sardonically to himself. *Completely forgot about Kyote taking it off him. Well, at least he won't shoot us in the back with it. That... that would have been fitting with how everything's gone down tonight.*

When heavy footfalls stomped across one of the southern rooms, Flynn checked his firearm, ensuring that the safety was off and that the first round was chambered.

He held back as the first man charged into the foyer. As the well-dressed Tirean skidded to a stop at the bottom of the steps, Flynn recognized him as his tail.

When a second assailant joined him, they began to march up the steps. Kyote popped out and fired off two rounds, neither of which hit their mark. One whizzed past the Tirean's head while the other knocked a chunk out of the bottom tread.

The men fired salvos in response. Bullets perforated the back wall as Kyote dropped back behind cover.

At this, the new arrivals scrambled for cover. The other three men hastily scurried into hiding behind open doors and the corner of the adjacent hallway.

During the frenzy, one man shouted to his allies in a tongue that Flynn immediately recognized as Tirean. While he wasn't fluent, he identified the syllable clusters and the rapid-fire way in which the language was spoken. Was it possible that members of organized crime in Tir were interested in the Eye? If so, was it even safe for Flynn to transport? Or, more importantly, relinquish to Wallowrich? Maybe it wasn't the Eye, but something else Pourrie owned. Perhaps they merely wanted Pourrie for questioning.

No, don't do this, Flynn admonished himself. *Don't start imagining this is deeper than it might be. They're probably mercenaries, just like you are. Hired by someone who also wanted the Eye. Someone who didn't mind if a lot of people died to get it. If you start thinking these guys are part of something bigger, you'll never stop looking over your shoulder. Just get out of here alive, hand the Eye to Wallowrich, and be done with all this.*

Flynn overheard another man call out in Common.

"Watch out for more! There should be three of them!"

Soon, the attackers opened fire. As they did, Flynn squeezed off a few rounds of his own, none of which did anything but call their attention to him. Return fire sent a scattering of plaster into the air. A chunk glanced off of his cheek, leaving a small gash just below his eye. Flynn dabbed at the trickle of blood.

As he rubbed at the scrape, Flynn felt a short flare of anger. He fired a couple of poorly-aimed shots. A barrage peppered the nearby wall in response. One slug punched through a framed print, shattering the glass.

The fight devolved into a chaotic back-and-forth that only wasted ammo and wrecked the house's interior.

Kyote was frustrated. The longer the fight, the worse their odds.

Bullets pelted the wooden furniture behind him. The impacts vibrated against his spine. A portion of the cabinet exploded into a spray of splinters. Kyote recoiled as he shut his eyes tightly. A few slivers lodged in his hair and beard.

Son of a bitch. Automatics eating up the hardwood like it's nothing. What little advantage we had isn't gonna last, especially if they've got a few extra mags. At least they ain't got grenades. Small comfort, I guess.

He glanced at Flynn, who was pressed against his own quickly-deteriorating cover. Flynn's eyes were rolled upwards, as though he was looking into his brain for a plan. Kyote hoped he felt like sharing one soon. Their situation was not improving.

Behind Flynn, Rolde huddled against the entrance to Pourrie's office with the crate clutched tightly in his grasp. From time to time, he nervously glanced over his shoulder, as if someone might come down the stairwell at the far end of the hall.

When Kyote returned his gaze to Flynn, the two men's eyes locked.

"You got anything in mind?" Kyote asked as ammo punched through part of the nearby banister. " 'cause I don't know how much longer Pourrie's furniture's gonna hold out."

Before Flynn could respond, a voice called out from below.

"Charge them, you idiots!" one of the men bellowed angrily, attempting to take command of the battle. At this order, a group of attackers rushed out and fired at the top of the staircase.

"Forget I asked," Kyote muttered. *I guess they're feeling the need to be on their way as well. Pressed for time, what with fighting Pourrie's men in the yard. I figure they thought they could waltz right in. I bet they're pissed that we ruined what should be easy pickings by now. Feeling the need to hurry it up.*

Kyote ducked down as another attack pounded at his cover, sparking irrational anger.

At first, his bloodlust was a tiny voice that begged him to drop all civility, to throw himself into the fray with wild abandon. The whisper clawed its way to the forefront, overriding his conscious thoughts. At some point, Port Nym's constables would come to the mansion. When they did, he didn't want to be around to explain what had transpired. He knew he could put an end to this, before they ran out of ammo, if only he would unleash the wild part of himself.

Aw, fuck it…

Kyote curled as the muscles along his back and shoulders constricted. His peripheral vision blurred and he heard his heartbeat pounding loudly in his ears. Short, rapid breaths blew out through his nose as a flare of orange lit up his irises. In seconds, the rational part of his mind receded, as the feral thing that reveled in the thrill of battle came forward. Now, all that mattered was that someone was shooting at him.

As he looked up, he spotted Flynn, who had pressed himself against the nearby wall. With his distorted eyesight, Kyote saw his ally as a hazy blur, amber light haloing the man's silhouette. Kyote knew not to lash out. Flynn had the right light; he was not the enemy.

Not when five men below them glowed red. They were noisy and filled with violence and he needed to silence them.

Tearing a feral howl from his gut, Kyote rose from his crouched position. As the bellowing roar echoed, some of the combatants recoiled. He loped like a beast towards the stairs.

As he leapt from the top step, Kyote fired down on the men. Some scattered for cover to avoid the hail of gunfire. Out of the dozen shots, only two struck their mark—one hit a man squarely in the throat while a second grazed another's leg. The first body dropped to the ground, grasping futility at the gushing wound and gurgling a few final breaths.

Even as they clumsily clambered out of the way, some came to their senses and struggled to return fire.

Still midair as he flew downwards, Kyote didn't flinch when a bullet perforated his abdomen. Blood misted the air as the slug punched clean through. A second round struck him on the leg, just below his knee. Muscle fibers tore as lead glanced off the bone. At that moment, the injuries stopped him no more than insect bites.

One of his attackers stood dumbstruck at the first step, gun held impotently at his waist. Kyote slammed into him with such force that both men were thrown to the ground. Tangled together for a brief moment, the two men bounced off of the floor as they tumbled backward. Kyote drove the back of his fist into the man's head, knocking him unconscious with the blow.

Kyote dropped the empty pistols and quickly went for the man's machine gun, which had bounced a meter away. The remaining men kept shooting, continuing to poke holes in the surrounding flooring.

With their attentions aimed at Kyote, the assailants were unprepared as Flynn stepped out from cover and unloaded on them. Two hits to the torso dropped one man; he fell lifelessly to the ground with a bloody grunt.

Joy lit up Kyote's face as he collected the weapon and flipped over onto his back. This put him facing one gunman who'd taken shelter in the nearby corridor. As the firearm jerked in his hands, Kyote shot a spurt of lead that arced upwards. Rounds punctured the assailant; as his body fell over, a dull groan escaped as the wind was pushed from his lungs. Another four bullets slammed into the ceiling and made stucco rain down.

Even as the dead man slumped lifelessly, Kyote flipped about. Though faint echoes of pain pulsed from his injuries, he was too into the moment to care. The surge of fury muted everything else. He could hear the movements of one more foe in the doorway to the dining room.

To Kyote, the next events played out in slow motion. He could see the man's every stride. He saw the face tighten as he shifted his weight and raised his weapon to fire on Kyote.

He said something that Kyote heard as a blur of incoherent mumbles.

Kyote rolled to the side and attempted to get his feet under him. Unable to stand on his compromised leg, Kyote wavered as he leveled the machine gun at the last man. A squeeze of the trigger sent a poorly-aimed spray. Still, three rounds peppered the assailant's chest, enough to turn the man into a fast-dying heap. The dead man's weapon skipped across the floor, coming to rest against the foot of the nearby grandfather's clock.

Moments passed in sudden silence.

Kyote stood in the foyer, hunched over, as he took quick, panting breaths of the cordite-rich air. Though blood leaked from both of his wounds, he paid them little mind.

After a few seconds, he let out a deep sigh, and his shoulders slumped. Now that his work was complete, the fury that had overtaken him quickly evaporated. As the sensation of pain, previously numbed by the animalistic rage, finally reached him, Kyote's stance faltered. His leg buckled, and he slumped down onto his knees. A hand went to his stomach and pressed at the open wound.

"Well, shit…" he groaned as the orange in his eyes flickered off. Now deep brown irises floated on bloodshot sclera. The rush of incoming stimuli and the overwhelming agony caused him to curl up tightly. Though he wanted to scream, he no longer had the energy to do so. What stamina remained would be utilized by his body for a healing process that automatically worked on his injuries.

With Rolde on his heels, Flynn charged down the steps to assess their situation. Blood and spent casings were everywhere. The walls were riddled with holes. He quickly counted five men down, probably dead. If Rolde's appraisal had been accurate, there wouldn't be any more with whom to deal. Still, Flynn cocked his head and listened for a moment.

Except for the roar of the throng partying a few blocks away, there was nothing to hear. The neighborhood itself was deathly still. Now that gunfire had ended, Flynn wondered how long that would last. They needed to be gone. He would have to be quick if he wanted to find evidence of who had sent the machinegun-toting crew. All he knew right then and there was that some of the men were Tirean and that they'd been trailing him.

Flynn saw Rolde kneeling beside Kyote. The medic didn't appear to be concerned about Kyote's wounds.

Flynn quickly went down on one knee and patted down the nearest body. Moving quickly, he rummaged through the pockets, only to find a few coins and a key. He cast these aside and moved on to the next man.

"What are you doing?" Rolde inquired as he looked up. Kyote rested against the bottom steps. Though still bleeding, Kyote was already on the mend. Rolde had seen the after-effects of his fury before. With or without injuries, the rage took a toll on his body left him exhausted. Kyote's eyes glimmered amber as his recuperative gift did its work. The wound in his leg began to slowly close, as if the injury was occurring in reverse.

Rolde set down the crate and began to examine Kyote's gut. With a finger, he poked the hole that had been punched through his dirtied shirt. For a second, he considered applying pressure, but stopped short. In spite of his training, he knew that it was best to let Kyote's body do the work.

"Trying to see if any of these guys have some form of ID," Flynn noted as he moved onto the third. "I'd like to have some kind of idea where they came from. Who sent them. If only so that we can steer clear of them in the future."

"Oh," Rolde said as Flynn's reasoning eventually sunk in. "Find anything, then?"

"Unfortunately, no." Just as he was about to move on,

Flynn noticed a lump underneath the supine man's shirt, just below his throat. He uncovered a gold cord hung around his neck. Attached at the middle was a small carving that fit comfortably in his palm. The onyx idol was of a footless, blindfolded woman. Held against her chest in her left hand was a closed book.

Flynn tugged at the well-crafted icon until the chain snapped and coiled to the ground like a dead snake. He brought it up close to his face.

"What'd you find?" Rolde inquired. Though the stomach wound seemed worse than the leg injury, it too appeared to be closing. If they waited long enough, Kyote's injuries might be completely healed before they departed.

"Not… not entirely sure. Something to look into later," Flynn muttered, putting the miniature statue in his pocket. Something about the item was important, but the information felt just out of reach. With the madness that had been their evening, Flynn excused himself for being unable to recall the symbol's meaning.

After examining the other bodies, Flynn realized that he wasn't going to unearth anything of value. Except for the necklace, it appeared that none of them kept anything personal on them. This caused a knot to form in his stomach.

Though the lack of information made him uneasy, Flynn turned back to Rolde.

"So, uh," Rolde started as he glanced up the staircase. "What do we, uh, *do* with Pourrie?"

This gave Flynn pause. It was a good question, the answer to which had changed in Flynn's mind since their arrival. Pourrie could identify them. They'd left a lasting impression on the man who was, hopefully, still hidden in his office. Flynn had to hope that fear motivated Pourrie more than anything else.

"We... we let him go." It felt like the right option.

"Say *what?*"

"He's gonna run," Kyote feebly noted as he struggled to sit upright. His arms were weak, and more than once he teetered. Though exhausted, he'd finally recovered his wits. A mixture of emotions played on his face, everything between delight and regret. Pain and discomfort showed in the corners of his eyes and his tightly-clenched jaw. "Look at this place. His own men are wiped out, and two different sets of guys came here. We came for the Eye. Them? Who knows? Maybe he's got other shit up there worth taking. Maybe he owes money. He ain't sticking around. He's… uh, he's gonna pack up what he can and get outta town."

"Exactly," Flynn added. "Right here and now, he doesn't have a protection detail. Even so, they didn't exactly hold these guys off, and the property's outer wall is probably a mess. Not exactly the stronghold he expected it to be. He was scared shitless when we ran into him, and that was before the fighting made a mess of his home. If Port Nym's law enforcement agency doesn't get a hold of him for questioning beforehand, he'll disappear. Probably hope to hide somewhere else, before he's tracked down again. Though…" Flynn trailed off as he considered something.

"Flynn?" Rolde inquired as he looked into Flynn's pensive features.

"The Eye. Maybe, he thought someone would come for it. Maybe he has something else. He may just owe money to someone."

"Whether he does or not…" Kyote mumbled, struggling to keep himself conscious.

"Doesn't really matter at this point," Flynn finished. "Not for us, at least." He turned to Rolde as he motioned to Kyote. "Is he able to…"

"He'll need help."

Flynn held out a hand and beckoned to Rolde. "Give me the Eye. You take Kyote and get him out of here through the back gate. It *should* still be unlocked. I'll cover our retreat."

Rolde quickly handed over the crate and then slipped an arm around Kyote's back. After hooking a hand under his armpit, he lifted the man to his feet. Though Kyote was heavy, he had enough strength to help lighten Rolde's load. Once both were up off the floor, they began to lurch back through the house.

Flynn listened to the sounds of the city around them. The neighboring ward remained strangely silent, as if the occupants of the East Grove were in hiding.

Still no sign of Port Nym's finest, he thought to himself. Local law enforcement might have been too tied up with the crowds downtown to react to the gunfight. Flynn hoped that this was the case. He quickly dismissed more fanciful suspicions that the constables were paid to stay away.

When he heard the back door open, Flynn knew it was time to leave. As he headed for the laundry room, he heard footsteps upstairs.

Chapter 13

The Seventh of Shumond
The Marecale Valley

For a short while, fortune appeared to be on their side. The trio fled Pourrie's estate without further complications. After the noisy, violent chaos of combat, the silence that they left in their wake was eerie.

After a short stop to recover their gear, Flynn rejoined his allies as they hurried away from the scene. In the deep shadows of the adjacent alley, they trudged northward. Though he followed Rolde, who managed to keep Kyote upright and moving forward, Flynn's attention was split between his course and the surrounding ward. A dog howled from two blocks over. Nervous clatter escalated as neighbors, hopeful that the firefight had ended, ran out onto their lawns to investigate.

Even though they moved at a slow pace through the backstreets, they were out of the East Grove before the first of many constables turned up. Flynn paid particular notice as a fleet of motorcraft delivered a squad of uniformed men who promptly cordoned off the crime scene. It would be almost an hour before the trio stopped for a rest; a local greengrocer's fenced-in back lot served as a hiding place while they recuperated. Though exhausted, Kyote was eventually able to continue under his own power.

They avoided the most crowded of the night's festivities,

which gradually came to an end as the morning sun peeked over the eastern horizon. At the northern coach station, Flynn paid the transit fare for three to a ticketeer who was barely awake. Before long, they were on the first carriage out of town.

It wasn't until they were seated in the stagecoach, heading north to Chancel by way of Thelleerd'eth, that Flynn could finally relax. With Port Nym shrinking in their rearview by the second, he grew increasingly confident. Whether the VMF would find out about their activities was an issue for another day. Right now, the trio could enjoy a well-earned rest, even if only for a short while.

As the morning skies lightened, Flynn took note of the coming storm. The southern horizon met a wall of grey clouds that promised heavy rains later in the day. Flynn wondered if the impending squall would put a damper on Port Nym's festival finale. At least it would lessen some of the pervasive stench of debauchery from the carnival city.

Once he felt sure that they were safely away, Flynn's muscles slackened, and he slumped into his seat. A long, drawn-out breath whistled through his pursed lips. His thoughts returned to the previous night's events. There was a fair bit there he needed to sort through.

While their mission was technically complete and the Eye was in their possession, Flynn was dissatisfied. Bodies littered Pourrie's property. Pourrie himself could identify both Kyote and Flynn; perhaps he could pick out Rolde by the sound of his voice. Though they slipped under cover of night, there was always the chance that a neighbor, one who'd regained a modicum of bravery after the worst of the shooting was over, spotted them as they departed.

Flynn replayed their time in Port Nym in his head multiple times, trying to pinpoint the moment when everything went wrong. As he did, something he had overheard stuck out. It hadn't set off alarms in his head at the time because they were in a life or death situation.

"Watch out for more! There should be three of them!"

How was it that their opponents knew that? By the time the first man had reached the steps, Rolde was out of sight, hidden beside the door to Pourrie's office. In fact, at no point in time did the trio enter or leave the house together.

Flynn attempted to think about it with a rational mind. He tried to lay out the facts, to trace where and when they'd been compromised. That he knew of, their opponents—he wanted to think of them collectively as Tireans, but in truth only a handful were natives of Tir—attempted to follow him once. It was possible that he'd not seen earlier efforts. The fact that they stated Flynn was part of a trio hinted at previous reconnaissance.

How long had the third party been casing Pourrie? Did Kyote's rash action influence their plans?

As he thought about Kelvin's kidnapping, Flynn glanced at Kyote, who shifted about uncomfortably in his seat. His pallor showed that he was still on the mend. If history was any indication, however, Flynn figured the bloodshot glaze in Kyote's eyes would fade before the day was out.

To his side sat Rolde, who'd spent most of their exodus staring languidly out the window as the world passed them by. Noticing his compatriot, Rolde's countenance brightened.

"You feeling better?" Rolde inquired of Kyote, who was still rubbing the sleep from his eyes.

"A bit of pain and what's left of a migraine in the front of my brain," Kyote replied after clearing his throat. "But, I'll be okay. Not the worst I've felt before. Not by a long shot."

Rolde nodded knowingly. He'd been front row center when Kyote took a grenade blast during the war. He'd heard about what happened at Gran'palacio Imperial. He blurted out the question that came to mind.

"Man, I gotta know, but… can you even die?"

This elicited a sardonic laugh. "Dunno. Never tried. I imagine that's something I'll figure out when I get there. Not sure how far across the line I can get before I don't come back."

"Yet you keep trying, right? Did you ever consider… oh, I don't know… maybe dodging some of the bullets? Or at least not throwing yourself into the mix like a madman."

Kyote let out a chuckle as his head rolled limply back and forth. "Now you're just making shit up. Like I could *dodge* bullets."

"You could try to not get shot," Flynn suggested without looking up from the papers in his lap. This comment drew the attention of both men. Kyote's brow furrowed deeply as his jaw set.

"You really think I got the presence of mind to consider that when I'm… well, you know." Kyote quickly turned away.

Flynn understood, and had struggled in his own way. His gift, one he almost entirely refused to employ, came with a similar downside. Trapped and alone during the attack on Fort Biaa, he'd used his own fury to slaughter a squad of soldiers with horrifying results. Once unleashed, his version of what he termed "the gifted's bloodlust" made Flynn strike down an unarmed man, despite the general's efforts to surrender. He swore to himself he would never lose control like that again.

After a few seconds, Flynn replied. "Fair enough."

The trio fell into silence for a while. Flynn dug into his pack and unearthed some a book. He folded up the papers and replaced them inside a pocket. Kyote leaned his head back and closed his eyes.

Just as the rumble of the coach eased Kyote back into

slumber, Rolde leaned over and spoke into his ear.

"Dude, are you… are you okay? Like, I notice that you've gotten a bit an edge to you lately. Fighting angry, ya know," Rolde commented. "You weren't like this during the war."

For a moment, it seemed like Kyote wasn't going to respond. Eventually, his eyes opened to slits.

"Well, maybe I wasn't so mad at the 'rehzan soldiers. I guess it was hard to be angry at them. They never did me any wrong, personally. Just doing their job. Just like us."

The scowl on his face hinted that Rolde didn't quite accept the answer. "But—"

"We were there, fighting them in their homeland. They had the right to raise their guns at us. The only time I was ever pissed was when that bastard Ceosan blew up his palace." Kyote's lips pressed together as his face scrunched tightly. "Even at Yehntze, I only got bloody because… well…"

He didn't have to say anything else. They both knew that Yehntze was the first time they'd lost one of the 12th in battle. If he hadn't given into the fury, more would have died.

"I'mma go back to sleep, now," he announced. Rolde frowned as he turned back to the window. The first flash of lightning arced across the sky.

The Eight of Shumond
Thelleerd'eth

Once past the northern tip where the Horans and Southern Hadley Mountains met, the carriage turned eastward on a direct course for Thelleerd'eth. The township in the central plains was a quaint trading post populated by around two thousand people.

Surrounding the central business sector, which ran the length of the village, were small collections of quaint homes, many of which were constructed from wood and red clay brick. There was a bucolic quality, hinting at a pervasively-conservative lifestyle and a quiet nightlife. Most visitors recognized the village's archaic atmosphere for what it was: Thelleerd'eth was frozen in time decades back while other parts of Verenigen marched towards modernization.

Just as the afternoon's sunlight began to fade in the west, the last northbound carriage rolled in to town. Worn out from their time on the road, the trio disembarked, headed for the nearby inn, and quickly booked lodgings for the night. Since they planned to be on their way in the morning, Flynn didn't require more than a decent meal and a place to rest. His allies, though, were in dire need of a drink or two.

Their room was a simple, functional space, with floral wallpaper and rustic furnishings. The drapes were solid sheets of green-dyed wool, and the bedding was dull and smelled of soap. The mattresses themselves creaked noisily under any weight. Too tired to care, Flynn only grunted before he settled into one of the upholstered chairs.

As he reached into his bag, he overheard the conversation between Kyote and Rolde. Soon, they would seek whatever passed for nightly entertainment in town. Though he kept it to himself, he knew they'd be hard-pressed to find more than a few libations. Thelleerd'eth didn't strike him as ribald in any way.

While Flynn scratched some notes on a piece of paper, Rolde approached the table and opened the wooden crate. This was more than Rolde's usual curiosity at play. There was a magnetic pull from its contents that seemed to beg for attention. Rolde brushed some of the straw aside, reached in and withdrew the Eye. As his skin touched the stone's exterior, Rolde shuddered as a small jolt ran through his body.

"It's surprisingly heavy," Rolde noted as he hefted the ore.

Kyote peered at the massive gemstone as Rolde held it aloft. Glints of color reflected off the surface as the lamplight passed through it.

"I guess I can see how it got its name," Kyote noted after a moment. When Rolde looked over his shoulder with a furrow in his brow, Kyote motioned for him to turn the Eye. "Look at it longways. When the light catches it *just* right…"

Rolde did as he asked. It took a few seconds of peering intently at the object for Rolde to see what Kyote meant. His eyes bulged as his mouth dropped open.

"Oh!" Rolde exclaimed.

Flynn continued. "Because of the oblong shape, the indentations look like an iris when you hold it like that."

"Yeah, we got it just fine, professor," Kyote muttered under his breath.

"So, what would you put in the holes?" Rolde inquired as he rotated it back and forth. "I mean, I assume they would put something in them. Maybe it's just for decoration."

"One would think other ores," Flynn stated matter-of-factly. This caused both Kyote and Rolde to cast odd glances his way. While imbued ores came out of the earth as raw gemstones, most were tooled and polished into oblong forms that typically fit into the palm of a man's hand. From the ones he'd seen, most rare ores could fit into the Eye's indentations.

"And what would that do?" Rolde eventually asked. "I mean, why would someone want to do that?"

"Haven't the faintest of ideas," Flynn replied. "Without knowing what the Eye itself does, I couldn't even begin to hazard a guess. And since I don't exactly own a rare ore, it's not like I could test it out." He paused for a moment before adding, "Probably someone at the Library could determine it once they have the time to examine it properly."

"It's for the best," Kyote grumbled. "Let people with the time and means check it out. As long as we get it back to Wallowrich in one piece, that's all that really matters for us." He then looked at Rolde and nodded once. "You ready?"

"Hunh? Oh, oh, yeah." Rolde turned to Flynn as he deposited the Eye on the tabletop. It wobbled back and forth before settling into place. "Well, we're gonna go out and… try to enjoy what the town has to offer," Rolde said to Flynn. As he did, Kyote rose and made for the room's exit. "You interested?"

Flynn shook his head almost instantly. "No, not really. You go on without me."

"No surprise," Kyote mumbled to himself.

At this, Flynn looked over his shoulder. "One of us should stay here with the Eye, just to make sure no one, well…" While it could be paranoia, Flynn wanted to be safe. Port Nym had left him feeling unsettled. "Just try to keep from attracting too much attention. We—"

"Yeah, yeah," Rolde interrupted as he patted Flynn on the shoulder. "We got it. Don't pick no fights. Don't get the local law interested in what we're doing."

"We'll try not to kill anyone," Kyote sardonically commented as he flung the door aside and charged outside.

Though Flynn wanted to lob a barbed comment back, he swallowed it. Both he and Kyote were low on patience and had been since leaving Port Nym. Tired and harried from the attack, they'd both been in a foul mood. They needed to settle their nerves. Perhaps when this was all over, they'd take some time apart from each other.

Even as he focused on his research, Flynn felt something pull at his attention. At first, it was like a nagging itch somewhere between the back of his eyes and the base of his skull. The more he struggled to ignore it, the more insistent it became.

The shaking that had started in his hands became increasingly pronounced. The pen rattled in the tight grip of his fingertips.

He tried to press on with his reading and focused on the dense passage before him. The words made no sense. He tried again.

He swore to himself and slammed his palm against the open tome.

"Gods damn it," he seethed through clenched teeth.

Flynn looked up from his books and glanced at the Eye, which still rested on the nearby table. Rolde had not returned it to the crate. On the other side of the stone was a lamp, whose amber glow provided the only light in the room. Though his thoughts were on the recent tension and his inability to concentrate, he was surprised by what he saw.

The oversized ore sat at such an angle that he could peer into it longways. As the light shone through it, he spied a pattern within. Etched inside was a tightly-wound spiral that grew in width exponentially until it reached the outer surface. Flynn doubted it was a natural formation since the coiled carving was so perfectly made, yet he hadn't seen any manmade artifacts with that level of workmanship before.

Flynn rose from his seat and leaned in close. The carved motif was not impressed on the exterior itself.

He realized that he wasn't knowledgeable enough about ore lore to make any educated guesses. He would leave those concerns to whomever the Library dispatched to examine the Eye once it was in Wallowrich's collection.

Well, at least something good will come out of this.

As he continued to turn the Eye over in his hands, Flynn

noticed the same soothing sensation he had felt in Pourrie's office. His irritation washed away, and Flynn felt relieved.

In fact, all the concerns that nagged at him were just gone. He observed the ore warily as he held it out at arm's length. While he wouldn't consider it sinister, the way it beckoned and manipulated him felt intentional. Once he made physical contact, the Eye seemed all the more precious.

It wants to be held. Flynn shook his head. *No, that's foolish. That would be attributing sentience to an object.*

From his experience, all imbued ores contained some form of energy. Aeustes served as a consumable fuel source to light cities and power machinery. While it may have had other uses, iolide was deemed an excellent explosive, with an impressive detonation yield per gram. That he knew of, no one had attempted to determine iolide's viability as an energy resource. That was likely due to its volatility and the prevalence of aeustes. Though he knew very little about the specific artifact, O'mas had carried a bullet-deflecting ore with him during the war.

Flynn had little idea of what the Eye's uses might be. The comforting radiance combined with the subtle feeling that it demanded reverence caused Flynn to be suspicious.

Flynn felt an anxious flutter in his chest.

Though he struggled briefly, Flynn eventually replaced the Eye inside the crate and closed the lid. This seemed to muffle the ore's call. The fog that clouded his brain slowly lifted. As it did, he picked up the box and moved it to the far side of the room. He jammed it in the back corner and piled their luggage on top.

He returned to his seat and collected his reading.

Though he occasionally glanced back to where he'd left the Eye, Flynn felt he was himself again. At that moment, with his head clear, he desperately wanted to hand the Eye to Wallowrich so he could be free.

Chapter 14

The Fourteenth of Shumond
Norte'wald

As they continued their return trip, Flynn's nerves were frayed thin. This feeling was exacerbated by the pervasive tension between himself and Kyote, who'd only replied to Flynn's questions with sullen barbs.

The monotony of their trek did little to ease his mental fatigue. Each man fell into a routine. While Kyote often slept and Rolde watched the passing scenery through the carriage window, Flynn pored over his readings. In truth, this was for the best. Any conversation devolved into petty spats as frayed tempers got the best of the pair.

At every stop along the way, events played out the same way: Kyote and Rolde went off to entertain themselves with food and drink while Flynn was left to guard their prize. Flynn and Kyote spent very little time alone together.

To make matters worse, the Eye emitted a constant buzz that rattled in the back of his head, demanding Flynn's attention.

During the hours in which he was alone with the ore, Flynn struggled to resist its alluring aura. When all three men were together, the Eye seemed to sleep. Perhaps it wanted to wait until it was alone with him. Flynn wondered if the stone was somehow plotting against him. The idea that the ore knew when he was on his own struck him as particularly sinister. After mulling over such notions, he roundly dismissed them as paranoid, as the products of an overtired mind in need of rest.

Though Flynn briefly considered broaching the matter with his allies, he ultimately decided against it. There was nothing to be gained by raising a topic that might set already-threadbare nerves even further on edge. He knew that Kyote would question his sanity. Rolde might be more receptive, considering his curious nature. In the end, Flynn kept it to himself.

In truth, he hoped to maintain the status quo for as long as possible. He was grateful for the uneasy peace during the last leg of their trip and wanted to hold onto it for a few hours more. Once their delivery was complete, he expected to be done with this all. Hopefully, he'd never have to think about the Eye again.

When his thoughts turned to the future, Flynn knew that any long-term arrangement for the trio was out of the question. Wallowrich's mission had driven a wedge into the already-existing divide.

It wasn't hard to predict what awaited each of them. Kyote and Rolde would head for the nearest township to indulge their baser desires for a few days. They might disappear into the southern wards of Chancel, where they could stumble from bar to bar until they were out of coin. He, on the other hand, just wanted to travel back to Kit'abana, where he'd bury himself in research for as long as the staff would allow.

Besides their unraveling relationship, there was another reason to part ways. They'd certainly run afoul of some other group in Port Nym. Flynn figured it was best to lay low for a while. Though he kept watch on their surroundings as they continued the lengthy journey northward, Flynn saw no evidence that they were being followed. Still, once they handed over the Eye, he wanted some time and distance between himself and the events at Pourrie's mansion.

The closer they traveled toward Norte'wald, the more conflicted Flynn became. While he was anxious to be done with their job, ambivalence about his return caused his stomach to roil. He had no interest in seeing Stellan a second time. His mother's pearl brooch, still tucked into the bottom of his pack, was the only token he wanted from his parents' home. As horrible as the notion might sound if spoken aloud, Flynn would feel relief if he never had to see the man again.

Only once, as he dug around for some of Wallowrich's books, did Flynn's attention fall to the onyx idol he had pocketed. As he removed the tiny statue, which had hung around one of the attackers' necks, his thoughts turned to its meaning. It irritated Flynn that he couldn't place what the symbol represented. Though currently focused on their own mission, Flynn felt the need to understand its significance.

Maybe ask around once I've revisited the Library. Make some inquiries with who are far better educated on such things. Perhaps arrange a meeting with whoever's in charge of identifying historical iconography now. This feels like it has some kind of meaning to it.

He pushed it back beneath a bundle of unwashed clothes as he rooted about for something to distract him. Wallowrich's books struck him as tedious. Right now, he wanted to find comfort in the familiar.

It was midday on the fourteenth when their coach pushed through the final acre of dense forest and past the southern entrance of town. Very little was said as the trio disembarked and collected their gear. Tired from the venture, even gregarious Rolde had turned morose. There was no joy to be had here; their success had come at a cost.

Their return to Norte'wald was virtually ignored. This time, no one rushed out to greet them. The war hero was now an errand boy. No one stopped them as they left the station behind and marched through the center of town.

For Flynn, this was for the best. He didn't want to waste any more time in town than necessary. The sooner they delivered Wallowrich's prize and collected their pay, the better. Any comment to the locals could turn into fast-spreading gossip.

Once on the north side of town, they made a beeline for the path to Wallowrich's estate. As they trudged along the winding trail, Rolde glanced at the darkening skies on their left. Thick clouds promised rainfall. A brisk wind rolled across the waters of the North Sea and battered angrily against the cliffside. A haunting wail blew through the surrounding copses.

Wallowrich's lawn was still untended and wild, with tall grass that swayed in the breeze. Flynn glanced at the overgrown topiaries as he strolled along the main lane.

While he took all of this in, questions occurred to Flynn. *Why does Wallowrich stay here? It's clearly too much house for one man, and it's not like he's paying for additional staff beyond his manservant to keep up appearances. No one's working on upkeep for the exterior or the yard. How many rooms does he even use anymore? The kitchen, his bedroom, his office, and the one where he keeps his collection…* Most likely, Wallowrich stayed because he didn't care to move his precious curios. Beyond even his wellbeing, the man cared for his collectibles more than anything else. Flynn felt a pang of sorrow at this realization.

Flynn decided to abandon this line of thought. They were here to resolve their mission and get paid. He'd be relieved if they managed to accomplish that without further complications.

Flynn felt the first drops of the storm splatter on his scalp as he reached up and banged on the front door. Annoyed, he swatted at the wet patch of hair.

After a few seconds, Kyote moved in and hammered his knuckles on the entryway. A soft patter of rain began to beat on the path behind them.

"Man needs to hire himself a doorman," Kyote grumbled as he raised his hand. Just as he was about to pound on the wood yet again, the rattle of the handle caused him to stop.

The door opened slowly to reveal the face of Gohn, who paused for a moment to examine the visitors.

"Good day, gentlemen," Gohn spoke in a tone that revealed no emotion. His eyes subtly moved to the crate in Flynn's hands. "I see you've returned from your mission abroad. Successfully, I assume."

Flynn ignored the comment as he shifted the box from one arm to the other. Its weight felt increasingly unwieldy, like a burden he would soon be unable to bear. "Is Wallowrich in? We've come… well, you know why we're here."

"At this time, the master is in his office. He's been under the weather as of late, what with the change in the seasons, so you'll excuse him if he doesn't greet you with the same vigor as before. Please, do come in." With a sweep of his hand, Gohn directed them to the stairs at the other end of the hall.

"Thanks, pal," Kyote said with a nod as he and Rolde pushed past the manservant. With an elegant sidestep, Gohn swung out of their way.

Flynn lingered for a moment as he drew in a long breath. Though he was tired, the final leg of their trek was before him. All Flynn needed was enough strength to cross the hall, climb the steps, and march into Wallowrich's office. If the man was unwell, he'd be more likely to wrap up their business quickly.

Before he could step forward, Flynn found himself crowded by Gohn, who'd moved in uncomfortably close. The scent of talcum powder hung in the air around him. He cocked a single brow and glanced at the servant.

"I take it that package is intended for Mr. Wallowrich. The item he's been expecting, yes?" Gohn inquired before Flynn could comment on the virtues of personal space.

"Yes."

With hands extended toward him, Gohn offered to take the crate from Flynn. "If you wouldn't mind, I will relieve you of the ore. Mr. Wallowrich already has a place reserved in his collection for it. Considering his current health, I thought to arrange it for him so he could view it once you completed your business. I doubt his hands could properly set the piece. He hasn't gotten out of his chair all day today."

Flynn handed the box over and felt an immense wave of relief. Strangely, his body seemed lighter. A thin smile cracked his lips.

"Thanks," he said to Gohn before catching up with Rolde and Kyote.

Gohn replied with a faint smirk and a nod of his head.

Despite their haste, Flynn was able to catch up with the others before they'd ascended the stairs. It was there that he halted for a moment with a foot on the bottom step. There was a smell that he'd not noticed during their previous visit to the mansion. An odd aroma, that of black tea leaves, wafted past him. Though he didn't know Wallowrich intimately, he did know that the man preferred a stout cup of coffee over tea, a traditionally Tirean beverage.

Flynn shook his head and scaled the staircase with long strides. Norte'wald was not somewhere he wanted to linger; that they had to wait for the first stagecoach out of town the following morning was frustrating enough.

As they crossed Wallowrich's collection room, Flynn's pace

once again slowed. It wasn't the sound of rain on the floor-to-ceiling windows to his left that caught his attention. Though he'd been here many times during his youth, his memory of the room's current arrangement was hazy. When his gaze fell on an empty display case in the back corner, it took him only a few seconds to realize that one of Wallowrich's recent additions, the Cerulean Visage, had been removed. The glass door was ajar.

Maybe he wanted to look at it in his office, Flynn thought, though the odd feeling persisted. The Wallowrich he knew always commented that the artifacts were fragile, and he wanted to protect them from destruction. As he'd said before on many occasions during Flynn's youth: time was already enough of an enemy.

Kyote cleared his throat pointedly.

"You coming? Or, you wanna piss away more time gawkin' at his collection? You got all the time in the world to dick around once we're done," Kyote hailed from the back door, where he and Rolde waited. When Flynn met his piercing gaze, Kyote added, "I figure it's best if you go in first. You speak the man's language. I doubt he cares to talk with the labor."

Flynn offered a pained grimace as he joined them.

"Hey, wait a minute, where's the Eye?" Rolde glanced at Flynn's empty hands.

"Handed it over to Gohn. He offered to place it in the collection for Wallowrich." Flynn gazed over his shoulder, only to discover that they were alone in the room. *Guess he'll be along in a moment. Even if he is unwell, I imagine Wallowrich will want to see what his coin purchased.*

"To-daaaay…" Kyote growled with his hand on the knob. This drew Flynn's attention back to the entrance to Wallowrich's office. After Flynn turned back around, Kyote opened the door and stepped aside. With a wave, he motioned for Flynn to enter before them.

Though irritated, Flynn did. As he slipped past them, he announced their arrival.

"Mr. Wallowrich, it's Flynn. Flynn Earrele…" He shot a sideways glance to Kyote. "…and his associates. We've returned from Port Nym bearing gifts." He let out a hollow chuckle. "We've returned with the Eye. Your man, Gohn, said you were feeling under the weather, so we…"

He trailed off as he spotted the body slumped in the desk chair. At first, it seemed that Wallowrich was asleep, but the man's chest wasn't moving.

Flynn dashed across the room. He clumsily dropped his rucksack onto the desktop, which knocked a stack of papers to the floor. He leaned in checked Wallowrich for signs of life. When Flynn saw the pallor of his skin and the loose way his mouth hung open, any hope that Wallowrich could still be saved vanished.

Before Flynn's fingers could reach the man's plump throat, he saw the bloodstains coating the lower half of his vest. The dark velvet was discolored brown.

"Shit…" he swore under his breath.

"What? What's up?" Rolde inquired as he dropped his pack by the open doorway and moved in beside Flynn. When he noticed Wallowrich, he stopped short. "Is he—oh… oh, that ain't good. That's, well, that's fatal."

"Is he dead?" Kyote inquired from a few paces behind the pair. There was a sanguine odor, like that of raw meat, in the air. Someone had bled recently, a lot. His nose curled as he drew in another whiff.

"Uh, yeah," Rolde replied without looking back. "He's a bit more than under the weather, I think."

Flynn ignored the exchange and leaned in. With a fingertip, he opened up the thin slit in Wallowrich's shirt to reveal the wound. Though the weapon was nowhere in sight, Flynn assumed that the deep laceration just below his ribs had been the cause of death. He took a step back and glanced down, where a puddle of crimson fluid was still tacky.

Somewhere beyond the patter of rainfall on the roof and the rustling of tree limbs in the ever-increasing wind, Flynn heard the approach of hurried footfalls. The heels of dress shoes tapped loudly on the parquet. Someone was approaching the office, and in a hurry.

It must be Gohn coming, he thought as panic began to settle in. *If he sees this—*

It didn't surprise to Flynn when Gohn barged through the still-open doorway. He still clutched the Eye's crate. Gohn's gaze danced from one man to another. His eyes narrowed as he focused on Wallowrich's corpse.

"Oh my, what have you done to the master!?" Gohn was performing an emotion he clearly did not feel. Though he spoke loudly, he did so without real alarm. As the trio turned to face him, the manservant slowly backed away.

"Whoa, whoa, w-wait a moment," Flynn called out from where he stood. "We just found him like this." It felt as if acid boiled upwards from his stomach.

Flynn's gaze went to the box in Gohn's hands.

"I fear, gentlemen, that I must report you to the authorities," Gohn announced with what might have been joy on his taut face. "I'd ask that you wait for this to be properly sorted out, but even before you perpetrated *this…*" He motioned to Wallowrich's slumped form. "It had recently come to my attention that the three of you are wanted men. It is my duty, as a citizen, to see that you're arrested and brought to justice. Wallowrich's murder is only the most recent of your crimes."

Kyote snarled as he turned towards the servant. "What the bloody—"

"What are you on about?" Flynn interrupted as he stepped away from the desk.

"Well, have you not heard? Apparently, three armed men stormed the Pourrie estate in Port Nym, gunned down his men, and then killed him in cold blood. The VMF was provided a description of the perpetrators by some witnesses and are now awaiting them. That they would turn up in Norte'wald so soon after their attack is troublesome for the local citizenry. I doubt the town's constables will be able to detain such brutal murderers."

"That's not how it happened!" Rolde barked as he glanced at Kyote and then Flynn before returning his gaze to Gohn. "You're full of sh—"

"It's a set-up," Kyote announced with a grim sneer. He refused to look away from Gohn.

News travels fast, Flynn thought as he nodded in agreement. *Faster than should be possible.* "Well, at least we know who hired the goons that attacked the property," he eventually added.

"Why, whatever do you mean?" Gohn pretended to be shocked. His free hand went to his mouth. Then his shoulders slumped as he grinned. "I would like to take credit as if this was some masterstroke, but Wallowrich did me a kindness by hiring Mr. Earrele. Once I discovered he intended on extending the contract to three former soldiers who were unlicensed and still wet behind the ears, it was a matter of waiting until you made your move."

Kyote shifted his weight.

Without taking his eyes off the trio, Gohn retreated through the open doorway with unexpected speed.

"He's bolting!" Rolde cried out.

"No, he ain't." Kyote could hear multiple sets of feet on the distant stairs.

Without another word, Kyote dashed from the office. When Gohn moved deeper into Wallowrich's personal museum, Kyote was quick on his heels. Flynn and Rolde chased both men into the next room.

Instead of making a break for the exit, Gohn danced around, enjoying the game of cat and mouse. When Kyote attempted to get in close, Gohn would slip to the side and put a cabinet or display case between them. Even the entrance of Flynn and Rolde did not send him fleeing.

Instead, Gohn taunted them. "I'm afraid that in lieu of the local law—who I'm certain won't handle this situation to my satisfaction—that some associates of my own will have to deal with this unpleasant state of affairs."

"Ya know they're not gonna be able to hold us, right? Don't matter how many you brought with you," Kyote barked as he cut across the aisle. Gohn scampered backward, just out of his reach.

"They don't have to. It'll be far easier to turn over the murderers of Mr. Wallowrich when they are also dead. I'm certain that with a few inquiries to the VMF about your recent activities, it'll also be discovered that you were also connected to the deaths of Mr. Pourrie and his men."

"But Pourrie—"

Flynn held out a hand to cut Rolde off mid-sentence.

Gohn reached the double doors at the other end of the chamber. As he did, he glanced to each man.

Flynn attempted to look Gohn dead in his eyes, to divine the truth from the words he spoke. "You had him killed after we left, didn't you?"

Gohn's only reply was a thin smirk.

From behind Gohn, the doors opened, and four armed men poured into the chamber, as if on cue. These goons were dressed like the ones they fought in Port Nym had been; well-tailored black suits that hugged their muscular frames disguising their deadly purpose.

At the fore stood a barrel-chested man of Azzotian descent with a thick beard and an impressive cudgel made of wood and painted matte black. At his side was a raven-haired thug armed with a pair of knives that he waved back and forth, as if he was preparing to carve up the evening's roast.

The other two suited men brandished their own batons. When one of their jackets flapped open for a moment, Flynn spied a holstered firearm.

"Effee," Gohn addressed the bearded leader. "Please tend to our problem. I'll be heading onto the coach station. Meet me there when you're finished here."

Effee nodded.

Flynn's hand went to where his pack should have been. It still rested on Wallowrich's desk where he'd cast it aside. This was a problem, as his pistol was still tucked inside. Both Kyote and Rolde had also packed their firearms, hiding them beneath dirty laundry in case they were inspected by law enforcement during their journey.

Before he could do or say anything else, he saw Kyote crouch down.

"Of fucking course. I guess it's up to me to deal with this," Kyote swore. Without another word, he threw himself forward.

Chapter 15

The Fourteenth of Shumond
Norte'wald

At first, Kyote's charge caught their adversaries off guard. Perhaps they'd planned to toy with their opponents before the melee made a mess of the room. Instead, Gohn's men found themselves immediately under assault.

Shocked, all but Effee recoiled.

If his mind wasn't so busy devising ways to extricate themselves from the situation, Flynn might have chuckled. While Kyote's unpredictability had, on many previous occasions, irked him to no end, in this circumstance, it was their only strategy.

As Kyote closed the distance, another man regained his wits and stepped forward, intending to intercept Kyote with a blow of his knives. Shifting his upper torso as he ran, Kyote let his rucksack drop from his shoulder. When the strap landed in his open hand, he flung the pack directly into the approaching attacker's face. The impact caused him to stagger just long enough for Kyote to slip past him. His blades dropped to the floor and skidded to a halt, just out of reach beneath the nearby furniture.

Seeing this, Effee barked out terse orders as he hunched over and readied himself.

"Houn, take care of blondie. Rowe, you got doughboy.

Mattris and I'll deal with the wild man."

As the other two men set out toward Rolde and Flynn, who stood by the entrance to Wallowrich's office, Effee strode to meet Kyote's charge head-on. He brought his fists up like a well-trained pugilist.

Rather than evade the burly man's reach, Kyote lunged. Effee's broad arm struck Kyote across the shoulder. The impact sent him spinning into the nearby display case. Shattered glass rained to the floor as Kyote slammed into the base with a stunned grunt. Before he could recover, Effee closed in and began to whale on him. Kyote drove himself into the man's abdomen, knocking the wind from his lungs for a second.

As they tangled, Kyote's nose filled with the scent of black tea.

On the far side of the room, Flynn moved quickly to intercept Houn. The lean figure stepped tentatively towards Flynn. As he did, Flynn was formulating his plan. Out of the corner of his eye, he watched Rowe stalk Rolde.

While it wasn't the most intricate tactic, he knew he'd only get one shot for his gambit to work. He needed to distract Rowe, who slowly approached Rolde with his baton extended. Unlike Rolde, who was not much of a fighter, Flynn had some combat skills. On top of his Gendarmery training, martial arts made up a part of his Evisran studies.

Flynn hoped that hoped that his plan could both shield Rolde from combat and free him to chase Gohn, who'd already fled the immediate scene.

While Effee clutched his sore abdomen, Mattris launched himself at Kyote. Since Mattris' blades were lost earlier in the fight, he used gloved fists. After delivering a few blows to the ribs, he lifted Kyote off his feet and drove him into another case. Though the shattered glass and wood jabbed him in the back, Kyote clutched Mattris by his jacket. As he forced them backward, he yanked Mattris off his feet. The pair tumbled in a mass of limbs, flipping towards the north-facing windows.

As Kyote landed flat, he drove his knees firmly into Mattris' hips. This, coupled with his own momentum, threw the man through the windowpane with a violent crash. Large shards hit the floor with a nerve-wrenching clatter. One sliver slashed Kyote across the cheek. Another opened a long gash on Mattris' forearm.

Kyote scrambled to his feet and rushed headlong at Mattris before the man could recover. Though Effee moved in to cut him off, Kyote pulled Mattris up and slammed him against the balcony's banister. The heavy rainfall quickly plastered his hair to his bloodied face.

Before he could deliver a blow, Kyote felt a hand tug at the back of his jacket. As Effee yanked him off Mattris, Kyote flailed wildly. His balled fist missed Mattris' nose by centimeters. When Kyote swung his right leg, the toe of his boot caught Mattris under the rib cage. The impact lifted the man off of his feet. Mattris once again rammed into the railing and tottered precariously for a second.

Mattris' eyes bulged as his weight inevitably rolled backward. His hands grasped the empty air as his arms thrashed about. His fingers slid on the wet railing.

"Oh, shi—"

Mattris flipped over the balustrade. His grip held for only a second. As he dropped off of the mansion's second-story balcony, his words became a scream. Soon, he was silent.

"Oops," Kyote muttered, grinning.

Effee chucked Kyote out of the way and sprinted to the banister. When he saw that Mattris was gone, Effee turned back to Kyote, who was brushing water droplets from the shoulders of his jacket.

On the other side of the chamber, Flynn was embroiled in a struggle with Houn, who attempted to cut him off from the rest of the fight. As he bobbed just out of the man's reach, Flynn glanced at Rolde, who struggled to keep distance between himself and Rowe. Rolde's lip was already bloodied.

As he watched Rolde back down the adjacent aisle, Flynn knew he had to make his move.

Flynn predicted the courses of all four men as they danced about between the rows of curio cabinets. If he could time it so that Rolde's pursuer came toward him just as he was engaged with Houn, he could force them into each other.

As the seconds passed, Flynn could feel his pulse race.

When the countdown running in the back of his mind hit zero, Flynn came to a complete stop. He bobbed forward for a second to bait Houn. Already fired up, Houn responded. He swung his baton in a wide arc as he lunged. Flynn shifted his weight as the cudgel came towards him, arcing diagonally at his neck.

Flynn twisted as his hands shot out. He grabbed Houn's arm mid-swing, and pulled hard, dragging him off balance. With a sharp snap of his hips, Flynn yanked Houn around. Unable to remain upright, the attacker fell into the nearby cabinet. Houn toppled over the waist-high display into a heap at Rowe's feet. Rowe stumbled to a halt, gawking at the collapsed form of his ally.

"What the f—"

Rowe didn't notice Flynn until he leapt over the exhibit and kicked Rowe's legs from beneath him. Rowe screeched as he went face-first into the heap that was Houn.

Flynn glanced over his shoulder at Rolde.

"Go. Get after Gohn before he gets away," he ordered as he turned back. The pair was tangled up and too angry to unravel themselves properly.

It took Rolde a second to process his instructions, but then he nodded.

"Got it," he said as he scurried off.

Good, at least that's done. Now to—

Flynn's thoughts stopped as Rowe plowed into him with his shoulder. Full of rage, Rowe drove him hard into the counter. Briefly stunned, Flynn raised an arm as a pair of blows rained down on him.

In between grunts, Rowe swore under his breath. Flynn could tell the man was growing more reckless by the second.

After snarling through his clenched jaw, Rowe drove an elbow into Flynn's chest, forcing just enough space between the two men. Rowe dug into his jacket for the holstered pistol. Flynn sprung forward and went for his hands. He knew that he needed to overpower Rowe, right then and there.

Their struggle sent the knotted pair into a table lined with ancient nautical equipment. Though the impact jarred Flynn, he maintained his grasp. Rowe, on the other hand, lost his balance and stumbled.

Sensing the shift, Flynn sharply twisted Rowe's wrists, wrenching the weapon away from him. Rowe's ruddy face went pale as he fell backward. His brown eyes bulged as his gaze fell on the matte black pistol.

Flynn fumbled with the firearm for a second before he turned it on Rowe. Instinct took over, and his finger squeezed.

A few pops later, his assailant slumped to the ground, clutching at the bleeding holes in his abdomen. One round struck just below the ribcage on the right side.

Before he could even take a breath, Flynn looked around. It took only a second to locate Houn, who was just now getting to his feet. Houn reached inside his coat. At he did, Flynn leveled the gun at his head.

"No, no, no," Flynn called out in a tone that was as much a command as it was a warning. This caused Houn to stop mid-reach. "Don't go for it. You might live through this if you keep your head."

Seconds passed as Houn appeared to ponder his situation. As he did, Flynn's posture shifted. He brought a second hand up to stabilize his aim. When his feet moved into a firing stance, this forced Houn into compliance. He raised his arms and grinned sheepishly.

"Ya gots me, man," he spoke as his back straightened. "Dead ta rights. But, ya can't hold me here all day and ya know it."

"Don't plan on it," Flynn dryly replied as he moved in close.

"Izzat so? What you—"

Flynn whacked the side of Houn's head with the butt of the pistol. The first blow dazed Houn enough that his limbs wobbled. Though Houn fell to the floor, he was still conscious. Flynn leaned in and thumped him a second time.

"This'll hold you long enough for me," Flynn noted as he reached in, took Houn's weapon, and pitched it aside.

Flynn turned his attention to the north side of the room, where Kyote and Effee were locked in their violent conflict. Kyote's savage, chaotic fighting style was matched by Effee's sheer size and brute force.

Flynn wondered whether he should involve himself in the brawl, but decided against it. Their biggest concern was Gohn. Though he'd just dispatched Rolde to go after the man, he knew it was best to join the chase.

Flynn briefly caught Kyote's gaze. In that flicker of a moment, Kyote winked at him with a nod. Seeing this, Effee glanced over his shoulder.

While Effee was distracted, Kyote landed a right hook on his bearded jaw.

As Flynn charged out through the double doors, Effee countered with a blow that tossed Kyote back on his heels.

As he sprang out of the mansion, Rolde wasn't confident he could catch up with Gohn. The man had a lead of at least a couple of minutes. Rolde figured that, on a good day, Gohn could outrun him. Gohn had long legs, and Rolde was not exactly in the best shape. To make matters worse for Rolde, the relentless downpour reduced visibility. No matter how hard he squinted, he couldn't see the manservant. It seemed that Gohn was no longer on the property.

After drawing a long, resigned breath, Rolde scampered for the front gates. Once out from under the shelter of the porch's eaves, Rolde was instantly soaked by the driving torrent. With every stride, he felt his clothes growing heavier. Rolde reached up and brushed droplets from his brow.

It didn't take long for him to realize the futility of his effort. A stiff wind blew toward him, throwing even more moisture into his eyes.

"He's gonna get away 'cuz I can't see sh…" Rolde trailed off as he came over the nearby rise. Below him, Gohn sauntered as if he was enjoying a casual stroll. Tucked under one arm was the Eye's crate. Slung over the other shoulder was a weighty leather satchel.

"You gotta be shittin' me," Rolde muttered incredulously. Either the man was confident, crazy, or had no cares in the world.

It didn't really matter to Rolde.

"Hold up, you scrawny asshole," Rolde called out as he slid down the pathway after Gohn. The rain continued to pelt him as the muddy ground shifted beneath him. He was already struggling to breathe. If this chase lasted any longer, he'd run out of steam.

At first, it didn't seem as though Gohn heard him. He continued to stride along, seemingly indifferent to Rolde's approach. Rolde wondered if he could tackle Gohn before he even noticed his presence. Gohn tilted his head towards the satchel, listening to something inside.

Fine by me, Rolde thought. *I'll drop his ass all the same. Don't want to hit him too hard, though. He seems like he'd break—*

Suddenly, Gohn came to a sudden halt and spun around. Still charging forward, Rolde stumbled as he attempted to stop. His footing slipped, and he briefly lost his balance. Taking advantage of the opportunity, Gohn swung out an arm and drove his fist into Rolde's throat.

Rolde's eyes bulged as agony stole his breath for a moment. A sharp pain flared in his head, where it pinged across the base of his skull. His fingers immediately went to his esophagus. Rolde dropped to his knees.

"Appears you've slipped past my men, yet again. Once in Port Nym and here again. Let me rectify that."

With his free hand, Gohn reached in and lifted Rolde up off his feet. Shock and horror painted Rolde's features at the sheer improbability of the man's strength. Gohn manhandled Rolde like he was a child's doll.

Rolde tried to speak, but his words emerged as in a raspy croak.

With Rowe's pistol still in hand, Flynn sprinted from the house. Even if he had noticed a trail of footprints in the swiftly-eroding mud before him, he was far too intent on catching up to examine them. There was only one path from Wallowrich's mansion to town. Sure, someone could disappear into the forest if they were so inclined, but he hoped that Gohn wasn't the kind of man to do so.

The rain needled Flynn's face as he pushed through the half-open gate. A clap of thunder sounded overhead. The loud crack caused him to flinch.

Going to get struck by a bolt of lightning the way things have been going. Won't that beat all?

Flynn skidded to a stop at the top of the rise. The heels of his shoes dug into the sodden turf. Through the haze, he spotted Gohn, just as the man lifted Rolde off his feet. Rolde was not small by any metric, and Gohn was slender, almost gaunt. Flynn's heart skipped a beat.

Flynn realized that his friend was in serious danger. Rolde's feet dangled a few centimeters above the water-logged pathway. Rolde pawed in vain at Gohn's arm as he tried to pry the man's long fingers from his throat. He swung a boot forward to kick himself free, only for the blow to glance off Gohn's hip.

"Hey! Hey, you! Turn him loose!" Flynn yelled, but the angry storm drowned his words. When that failed to garner Gohn's attention, he raised the pistol and aimed it at the man's chest. Though Flynn doubted he could hit Gohn from this distance, a warning shot might startle him enough that he would release Rolde. At that moment, Flynn wished that he'd been more vigilant during his firearms training with the Gendarmery.

He squeezed the trigger, and the gun kicked in his hands. Moisture on his palm caused the weapon to slip in his grip. As he predicted, his aim was off, and the round flew past Gohn's shoulder. The man never flinched at the sound.

A second later, Gohn's head turned ever so slightly in Flynn's direction. Their eyes locked, and Gohn's grayish mouth smirked at him. As Flynn began to charge down the path with the gun still leveled at him, Gohn shifted his stance. For a moment, Flynn thought he intended to use Rolde as a human shield.

At seeing this, Flynn lowered the pistol. He'd have to convince Gohn to release Rolde.

Ready to negotiate, Flynn came to a stop. He held the firearm against his hip and pointed it at the ground. His mouth dropped open as the first words of his appeal formed.

Gohn did not speak, but he acted. With a single sweeping motion, Gohn tossed Rolde over the side of the cliff like a piece of trash.

"NOOOOO!" Flynn screeched in horror as he watched Gohn casually end man's life in what felt like slow motion. The sound of his scream could not cover Rolde's terrified shriek as he disappeared over the rocky edge and plummeted to the waters below.

Flynn whipped the pistol up suddenly. Before he could get a bead on Gohn, the man shifted to the side and flung the wooden crate at Flynn. The box smashed against his face with such force that Flynn staggered.

Flynn squeezed off a few errant shots as his free hand went to his head. He saw stars as the pain along the bridge of his nose and around his eyes briefly overwhelmed him.

Get it together, he told himself as he stumbled about for a moment. He could hear the splashes of footfalls near him on the sodden pathway. Though he knew Gohn was moving in on him, no amount of concentration would get Flynn's sight to comply. His visual field was a greyish blur with white flares that flickered back and forth. He swung the gun in the air and fired off another barrage. *Can't let him—*

A sweep across Flynn's knees knocked him over. He dropped with an inglorious grunt as the fall rattled him to the bone. When his right hand hit one of the stone pavers, his grip on the pistol faltered, and the weapon bounced out of his reach. His index finger pointed out at an odd angle.

As Flynn struggled to prop himself up, his eyesight slowly returned. He spotted Gohn's silhouette as the man picked up what remained of Pourrie's box. Packing straw stuck out from two shattered sides. He withdrew the Eye and tucked it under one arm before turning back to Flynn. Even with his compromised vision, Flynn could pick out the glowing mass of the oversized ore.

Before Flynn could even raise an arm in defense, Gohn ran towards him. Gohn raised the remnants of the crate and smashed them across Flynn's skull. A gash opened up along the top of his head, and blood streamed down from his scalp. Though dazed, Flynn was able to hold onto consciousness.

Flynn swatted at the surrounding pathway to locate the gun. When one of his muddied hands gripped the barrel, he pulled it closer. Flynn fired off another salvo, praying that he would at least drive Gohn off. Each recoil sent a shock of pain from his damaged hand up the length of his arm.

After the last round was fired, the gun clicked impotently. He swung it in the air for a moment, like a cudgel, but Flynn's body finally gave up. His head slapped backward into a puddle of dirty water. As he released the empty weapon, it skipped across the wet pavers.

As he sprawled helplessly on his back, Flynn listened for

any sign of Gohn. His limbs refused to respond to his mind's panicked directions.

Seconds passed as nothing happened. Though the pain in his head was overwhelming, Flynn's hearing was sharp. For a moment, all he heard was the howl of the wind and the rumble of distant thunder. He then heard the pitter-patter of Gohn's dress shoes on the wet stone-laid path.

Once these faded, Flynn knew he was alone.

Eventually, Flynn sat upright as he wiped the blood from his face. Even though his vision was still blurred, he could see the broken fragments of the crate strewn around him. He assumed that the spray of gunfire had finally driven Gohn away.

Probably had a carriage to catch, Flynn sardonically thought as he struggled to his feet. *Didn't think I was worth the couple seconds delay it would take to put me down after I ran out of bullets, I guess.*

His brain throbbed in his skull, and the driving wind and rain abraded his facial injuries. It took a few moments for him to remain upright because his legs kept wobbling. Flynn couldn't close the fingers of his right hand into a fist without a sizeable amount of discomfort.

Once he was able to walk, Flynn went to the cliff's edge and peered over at the darkened surf far below him. He knew what he'd find there, but he needed to look all the same.

At that moment, Flynn's heart broke. Like a glass ornament that had dropped to the floor, he could feel it falling apart and scattering. Gohn no longer seemed to matter. He slumped to his knees and gazed at the roiling waves as they violently beat against the rocky shore. While there was no sign of Rolde, this drop was not one that someone could survive. His body would be swallowed up, dragged out to deeper waters by the undertow.

Flynn didn't know how long he sat there. As it splattered

against his face, rain mingled with the tears as they slipped away from his eyes. The torrent pounded his bloodied scalp. His chest heaved in a herky-jerky manner, but otherwise, Flynn was motionless.

Despite his overwhelming shock and sorrow, Flynn willed himself to rise. He couldn't remain in this precarious position for too long, unless he wanted to join Rolde in the icy waters of the North Sea. Though his head spun, Flynn looked around. Gohn was completely out of sight. Apart from the broken box, all evidence of his presence had already washed away, hidden by the muddy puddles between the stone pavers.

Flynn had no desire to hunt Gohn. He was done with, not only this mission, but this whole way of life. Chasing Gohn had already cost Rolde his life. That Flynn had survived his own brief encounter with Gohn was a small miracle; he shuddered when he thought of Gohn's unnatural strength.

What about Kyote? Flynn glanced back up the hillside. He'd left him to handle the last of Gohn's men on his lonesome. The fight was likely over by now. Flynn had little doubt that the man had survived. A part of him figured Kyote would outlive them all.

After a few seconds spent staring at the waterlogged pathway, Flynn recovered the pistol and took off for Wallowrich's estate.

What had once been a place filled with pleasant memories was now a place of pain. Wallowrich was dead. The Eye was gone, and so was any possibility that they'd receive payment for their troubles. There was also a good chance that Flynn and Kyote were wanted by the VMF for, at the very least, questioning.

Rolde's death left him hollow on the inside. Flynn had to

force himself to march back through the storm to find Kyote. His head throbbed, and his eyes still struggled to focus. Once reloaded, Rowe's pistol might fend off any direct assaults, but he couldn't hit the broadside of a barn at any distance. If Gohn's men had somehow managed to subdue Kyote, Flynn doubted he'd be able to help.

Once inside, Flynn was relieved to be out of the rain. Though it had tapered off, the wind still blew with some force. Trees swayed as the last bands of the storm battered the coastline.

He noticed that a puddle collected around the still-open entrance. *No one will be here to tend to the damaged parquet.* With a flick of his hand, he brushed the water from his hair, casting a mist of bloody droplets to the floor around him.

Except for the noise of the gale outside, all was silent. There was no grunting, no yelling, and no smashing of glass or wood.

Kyote must be alive. He's too… resilient to die. Too much of a pain in the ass to die, even if they unloaded their pistols on him. And I didn't hear any gunfire. For the best, probably. It would only have served to piss him off. Whether he's in any condition to get out of here under his own power or not is another thing.

Climbing the stairs proved difficult. He felt like a doomed man. With each step, his feet grew more leaden.

Eventually, he returned to the scene of the battle. Many of the furnishings were damaged or beyond salvaging. Wallowrich's curios were now buried under piles of wood and glass. Somehow, an ancient bronze sextant had lodged in the wall, not a meter from the entrance. It took him a moment to find Kyote amidst the wreckage.

Kyote sat on a pile that had once been a waist-high cabinet. Though bloodied and bruised, he seemed otherwise no worse for wear. As he looked out the window, Kyote shifted anxiously. Although visibly injured, Kyote's eyes were bright and his color was normal.

"Kyote? Where are the rest of Gohn's men?" Flynn inquired as he lingered in the doorway. Water dripped from his drenched clothes and puddled around him. Though now was not the time, Flynn wanted to strip down and wring out the fabric.

At the sound of the familiar voice, Kyote rose to his feet. Without turning from the view, he brushed the seat of his pants.

"Dead or gone, I figure. One of them's back there, face down in a display cabinet." Kyote hooked a thumb over his left shoulder. "Jumped into the fight. I guess you didn't knock him out good enough." He then pointed at the smashed window a few paces on his right. "A second is either laid out on the lawn or somewhere at the bottom of the North Sea. Not really my concern. I saw two of them make a break for it. Big Red and one of the others. The guy you shot. Don't know if he'll live because that shit looked fatal." Kyote paused as he wiped the blood from his busted lip with the back of one hand.

As he looked around, Kyote's brow furrowed. "Hey, uh, are you okay? You've looked—wait a minute… uh, where's… where's Gohn? Did you catch that bastard? Don't tell me… Did Rolde… Wait. Wait a minute. Where the *fuck* is Rolde?"

Flynn's face tightened at the mere mention of Rolde's name. Even beneath the swollen bruises, Flynn grimaced at the answer he was about to give.

"Dead," Flynn replied coldly, trying to hide the sorrow he felt. He was still shocked to his core, hoping that his memory, rattled by the beating he'd received, was faulty and Rolde would come running in out of breath.

"*What?*" Kyote's eyes bulged.

"Gohn… Gohn, uh, tossed him off the cliff." Flynn muttered as his chin dipped into his chest.

Rage quickly consumed Kyote. His face flushed as he stormed over to where Flynn stood just inside the room. As his jaw clenched tightly, he grabbed Flynn by the shirt. Liquid seeped onto his fingers as it was wrung from the fabric. "And Gohn? Did you—"

"He got away," Flynn said as he batted Kyote's hand aside.

"You *let* him get away!" Kyote was seething. His words were a feral growl. Flynn recoiled from the hostility that roiled off of Kyote in waves.

"I was concerned… I ran to… I-I went to the cliffside to see if Rolde…" Flynn sputtered as his mind started to spin. His head hurt too much. He wanted to recount the events just as he'd witnessed them, but Kyote was too impatient. "I lost track of Gohn after—"

"We gotta go," Kyote snapped. "That bastard's gotta die. Ain't no other way about it."

Before Kyote could stomp out of the room, Flynn reached out with his broken hand and snagged him by the sleeve. The tug was enough to send a spike of sharp pain up his arm. Though he grimaced, Flynn attempted to hold on.

"Wait a damn minute. Rolde's fucking dead and all you care about is going after Gohn?"

Kyote shrugged him off. "Shouldn't you? What else is there to do? Ain't you wantin' a piece of them? Or don't you give a shit what they did to Rolde?"

Flynn raised an accusatory finger at Kyote.

"No. You don't get to do that. You don't get to pretend this—"

"Oh, fucking get down off your high horse, you righteous ass. You were never in this for anything more than the coin. Just go ahead and admit it."

Through clenched teeth, Flynn fumed. "What else was there? Glory? Good times? Your ENTIRE PITCH to me in Chancel was about earning enough coin to live comfortably. Wasn't that the point of it all? By all the gods, we're *mercenaries*. By our very nature, working for coin is what we do."

"This stopped being about the coin when they screwed. Us. Over! When they set us up like rank amateurs—"

"That's what we are, you dolt! That's exactly why we were hired. We were incompetent patsies that Gohn fully intended to set up using Wallowrich. From day one! That we didn't do him the favor of dying in Port Nym screwed up his original plan. Pretty certain that he didn't even think we'd turn back up. It's easy to blame anything on a dead scapegoat."

This enraged Kyote further. He began to pace back and forth, muttering under his breath. Kyote howled as he swung a balled fist into a cabinet's glass panel. Lacerations across his knuckles began to bleed as he retracted his hand and stomped past Flynn, who was more than willing to step aside. He no longer cared how this played out as long as it ended. If Kyote wanted to chase after Gohn, he could do so.

"Reason this all away with your talkie bullshit," Kyote continued. "We gotta go after them. Standing around here any longer running our mouths is just letting them get away. Try to convince yourself of whatever you got to do to drag your useless ass out that door, but this became about getting revenge. They gods damned killed one of our own! I want blood and I want it by the liter!"

"That's because violence is all you know."

Kyote spun about on his heel. Kyote's eyes burned as they bored into Flynn. There was a momentary flicker of orange around his irises. Before Kyote could respond, Flynn again leveled a finger at him.

"You're on your own, you madman," Flynn snapped,

waving a hand in the air. "You've already gotten Rolde killed. Your special little gift hasn't made the people around you impervious to harm. Being around you any longer is only going to end in my own death. If you had half a brain, you'd realize that we're fortunate to walk away from this now with the two of us alive. Go after Gohn if you have a death wish."

"What about Rolde, you chicken shit?! He don't mean dick to you?"

"No amount of killing is going to bring him back. Go after Gohn, then. See where that gets you. I won't be the next sacrifice on your altar of revenge."

"Oh, fuck you!" Kyote snarled as he stomped out of the room and down the steps. The heels of his boots pounded loudly on the wood. As he crossed the main hall, Kyote called out one last time. "Crawl in a hole and die, you fuckin' coward!"

Flynn bit his tongue. The anger he felt did nothing to ease the pain in his head. He paused and took a few soothing breaths as he balled up his uninjured hand and tried to squeeze the rage out of his system.

Eventually, his throbbing ire slowly ebbed. Once he was able to think with some clarity, Flynn became overwhelmed with feelings of regret. He'd lashed out and said things that no man should utter to his brother-in-arms. In a fit of temper, he pushed Kyote to chase after a dangerous man who was long gone. Even worse, he hadn't had the chance to warn him about Gohn's freakish strength.

He needed to stop Kyote before he got too far away.

Damn it all, he swore to himself. *I can't just let him run off like this.*

"Kyote, don't!" Flynn called as he rushed down the steps. He hurried to the front door, hoping he still might catch him.

"Gohn's already…"

Flynn sighed as his gaze passed across the storm-battered acreage. The rain had finally petered off, and faint slivers of the evening sky peeked through the dark cloud cover to the north. Kyote was nowhere to be seen.

"You're not going to catch him," he said aloud. Nothing could be more true.

As he leaned against the doorframe, his body went slack. Physically and emotionally drained, he slipped to the floor, and struggled against the overwhelming urge to cry. There was so much to process that he didn't know where to start. In the back of his head, beneath the noise of a possible concussion, reason advised him that he couldn't linger here.

Eventually, he collected himself and moved toward the second floor to gather his belongings. While he was there, he would grab Rolde's pack as well. Perhaps there were personal effects that he should return to Rolde's family, not that any possession would soften the bad news that Flynn had to deliver.

The last effects of adrenaline finally wore off. His face throbbed, and the swelling around his left eye threatened to close it. There was a sharp pain when he moved his right hand. It was likely more than just the finger had broken. From time to time, his vision blurred along the edges.

He returned to the room that was once Wallowrich's pride. Once there, something caught his notice. Amongst the wreckage were what remained of the collection of ores. Flynn immediately noticed two that could not have been more different: one was a brilliant green that seemed to generate its own radiance while the other was a matte obsidian that absorbed all the light around it.

Flynn brushed some broken glass aside and retrieved both. He cupped one in each hand and focused on the feel of the stones against his skin. There was a faint buzz from within them. He couldn't identify either stone, not without first recharging them and checking with the Library.

Flynn began to wonder why that, with all the time he had alone with Wallowrich, Gohn and his men had not stolen other artifacts. There were a fair number of rare and irreplaceable items in Wallowrich's collection that could fetch a reasonable price on the open market. Except for the Cerulean Visage, which he noticed missing earlier, it appeared that the only item Gohn took was the Eye.

A lot of priceless stuff is mostly just broken junk, now. What a shame.

He pocketed the ores before he left. Despite the lurch his stomach gave at the thought, they would have to serve as some sort of payment.

Interlude

The Twenty-eighth of Semmond
Vertegarte

Much to O'mas' relief, Cal Farber and his fellow craftsmen had performed their work admirably. Even though his specifications were nothing like those of the average home in Vertegarte, they'd executed his peculiar plans without question. Though he was aware of the Naturalism that the locals practiced, he had more practical needs for his place of retirement. That the builders had not openly disagreed with his designs for philosophical reasons was a pleasant turn of events.

O'mas' house was a modest three-room abode erected in the midst of the forest with only a dirt path connecting it to the village's outskirts. Except for the front door and the skylight in the back room, which served as office and living quarters, there were no other ways to enter the home. This was done to provide O'mas with privacy that even he knew bordered on paranoia.

In moments of honesty, he admitted to himself that this level of security was almost assuredly pointless. He suspected no one would come looking for him. Not even the recently-renamed VMF wanted anything to do with him. He was a relic of the Gendarmery, a clear reminder of the sacrifices they'd made to shorten the war. The Verenigen Congress and the VMF administration were now delivering a new message to the populace. They were looking forward to the future with the hope that everyone could quickly forget the past, and an aging spymaster was definitely a part of that past.

Even if someone did come to visit, O'mas doubted they'd find anything of worth. Except for a copy of personal files that he'd chosen to retain, there was nothing of value to which the VMF's Intelligence Division didn't already have access. He'd made sure to leave anything of note with his successors before signing his retirement papers.

Surprisingly, his retreat from the modern world had taken more effort than he'd initially expected. There were numerous discussions to be had and contracts to be finalized. When the last of his personal belongings were delivered to his new domicile, O'mas ended the lease to his apartment in Chancel. The only place outside the Vale with a ready bed for him was Ethvarth's residence in Port Hadley. It hurt O'mas not to visit his dear friend more often, but the proximity to Fort Granic made him uncomfortable.

O'mas' move had provided him with all the privacy and alone time that he could ever want. Not only was he hidden away in a place not many wished to visit, but he was considered an outsider by the locals. Except for the rare few, like Cal, the residents shied away from him as if he reeked of industrialism. He was okay with that.

The only drawback was that it left plenty of time for him to fret about unfinished matters. Without the constant distractions of tasks and missions, he filled many an hour considering the choices he had not made. Decisions he had made throughout his life now came back to haunt him. Because these feelings persisted as time passed, O'mas felt compelled to address one matter of unresolved business. The lack of resolution was a thorn in his side, one that consistently pricked when his mind wandered.

Part of his mission during the war had been to uncover the Grymore Foundation's involvement in the conflict. While he suspected that the industrialist, Etremaus Grymore, was peddling weapons and gear to the Moa'rehnzan government, he had no concrete proof. With the outcome of the conflict in Gran'rehnza already at its end, there was no hope of furthering his reconnaissance there. To make matters worse, the members of the High Council had been immediately taken into custody by the NDP resistance forces. Any information they had on the subject was well out of his reach. Jude Brandich, the lone councilman that the 12th captured, had been too new to the regime to know anything about deals between Ceosan and the Foundation.

His investigation was complicated by the fact that Etremaus Grymore had been reported lost at sea. After learning of Grymore's demise, O'mas had considered packing up the last of his files for good. The Grymore Foundation went into lockdown, meaning that there would be a review of its outstanding contracts and projects. It occurred to O'mas that, as soon as the elder Grymore's death was announced, those who knew anything of value would purge questionable data from the company's files.

O'mas hoped that the organization might evolve under new management. There had been an assumption, however brief, that with Etremaus gone, the Foundation's influence in Trone Stenan would wane. After a year of his son Zane's control of the company, this hope proved to be fleeting. In fact, from the leaks to which O'mas was privy, it sounded as if the Grymore heir took after his father.

This left O'mas conflicted. He was tired and wanted to be done with the outside world, to be left alone with his studies in a house without windows. Still, his need to see the matter to some kind of end dogged him.

While he had no desire to involve himself with the VMF, he had to find out just how dangerous the Grymore Foundation was. He'd never have a moment's peace if the unanswered questions rattled incessantly in the back of his mind.

His renewed investigation started with a few well-placed bribes that yielded information that could barely be classified as second-hand gossip. A stevedore in Eithos Los knew of a sailor who once worked for the Foundation. There was an administrator in Port Nym who'd rubberstamped a shipping manifest that was clearly forged. There were tiny crumbs of evidence scattered across the continent that would take years to collect. He would be painting a picture, one brushstroke at a time, for what might be the remainder of his life.

Now, without the burden of the Intelligence Division's day-to-day slog, he felt that he could invest his time. It would be a long game, one that realistically could take a decade before to bear fruit.

Of a more pressing matter was the need to bring order to his new home.

The final delivery from Chancel still sat on the floor of his office. Stacked two high in places, the wooden boxes were filled with the remnants of his previous life. The apartment in Chancel had not been a place where he rested for long. In fact, he was rarely stayed there for more than a month between trips.

As he examined the various crates, many of which were still packed full, O'mas let out a sigh. This was a daunting task, and he wasn't as spry as he'd used to be. Still, the work was not going to perform itself. A home that looked like a warehouse was not what he had planned.

He opened the first container and began to remove its contents. One by one, he sorted his possessions as he moved them to their new places. Clothes were stacked on the cot at the back of the room. Cooking utensils, including a set of cast iron pans, were noisily carried to the kitchenette. An engraved glass mug, a present from Ethvarth, was set on a nearby bookshelf.

After two hours of this, sweat drenched the collar and back of his linen shirt. While gulping down a glass of water, O'mas admired his progress. He dabbed at his brow with a handkerchief before he returned to his work.

His efforts ground to a halt when he uncovered a box filled with files. He removed a stack and set it on his desk. Decades' worth of mission briefings and personnel files had traveled with him. He liked the idea of revisiting the successes of his past.

As he flipped through the reams of paperwork, a thought occurred to O'mas. Instead of spending coin on the occasional lead, he might be better served by hiring his own men. It would take some time and effort to recruit people he could trust, but he knew that having an asset of his own within the Foundation was the best option. Indeed, he'd have to take great care. Neither the VMF's Intelligence Division nor the Foundation itself would take kindly to his investigation.

As O'mas examined the spiral-bound report, the pounding of knuckles on wood broke his concentration. O'mas looked up with a scowl that caused the lines in his forehead to deepen. He exhaled in exasperation. He wasn't exactly in the mood to entertain guests. His home wasn't in any condition for him to do so, either.

After another trio of raps sounded at the front door, O'mas rose from his seat and headed for the sitting room.

Just as he reached for the door handle, O'mas thought about his pistol. He still felt naked without a weapon. His service pistol, a black 9mm in its holster, was hidden beneath his cot.

Resisting the pull of a habit decades in the making, he shook his head, drew in a deep breath, and opened the door.

On the other side was a teenage boy who, at first glance, appeared no more than sixteen years old. His skin was oily and dotted with acne. His brown hair was ratty and in dire need of a trim. A thin layer of fuzz on his upper lip barely counted as a mustache.

"Can I be of some assistance?" O'mas inquired sharply.

"Uh, uh," the teen stammered for a second, stepping back in retreat.

Rather than wait for the youth's response, O'mas glanced down to the twine-wrapped package in his hands. "Is that intended for me?"

"Oh, uh, yeah." The boy nodded as he quickly offered the bundle. "Postal delivery for you. Mr. Barger told me to make sure you got this. Said he was paid to make sure."

O'mas knew the name. Arbis Barger was the head of a trade caravan that made regular trips into the Vale. He'd used his services before to transport some furniture. O'mas had a fair idea of what to expect. Unable to meet or get away, one of his contacts had uncovered something of value and sent it his way.

"Thank you," O'mas said as he relieved the boy of the parcel. Before he could add anything else, the teen turned on his heel and scurried off. O'mas was, again, okay with this.

He flung the door closed and unraveled the twine. Once back in his office, he slumped into the desk chair and scoured the stack of notes. While the opening letter was signed by someone named "Shiner," he knew this to be a pseudonym. Shiner was a mid-level administrator at the Trone Stenan docks who had family members working in one of the Foundation's assembly factories. The man had just enough information to provide the first clue about the Foundation's dealings.

Once he reached the end of the missive, O'mas nodded knowingly to himself. While there was a lot of vague language in the cover letter, Shiner's assumptions fell in line with his own. O'mas flipped through the pages, many of which were copies of invoices and shipping manifests.

Before long, the information convinced him that his interest in the Foundation was warranted. He was right to suspect that the corporation was up to no good.

The Foundation was still pumping out munitions as if the war had never ended.

Now he just needed to gather indisputable proof.

Chapter 16

The Twelfth of Sehbienimond
Dulton

It wasn't so much that Kyote lost track of the days, but that he slipped into a stupor that transformed time into a meaningless distinction. Sunset and sunrise were only changes in the light. The sights of faces and places flickered in his vision. In pursuit of Gohn, he'd spent the last four months on a trail that had quickly turned and stayed cold. His confusion and exhaustion now bordered on life-threatening, and his rage had been all but subsumed by grief. Kyote found himself unable to keep the manic pace.

Ultimately, all hope was depleted, and acceptance of his failure came like a swift blow to his heart. Crushed, he collapsed, plagued by regret in his few waking moments. It would take days for him to find the energy to rise and trudge on.

Broken by his failure, now he wanted to drown himself in booze.

Kyote crawled into one of Chancel's many taverns and held Rolde's wake alone, drinking until he couldn't think straight. Only when he woke up on a street corner, still intoxicated, still sad, and with the world's worst headache, did he accept his new reality. No amount of liquor was going to make his grief go away.

Now, with his partnership disbanded, his closest friend dead, and his desire for revenge thwarted, there was only one option open to him. At some point, he dragged himself onto a coach headed northward.

Kyote's memory had not failed him; Dulton was the same bleak stretch of gray earth that he recalled. The mining town, which sat in the shadow of the Northern Hadleys, was dogged by overcast skies and a dreariness that sapped all joy from its residents. The air itself stunk of burning oil. Machines from the nearby quarry clanged away at all hours. The grayish streets might as well have been paved in soot. More than once, he stopped to kick the dirt from his boots; it clung desperately to him, hoping he might carry it elsewhere.

As he lurched through the center of the town, Kyote scanned the faces on the surrounding streets. Many strode with heads down and hurried to their destinations with purpose. Groups of friends or families spoke to each other in brief spurts.

Briefly, he wondered if any of them recognized him. He recalled the fanfare that Flynn's arrival to Norte'wald had generated.

It didn't take long for him to realize that there would be no such welcome here. Despite his time at the orphanage, none of Dulton's populace gave him a second glance.

Worn from his travels, Kyote paused to rest against a brick wall as miners fresh off their shifts shuffled back into town. Once he gathered enough strength to go on, he began to make inquiries. Somebody could point him in the right direction.

Any information that could save him the laborious hike to the Dulton Home for Wayward Children would be appreciated. If he saw Miss Halliweil's smug smile, while in his current state of mind, he doubted that he could resist the urge to punch her.

Doing so would not improve either his situation or his mood.

It was late in the evening when a knock came at Celene's front door. She'd recently come home from the diner and was in readying herself for bed. The dull pounding came as a shock; occasionally, a neighbor stopped by for a bit of gossip, but she rarely received callers.

Nervously, she gathered up a threadbare robe and snuck to the entrance. Her straight black hair, which was tied up, threatened to unfurl. She paused for a moment as her hand grasped the knob. After a few breaths to marshal her courage, she turned it.

Standing before Celene was the phantom of a young man who had returned from the war two years ago. Since that time, he'd aged so much that she struggled to recognize him in the glow of the yellow lamplight. The lithe teenage boy with soft features was now a haggard man who'd regularly chosen booze over sleep. A thick beard lined his jaw, and an unwashed mane of tangled locks fell across his shoulders. Brown, almost black, eyes peered out from the deep pits beneath his brow. Sharp creases lined his forehead.

For a second, she recoiled out of something that might have been fear. While she knew him, his eyes were haunted, like something straight out of her nightmares. Beneath the apprehension, though, Celene felt pure joy that Kyote was still alive.

"Kyote?" She had to ask, just to be sure. Maybe it was a trick of the weak light. He might be a conjuration of her imagination, born from the regret that gnawed at her when she was alone with her thoughts. Or maybe, this was a dream from which she would soon wake.

"Yeah," he muttered in reply. His head bobbed weakly. "Celene… c-can I come in?"

The syllables hung in the air as the seconds passed. Celene recalled their last conversation, remembering Kyote's rage. The violence in his eyes had frightened her. She'd never seen its like before. As it had on many a cold, lonely night, his scathing statement echoed in her head.

"…*if you want to have a life full of dirty linens, then be my guest. I won't be sticking around. I didn't kill all those people— didn't nearly die—just to waste the rest of my days in the ass-end of the world!*"

Despite apprehension, she felt her heart lighten. In another life, where she had coin to spare, and they had loving friends and family, she would have assembled the most beautiful reunion party. She wouldn't turn him away a second time. She wasn't willing to lose him forever.

Celene softly nodded as she stepped aside. He ambled forward, too tired to maintain his balance. Scared that he might collapse, she reached out to provide some stability.

"I… I'm good," he said as he shrugged off her hand. Celene didn't take it personally; Kyote's stubborn pride prevented him from accepting help, even when he needed it.

As he passed, she noticed the state of his clothing. There were dark brown spots that she hoped were dried mud. The fabric of his coat was ragged. A series of gashes in the fabric piqued her curiosity. Perhaps in the future, he might be in a condition to explain.

He stopped in the middle of the main room and examined the meager furnishings. As he did, Celene closed the door. She waited for his sarcastic commentary about her shabby life. When he said nothing, she broke the silence.

"So, uh, what's…" she trailed off, unsure of what to say.

Celene had no clue where Kyote had been since he walked out the front door of the Dulton Home for Wayward Children. If his current condition was any indication, the past two years had been particularly unkind to him.

"Yeah?" he muttered as he turned in place. His slow movements revealed a deep weariness.

"What have you been up to? Since I last saw you?"

After a long pause that began to feel uncomfortable, he replied. "A lot. Not much of it was good, if I'm truthful." He then motioned to the lone chair. "You mind if I, uh… if I take a seat? Could use…"

As he wavered, Celene flicked her hand that she didn't mind.

"Yeah, yeah, go ahead. Make yourself at home, I guess."

She scrutinized his every movement as he dropped into the seat with flailing limbs. His shoulders drooped as the last of his energy was spent. A sigh passed through his pursed lips.

"Good," he muttered as his eyes closed.

Slowly, Celene moved a few paces closer.

"Kyote?"

While she knew from personal experience that the chair wasn't all that comfortable, in seconds, he was snoring loudly. The low growl of his breathing caused her to relax. When his face slackened, she could see signs of the boy he had once been.

Though she wished he didn't have to sleep in the dirty rags that were his clothes, she chose to leave him be. There would be time in the near future to get him bathed and changed. Perhaps once he recovered, he might be more interested in conversation. While there was a lot she wanted to know, she was most interested in learning the reason for his visit.

That night, she rested on her side so that she could watch

Kyote as he slumbered soundly in the chair. She woke more than once to see that he hadn't moved from his place. He would still be asleep when she headed for work the next day.

She returned the following evening to find him still in the chair. Even though she was relieved that he was still there, she'd never seen Kyote so despondent and had no idea of how to help him. He was awake now, but barely responsive. Every time she made an inquiry, he either ignored it or replied with a grunt.

Though she prepared dinner for two, she ate alone. Kyote's plate, which rested precariously on the nearby windowsill for an hour, went untouched. Frustrated, Celene quietly washed the dishes and headed off for her evening bath.

When Kyote cleared his throat, she paused and turned his way. As he stared at a blank spot on the far wall, Kyote slowly began to speak. His voice was low and flat. She had to concentrate hard to hear the words.

"Lost him somewhere around Chancel. Not hard to do. A lot of people can get lost around there. Big enough place like that is good for shaking any tail. I'm sure he knew that. Probably didn't even think I was still after him. Didn't even care."

Though she feared he was rambling to himself, she spoke up. "Who? Who was it?"

Without looking at her, he replied.

"Gohn. That bastard… he killed Rolde and thought he'd… well, I guess he did. He did get away. I guess the joke's…"

He grew silent again.

After a few seconds, Celene opened her mouth, but she didn't know what to say. Before she could utter a word, Kyote continued.

"Gohn had our number from day one. He could smell the stink of amateur on us. Probably why it was so easy for him to set us up. Make us out to be the guys who stormed Pourrie's place, killed his men, and then Pourrie himself. The only problem is that he thought… thought we'd oblige him by dying. Probably figured his men would kill us in Port Nym, and then they'd get rid of the bodies. If we never turn up again, they could pin both Pourrie's and Wallowrich's deaths on us."

Celene stepped up behind Kyote and placed a hand on his shoulder. As her palm rested on the taut trapezius, she felt him shudder ever so slightly. Eventually, his head fell against her arm as he let out a long, deep breath.

Celene struggled to keep her distance, since she felt compelled to wrap her arms around Kyote and cry with relief that he was back. She fully expected him to disappear once more, driven by a whim that would have him on the road again.

She wanted to make the most of this rare chance to feel close to him. If he only touched her skin for a few minutes, it would be more than she'd had in years. Before the ills of adulthood were forced upon either of them, they had been inseparable. Now he could vanish without a moment's notice.

What concerned Celene most was her growing desire to join him in his wanderings. Her life was a never-ending string of similar days. Working two jobs to pay for a small apartment that was barely worth the rent was not her dream. There were no prospects for career advancement in this town, and no available bachelors to court. After life in the orphanage, she couldn't see herself raising a family here anyway. While desperate to leave this all behind, she feared the unknown.

Though his ragged condition saddened her, Kyote's arrival had jolted her out of her rut. This time it wouldn't take much for him to convince her to leave Dulton behind. All he had to do was promise that hope existed somewhere beyond the city limits.

For the time being, Celene carried on with her day-to-day life. It was all she could do while Kyote recuperated. When she came home, she found him sleeping or staring at the ceiling. To her surprise, he never left her apartment, not even for a drink.

Kyote still sat in the chair and stared out through the window to the adjacent alley. Celene longed to bury her head in his shoulder, to comfort him and be comforted, but she held back.

Occasionally, he muttered the names of people and places about which she knew nothing. There was a story there, but she could not piece it together. She listened, hoping to hear the final hint that would make her understand.

If she could only wake up with him curled up beside her in the tiny cot. That would mean that they were alright, that the Kyote she'd known for most of her life was back. In truth, she wanted to roll the clock back to the time before the war. That was the last time she truly felt happy.

Celene was grateful that her shift at Olhweddy's was cut short. While it meant a smaller check at the end of the pay period, it also guaranteed that she could get home before the sun had fully set. For some reason, uneasiness had dogged her all day. Kyote had been a guest in her home for some time now. Every day, she feared that he'd disappear without so much as a goodbye. She didn't know how she would cope if he vanished a second time.

She quickened her pace as she hurried along the back streets. A cold wind out of the north buffeted her face. She clutched the fabric of her coat as a chill ran down her spine.

As she stepped into her apartment, a clatter sounded from the kitchen. Any apprehension she felt immediately melted away as the aroma of garlic and seared pork caused her mouth to salivate.

"Kyote?" she called, pulling the ribbon out of her hair.

His back was to her as he focused on the stove. In one hand was a spatula.

"In here," he replied without turning away from his task. "I picked up some groceries. Figured the least I could do was to put a meal together." There was a pause as he pulled the pan from the burner. "Go ahead and sit down. Get outta yer work clothes and into something comfy. Take a bath if you feel like it. I can... well, I guess I can keep this warm. Wasn't expecting you for a bit, anyway."

"I think I can wait until after dinner," Celene said with a soft chuckle. Though she kept glancing at the kitchen, she sat on the edge of the bed and waited. She was a little giddy at the prospect of having someone else prepare a meal for her. It was the first time in years that she'd enjoyed such a luxury.

Before long, Kyote arrived with two plates in hand. Sausages and peppers, atop a bed of mashed potatoes, were smothered in brown gravy. Celene thanked him as she placed the dish in her lap and dug in.

It tasted better than anything she'd ever eaten. Though the dish itself wasn't particularly spectacular, the richness made her warm on the inside.

While she continued to shovel the food into her mouth, she caught sight of Kyote as he partook. He was back in the chair and kept his eyes trained on the steaming plate of food.

As she finished her meal, Celene decided to ease into conversation. She couldn't pry too deeply for fear of poking around where Kyote did not want anyone to go.

"Are you… are you better?" she ultimately asked. It felt like such a childish simplification of a complex situation.

Kyote's fork hovered over his plate for a moment. He drew in a deep breath and shrugged his shoulders. After a few seconds, he set down the utensil and met Celene's gaze.

"I'll live," he admitted. "That's… that's just gonna have to do for right now."

While she wasn't sure she understood, Celene nodded all the same.

"I'm sorry. I don't want to pry—"

"In time," he interrupted her as he rose from his seat. "Just give me time, okay?"

Celene noticed the grimace which was barely hidden by his bushy beard. Before she could say another word, he went into the kitchen and dropped his dishes into the sink. She sat quietly at the edge of her cot, wishing there was something she could say or do to change things.

Kyote eventually broke the heavy silence.

"Hey," he called from where he reclined against the kitchen counter. When Celene met his gaze, she could tell there was something on his mind.

"Yes?"

"Look, I know you got a *thing* here," Kyote began. "You got a place and a steady line of income. Something that might even be a career—if it suits you—but… but, what about before? What about what we was talkin' about before I left for the war? Ya know, about trackin' down your parents? I've got the coin to make the trip. More than I had last time I was here. About the only thing good I can say came out of the last year. We can get on a boat as soon as we get outta here and be in Tir in no time. If… if you think… well, I don't even know."

"Kyote—"

"Look, I get that the last time I came back was a bit of bad timing. You didn't even know that I was still alive. I get that I didn't write you ta let you know how things were going, but—"

"How is now *any different?*" she snapped. Anger flared inside her. She surprised even herself at how quickly it came to the surface. Perhaps the same fear of the unknown beyond Dulton's borders still lingered within her, fueling this emotion. "You were gone for almost two years and then show up on my doorstep with the same pitch. This is just a repeat, except now we're a little older."

Kyote's eyes narrowed. "And in those two years, did things here in Dulton get better for you?"

This cut directly to the heart of the matter and extinguished her anger.

She averted her eyes as she spoke. "Those were… those were the dreams of a little girl. One who figured we could just sail a boat across the sea, show up on the shores of Tir, and people would happily point us in the right direction. I was naïve. I know that now. It was a rainbow-colored daydream that I held onto for as long as I could. Until my childhood was finally over. I know now any attempt to look for my family would be time wasted. Time better spent trying to make a life for myself."

"Any attempt to look for your folks is better than no attempt. You ain't gonna find anyone sitting around here." Kyote's mouth hung open for a second, as if he wanted to add something else.

"Maybe I don't want to know anymore."

"Really? That right? Or maybe you're just scared." He leveled a finger at her. "Sticking around here, sloggin' away at a go-nowhere job feels like some kinda comfort, right? It's safe and doesn't require you to take a chance."

The accusation stung.

"I… uh…"

Kyote crossed to where she sat and went down on one knee. He reached in and placed a pair of fingers on the tip of her chin. Though she straightened briefly, Celene eventually allowed him to touch her as he raised her head.

"Look, I'll be there the whole way. We'll do this together. In fact, there don't gotta be a time where one of us goes anywhere without the other. That was the plan, wasn't it?"

Even though conflicting emotions contorted her features, she nodded.

"I can't stay here in Dulton. You can see by the way the people walk. This is where hope goes to die. There's too much out there to be seen and done. Look, I got damage all my own, but it's not gonna get better sitting around here, grinding at a dead-end career. So, I say we pack up and go after your dreams. It's gotta be better than slaving away at the orphanage."

Celene no longer wanted to resist his pleas.

With a thin smile and teary eyes, she relented. "Okay."

Kyote wrapped his arms around her. Caught up in his embrace, relief and elation caused tears to stream down her cheeks.

That night, Kyote crawled under the covers and slept beside Celene. They struggled to fit comfortably, since the bed was barely big enough for her to lay flat on her back.

They rested there, side by side, face to face. She could tell by the scent of baby powder and flowers that he'd bathed recently. Celene felt nervous. He wasn't exactly the young man with whom she'd grown up. This version of Kyote knew of war and violence. He'd killed to save not only his own life but the lives of others.

Celene found herself wanting to speak all the questions she'd stored away since his arrival.

"So, what's it like out there?" she said. The tip of her nose brushed against Kyote's. "Out in the world. Outside of Dulton."

Kyote chuckled softly as a smile curled on his lips. "Different. Big. Small. You got places like Chancel and Trone Stenan that are so huge you'll never see it all. And then, there's places like Allhbienmark and Thelleerd'eth that ain't much different than Dulton. Just a little brighter and warmer since they're out from under the shadow of the mountains."

"And Moa'rehnza?"

This caused him to scowl.

"Never got to see it in a time in which people weren't shooting at each other. Probably had some nice places to visit, some good food to eat, maybe even a few nice folks. It's a shame that we weren't there for any of that." He bit at his lower lip before continuing. "They shipped us out once we was done. Well, once they could get us out of the south. Never really had the chance to enjoy the place. Don't know that I'd want to go back. Still too unstable to be safe."

After a moment, he snickered to himself.

"What?" Celene inquired.

"Oh, nothing. Just that thinking Moa'rehnza's any less safe than Verenigen gave me a laugh. I've been shot at far more times in the past year than I think I ever was as a part of the Gendarmery. Maybe it ain't too safe to stay at home either. Best for us to get outta here, for our safety. Ya know?"

This caused Celene to giggle.

Before long, the comfort of being in Kyote's warm arms helped her to slip pleasantly into sleep.

Chapter 17

The Twenty-first of Sehbienimond
Eithos Los

It didn't take long for Celene to pack up what she wanted to take with her. In truth, she had very little of worth and even less that held any sentimental value. She managed to squeeze a few changes of clothes into a backpack before they were out the door.

After leaving Dulton, they stayed in Scae'hale. Kyote was quiet and introspective. Worried that he'd relapse into his gloomy mood, Celene fretted over his well-being. It took some effort on her part to make Kyote reveal that Scae'hale was home to the Rolde family.

While she wasn't clear on the story's details, Celene knew that Kyote felt guilty about the loss of one who had presumably been a close friend. Realizing this, she chose to respect his boundaries. He would speak up if he wanted to discuss the matter.

Celene gazed in wonder at the township around them. This was the first time she'd ever been away from Dulton. She remarked that, while the Northern Hadleys were plainly visible to the northeast, it was nice to be out from beneath their shadow. More than once, she covered her eyes to protect them from the bright glare.

Kyote decided against a visit to Rolde's family. This

decision came after an internal debate that went on for some time. Until he could tell them that their son's death had been avenged, he would bring only bad news. Deep within him, he understood that he was a coward; facing them would be an admission of his own failure.

Little did he know that Flynn had visited months earlier and that the family had already held Rolde's funeral. They had begun to cope with their grief by having a small memorial service in his honor. If he had known this information, he would have been more inclined to call on them, if only to pay his respects.

Regret dogged Kyote even as they left Scae'hale on the westbound coach. His head was so filled with conflicting emotions that he struggled to sort them out. He pushed them aside to be dealt with at a later date, focusing on the practicalities of their journey.

With Celene by his side, Kyote wouldn't dive too deep into introspection.

At first, when they arrived in Eithos Los, Celene couldn't help but gawk. She was initially stunned by the sheer size of the city and the density of its population. The surrounding buildings towered over her. She succumbed to an initial bout of dizziness as she craned her head upwards. She felt small, like a rat scurrying through the city streets.

Even in the best of times, Dulton was not a busy town, and people rarely gathered in large crowds. Once they began their slow progress through the crowds and into town, she was quickly overwhelmed. As such, she moved in close to Kyote and took his hand in hers. Her fingers curled up tightly.

"It's okay," he reassured as he led her away from the eastern marketplace. His elbow drove a wedge through the swelling throng.

He understood her feelings. It was late in the afternoon, and the crowd was at its worst. The locals out to market caused foot traffic in the eastern wards to grind to a halt. Kyote's first experience with Eithos Los' daily shoppers had caused him similar anxiety.

After a few blocks, they stumbled across a westbound alley that pointed them deeper into the city. Soon they were surrounded by blocks of densely-packed apartments and townhomes. By the time they'd crossed a third unmarked intersection, Kyote had a fair idea of their location. They were no more than a fifteen-minute walk from some of the seedier parts of town, where people could get into trouble if they felt the inclination.

There was a moment, however brief, when Kyote considered visiting Den Six. He wouldn't partake of a drink or reconnect with old contacts, but would drop in on Hammerfeuer for a private conversation. Perhaps the man might have some additional information about their last job.

He ultimately decided against returning there. Any visit to Den Six would surely end in violence. Even if Celene wasn't traveling with him, that was trouble he didn't need to court.

I can't keep leaving a trail of broken bodies behind me, he thought to himself. *That the shit-storms in Port Nym and Norte'wald haven't caught up with me is a bit of good fortune. I go to meet Hammerfeuer and I figure I'm probably gonna try to rough him up before too long. If he doesn't beat me up then and there, he's gonna take it personally. And he's the kinda guy to send people after me. Pay for a hit out of his own pocket.*

The decision to press on felt right. It wasn't as if he didn't have enough on his plate. Though she stayed within arm's reach at all times, Celene was captivated by the city. She trusted him to play the role of guide.

He couldn't afford to indulge in distractions. Especially now, when, for some reason that he couldn't quite place, persistent foreboding caused Kyote's stomach to roil. While they made their way to the western harbor, he examined the crowd around him, trying to pick out familiar faces. Though no one followed them, his apprehension persisted. When they boarded the ferry for Issuhn on Tir, he exhaled in relief.

Once the boat, the *Daughti Jihnge*, set sail from Eithos Los, Celene slipped below deck to the passengers' cabin. She struggled with unexpected seasickness; she'd never been off land before, and the choppiness of the waves caused her some discomfort.

Kyote, on the other hand, chose to stay up top and watch as Verenigen grew smaller. He smiled to himself. He didn't know what the future held for them in Tir, but considering his past, he couldn't see himself ever returning.

As he rested against the railing, with the ocean spray pelting his face, Kyote's thoughts went back over the last few months. Rolde was dead, and he had to admit that he was at least partially culpable. That lump of regret throbbed like a broken bone. He could point to various moments along the timeline at which, if he'd altered his decisions, things would have played out differently.

Maybe when we knew that Flynn was being trailed, we should have pulled out. Or, at least waited and watched. When I grabbed Kelvin, we were forced to make a move on the mansion. Maybe when we saw Pourrie's men getting wasted, we should have bailed. Should have checked out Wallowrich's place when we came back. Made sure they weren't lying in wait. Made a right mess of it, being sloppy every step of the way.

One last thought occurred to Kyote.

Shouldn't have let Flynn send Rolde after Gohn. I didn't think of Gohn as much of a fighter but I knew Rolde wasn't good in a tussle. Should've had Flynn give chase. Flynn would have followed the man proper. Would've been smart enough to stay on the trail and track him to wherever he was looking to hide. Wouldn't've engaged unless he had to. Flynn would've done it right.

It hurt to admit that, but Kyote knew it to be true.

Flynn was the smart one. The one of the trio who thought of the bigger picture, made decisions based on knowledge. The very reason they'd brought Flynn on—that he'd be the rational one who kept them on task—became the same irritant that caused Kyote's animosity to grow. Truth be told, they were like oil and water. Without Rolde to act as a buffer, they would have been at each other's throats.

Their altercation in the ruins of Wallowrich's collection only made the end clear and irrevocable.

To make matters worse, Kyote was beginning to realize that his gift was also a curse. The fury caused him to be reckless, and as such, his temper grew shorter with every passing day. Since self-control eroded during the rage, he was capable of leaving death in his wake wherever he went.

At first, the ability served as a survival mechanism. During wartime, he needed every edge he could find. Freeing the beast inside saved himself, his friends, and his allies. Now, he began to wonder if, in some way, the feral thing which resided within him actually relished in the carnage.

Kyote couldn't discuss this with Celene. He'd just managed to get her back into his life. To reveal all the awful things of which he'd been a part would undo all the progress between them. He was concerned that it would send her back to Dulton, in fear for her life. She'd return to an empty life of dead-end jobs rather than stay with a man who had a tenuous grasp on his violent self. For now, all he could do was answer her questions with empty platitudes.

He turned his attention to the darkening panorama.

Once he could no longer detect any sign of Eithos Los on the horizon, Kyote moved to the fore of the vessel. Barring a few deckhands, Kyote was alone. Frigid wind occasionally blew ocean spray up on deck.

For a while, he kept his eyes trained to the west. He knew that the trip across the Dwyr Sea took only a few hours and that it would be some time before he spotted land. The time alone to sort out his thoughts was welcome.

As the sky darkened, only a nearby lantern illuminated his surroundings. Dense cloud cover blotted out the stars and moon above. The sounds of movement faded into a murmur of noise. Occasionally one of the ship's crew barked out something that might have been an order.

Though he had never been to Issuhn on Tir before, Kyote knew a bit about the capital city. He'd heard that the first sight of the city's lights on the horizon was something that shouldn't be missed.

When he saw the initial twinkling of white and amber in the distance, he slipped from the foredeck and went below. He spent a few moments looking over the crowd in the passenger hold. He weaved his way to where she sat and tapped her on the shoulder. She glanced up at him with a quizzical look.

"You okay?"

"Come," he said as he beckoned her with a flick of his fingers. Though briefly reluctant, Celene rose.

A cold gust blasted the pair as they returned to the deck. This caused Celene's cheeks to redden as she wrapped her coat tightly about her.

"Oof," she grunted as the icy breeze caught her by surprise. While she was used to late season weather in Dulton, this somehow felt worse. No longer sheltered by the Northern Hadleys, she thought the artic winds cut her to the bone.

"Yeah, a bit of a chill," Kyote noted as he placed a hand against her back. "But the view is totally worth it."

The city lights sparkled like a starfield pulled down into a rough shape no more than a few centimeters wide along the darkened horizon. As the boat moved in closer, the multi-hued radiance grew in size, spreading across the coastline like an untended wildfire. With every second that passed, the view of the city coalesced. A regal, tall, golden tower was surrounded by a forest of smaller grey obelisks.

"I, uh… wow," Celene sputtered as her eyes took in the metropolis. Before long, the capital of the island nation of Tir, formed by densely-packed wards that sprawled on for kilometers, came into focus. In the darkness of early evening, the glow flared like a beacon.

"Bigger than you'd thought it would be?" Kyote commented. He realized that Celene might be overwhelmed by such an impressive, and daunting, sight. While the trade city of Eithos Los was hardly small, it seemed like a suburb compared to the megalopolis that loomed before them.

"I'd, uh, I've read about Issuhn on Tir before, but I never really thought about how big it is. It seems to go on…"

"For kilometers? Yeah."

After a few seconds of silence, Celene spoke again. "What about… how does it compare? To other cities you've been to?"

"Hmm," Kyote mumbled as his eyes rolled up. "Without seeing how far the sprawl is from the coast, hard to say. Best guess? Bigger than either Trone Stenan or Chancel, though that's probably because their curtain walls kind *limit* growth, ya know? Both of those cities are kinda forced to grow up since they can't grow out." He moved his hands in the air to demonstrate what he was describing. "Gran'rehnza, on the other hand? Probably similar though not nearly as built up. Most of Gran'rehnza's… oh, what's the word? Oh, *ciduades.* Slums or shantytowns built up along most of the north. Even from here—" He pointed to the grouping of skyscrapers that grew more prominent by the second. "—you can see Issuhn on Tir's a *taller* city."

"So, how bad... how *full* do you think it's gonna be?" The question was open-ended enough to be about the crowd or the prospects of finding her family. She wasn't entirely sure which she wanted to know more.

He could feel her trepidation radiating off of her in waves. He put a hand over hers. "I'll be sure to stay within reach. Okay?"

"That doesn't answer…" she trailed off with a sigh. He never gave her a straight response. Eventually, she added, "Okay."

By the time the *Daughti Jihnge* arrived at the port, even Kyote was a little intimidated by Issuhn on Tir's size. The city seemed to spread out endlessly on either side of their point of arrival. Without a destination in mind, the pair waited behind the other passengers before they themselves disembarked. They followed the crowd along the docks into the adjacent marketplace.

Kyote realized that their brief stop in Eithos Los had not adequately prepared them for the over-packed metropolis that was Issuhn on Tir. Chancel, Trone Stenan, and Gran'rehnza seemed to pale when compared to the overcrowded urban landscape that was the Tirean capital. Even the widest streets were choked with signage, colored lanterns, and stacks of untended refuse. A thick aroma of human sweat, burnt oil, and regional spices filled the air. Bottlenecks caused the traffic to ebb and flow in a strange pulsing fashion. Those who didn't stop to talk or shop at one of the many stalls scurried off to locations deeper within the huge labyrinth.

Kyote glanced at the surrounding rooflines, searching for a shooter in the darkness.

His eyes narrowed as he scanned the crowd. He looked toward the hands of old ladies, only to find them filled with grocery bags instead of armaments. A group of teens rushed down the crooked lane bellowing joyfully to one another. When they merely brushed past them on the way to somewhere else, Kyote's vigilance eased.

A man reached inside his jacket, so Kyote shifted and nudged Celene in the opposite direction. When he produced a small sack of coins, the tension in Kyote's shoulders slackened.

This went on for some time until he realized that Celene hadn't spoken a word in what felt like an hour. He took a few deep breaths.

"You gonna be okay?" he asked as he leaned in close to Celene. It took a few seconds for the words to even register with her.

"Uh, oh, yeah. Well, I think so. Just, uh, just trying to get used to it," she eventually replied. After a few seconds of intensely examining their environs, she asked a question. "So, uh, do you have any idea of where we should start? I mean we've been walking around for a while now."

Kyote grunted as he smirked. He got the gist of her meaning. The metropolis wasn't kind to first-time visitors. Many of the signs were written in the old Tirean script, with no help for those who only knew Common. The few that were legible were of limited use to them. Street corners and intersections were unmarked, and most businesses were indistinguishable from one another.

The buzz of conversation around them was in a mixture of the two languages. Familiar words emerged in such thick accents that it took the brain a moment to decipher them. Kyote's head swam with overstimulation.

"I guess, uh, I guess we should get a meal and a bed for the night," he suggested. "Figure out what our next step from there is." In truth, he had no idea of where to even begin. They were at a clear disadvantage in more than one way. Without a firm grasp of Tirean, they'd struggle to get proper directions from anyone who wasn't bilingual.

If they could rent a room for the night, it would allow them time to regroup. Perhaps once away from the chaos of the streets, the pair could plan.

"Okay. Where to?"

His groan was muffled by the surrounding din. *Ugh, I wish I knew.*

Flagging down someone who could provide assistance took more than one attempt. An older gentleman, whose hands were covered with various hues of dried paint, directed them to an establishment that offered rooms. After swearing up and down that it was a reputable place, the Tirean gave them terse directions before he disappeared into the night.

From the outside, the inn looked like all the other three-story apartment buildings on the block, with pale wooden shutters and a slanted roof of red clay tiles. Once inside, the lady at the desk confirmed that there were indeed rooms for rent. After parting with some coin, they were escorted to a second-story chamber that was barely big enough for two.

Sparsely decorated and reeking of unwashed linens, the accommodations were not luxurious. Though they shared a few sour glances, they were too tired to voice their displeasure. They curled up on the lone mattress and fell asleep.

The following morning, they explored the surrounding ward. In this area, just outside of the markets of Raidon District's wharves, there was still a fair bit of foot traffic within the maze of interconnected alleys. Locals, engrossed by their daily activities, made no effort to interact with the pair unless they were approached.

They spent their daylight hours canvassing the area with little success. No one wanted to offer anything more than a view of their wares. Those who were talkative spoke in fragments of Common bookended by long strings of Tirean. Dispirited by the day's failure, they returned to their lodgings for the night.

They settled into a routine. Day by day, they widened the area of their investigation. By the twenty-fifth, they were making regular visits to adjacent wards. As they passed through Brómos District, the owner of a spice shop gave them their first real lead. She commented that she knew someone from the Kaize family, though that was decades ago when she was a child. She couldn't provide many details, but thought that they'd moved west. Whether the person she'd known or any members of their family were still in the city she could not say.

Kyote and Celene also found themselves drawn into the nightlife of Issuhn on Tir. As the sun set, the day-laborers and housewives went home and a younger subset of revelers headed to the city's taverns and gambling dens. Every street corner held people attempting to sell something to the passing crowd. Though they never stopped to pay the barkers any mind, Kyote knew the middle-men worked for the drug and sex trades.

By the twenty-sixth, they'd decided to move their base of operations to more western wards. Once they relocated to Neyong District, they renewed their search.

That evening, after a meal at the nearby noodle shop, they headed back to their lodgings. Tired from the day, Kyote had no desire to partake in the nightly festivities. It took all he had not to lose his temper at the inconvenience of the pulsing horde. The sun had only just set, and many partiers were already too tipsy to keep to themselves. The cacophony of self-indulgence that filled the streets grated on his nerves.

He forced his way through the crowd with all the grace of a bull. On occasion, he jabbed at people with an elbow. More than one screeched out in unexpected pain. Kyote only looked over his shoulder to verify that Celene still trailed behind him.

Kyote began looking for landmarks that would lead them back to the inn. When he spotted a glowing red sign in Tirean with a bird-shaped icon, he knew they weren't too far off. Relieved that they'd soon be able to rest, his shoulders slackened as his gaze fell to the surrounding mob. Awash in the garish glow of the vibrant signage, their features blurred into simple sketches.

Kyote came to a complete stop as he spotted a familiar face amidst the throng. As his heart pounded fiercely in his chest, he could feel his muscles tightening. Tiny tendrils of rage began crawling upward from his stomach and across his chest as his jaw clenched.

Even as he bobbed amidst packs of revelers, the tall, grayish man was instantly recognizable. Flanked on each side by a man dressed in a black suit, Gohn headed deeper into the ward.

"Kyote?" He barely heard Celene. He felt her tug at his arm. "What's wrong? Did you see some—"

Without a word, he shrugged off her grasp and charged off after Gohn. He pushed his way past one body after another. An open bottle of beer fell with a piercing crash of glass on stone. There were protests from those forced aside. Confused, Celene only attempted to give chase.

With each stride, he fell further and further behind his prey. Gohn and his men moved through the multitudes with ease, virtually unimpeded. Every time Kyote stumbled around the densest clusters of the night's partiers, the outline of the gray man was harder to see. Kyote took a corner and watched Gohn turn right just two blocks ahead. By the time he reached the same intersection, Gohn had vanished.

Kyote cried aloud with an incoherent howl. A pair of bouncers from a neighboring bar took a few menacing steps in his direction.

As she rushed up beside Kyote, Celene waved them off. Short of breath, she motioned with one hand that she had the situation under control. This was enough to send them back to their posts.

"Kyote!" Celene grabbed his sleeve. "What's… w-what's going on?" She placed a hand on her chest and gasped. Her face was ruddy from the exertion.

"It's Gohn. I saw him walking this way," he replied as he pointed to the adjacent alley. There was no sign that the man and his retinue had ever passed through. Kyote shifted from foot to foot, waving his hand wildly. "I just saw him not minutes ago, but it's like he disappeared into the back alleys."

This caused fear, dark and hard, to form in the pit of Celene's stomach. They'd fled to Tir, in part, to get away from Kyote's past, but it had followed them here. So far, their trip hadn't gone well.

Before she jumped to conclusions, she needed to consider that Kyote was tired. They'd been on the go since their arrival.

"Are you… are you sure it was him? I-I mean there are a lot of people in this city. You could have confused someone else for him."

He tapped at his temple with a finger. "Look, I'm not gonna forget that ashy bastard, no how. I got that skinny fuck's face tattooed to the back of my brain. Never gonna forget it."

He turned his attention back to the street.

Celene examined the harsh lines of his face. While his eyes were glazed over, she could tell he firmly believed in what he saw. For a second, his stance changed, and she feared he might run again. Celene knew that she needed to take control of the situation, for his own good, at least for the night.

"Kyote," she sternly said as she reached out. This broke his focus on the alleyway's dark entrance. When he turned back to her, Kyote noticed the knit in her brow. His posture shifted as he recoiled from her.

"Wha—"

"No!" she barked as she raised an accusatory finger at him. "You're not running off after someone you're not sure you're looking for. You're not leaving me alone in this city so that you can pick a fight with some guy who probably doesn't even know you."

"But, that guy…"

"Are you a hundred percent certain? Or is this just something you want to be true. That your mind isn't playing tricks with you?"

At that moment, he felt like a scolded dog. He hadn't considered that he might be chasing a phantom. Celene might be right. He'd not actually gotten a good look at the man's face. There was always the slimmest chance that it wasn't Gohn, but an unfortunate person with a similar appearance.

"I, uh…" He once again glanced at the backstreet.

"Are you… are you having doubts? That it might not be him? That maybe you just saw someone who looks like him and wanted it to be true?"

The more Celene spoke to him, the less uncertain he was that he had actually seen Rolde's murderer.

"Well, maybe you're right," he eventually admitted. He

didn't know that he believed it, but the apparition that might be Gohn left him with no trail to follow.

After a few minutes, Kyote allowed Celene to escort him away. That night, he tossed in their bed as he replayed the scene over and over in his head.

Chapter 18

The Twenty-eighth of Sehbienimond
Neyong District, Issuhn on Tir

Now that they had their base in Neyong District, Kyote and Celene renewed their investigation, hoping for improved results. Earlier conversations with locals along the wharf sector made it clear to them that they would be better served by heading west. Few knew anything of the Kaize name, but those who did mentioned decades-old interactions that had taken place further inland.

By the end of their first day in the new location, they came across more than one person who could provide details of interest. One remembered doing work for the Kaize family as a youth. For three years, he had been paid handsomely to tend the foliage around their property. When pressed for more, he noted that the former homestead had long ago been converted into a brothel. What remained of the once-luxurious abode was nearly unrecognizable since it had been remodeled multiple times.

It didn't take them long to realize that they'd moved to a seedier part of town. Their current lodgings rested on the edge of the Akayásen, which Kyote took to mean "red lantern district." By sunset, the streets were lined with ladies of the evening who beckoned to potential clients, many of whom tried to hide their faces as they pushed through the throng. Kyote regularly saw money exchange hands as newly-forged couples headed off to complete their business. There was a rank odor of bodily fluids and cheap perfume hovering over the ward.

On the corner nearest to their two-story motel was a home for wayward mothers. That they were relegated to such a place came as little surprise to Kyote. In his short time there, he'd learned that, in Tirean society, fathers were not responsible for children born out of wedlock. These unfortunates, if not taken in by their own families, were often cast out onto the streets. Such homes, referred to as Sheisiji Lodges, were privately-funded organizations that operated with sinister motives. The unwed mothers were turned into hostesses for the lucrative hospitality industry, while their children, when they reached the age of ten, were put to work in factories. The others less fortunate were forced to live as beggars and pickpockets. It was not uncommon to see packs of urchins huddling in back alleys or panhandling at major intersections. Though he hated to do so, Kyote often kept a hand on his coin purse as they passed through.

No one in a position of power cared to intervene for the greater good. There were no welfare programs to protect the vulnerable—not when the legislature was comprised of elderly Tireans who could trace their lineages back dozens of generations. Few saw reason to interfere in what was beneath them. Rare was the man who would provide for his mistress or girlfriend and care for an unexpected addition to their family. The people who benefited from the patriarchal Tirean society did not wish to see it change in their lifetimes.

Though learning of the more unsavory aspects of life in Issuhn on Tir did little to improve Celene's mood, she kept at the investigation. With every little scrap of information, she felt closer to a fresh lead, something that was less than a decade old. Celene was optimistically convinced that she was a single break away from finding a relative's current residence.

Unlike Celene, Kyote was often distracted, finding his thoughts returning to the night of the chase. Though he tried to convince himself otherwise, he could not shake the notion that it was really Gohn he'd spotted in the evening crowd. He kept a vigilant eye on everyone who passed them. More than once, Celene shot him cross looks at his inability to help her. At the end of each day, he felt no closer to an answer of his own.

Even with Kyote's attention split, they progressed, albeit slowly. Occasionally someone in Neyong and the neighboring Xenanto and Ilkabari Districts would know the Kaize family name. Tracking these leads almost always led to dead ends. The trails either went cold or pointed them out of the city to Tir's more rural regions.

An abandoned house on the edge of the warehouse sector was mentioned. It was said that, once the more unsavory elements of Neyong took over, the Kaizes had relocated to the property. The eldest Kaize male had no desire to be even tangentially associated with such business. A thorough investigation of this dilapidated dwelling unearthed only a placard with the family name, painted in Tirean, hanging beside the front entrance. Celene collected the sign and brought it back with her.

Each day, the pair returned to their lodgings worn out and dispirited. After a few days, Kyote knew he had to do something. He thought to lift Celene's spirits by taking her to a nearby bar.

It was a small hole in the wall, dark except for a few candles and some neon lamps on top of the bar back. He had no idea what the Tirean sign read, but the service was as he liked it: a waiter paused only long enough to take his coin and deliver their orders. There was no small talk. No one verified that they were of legal drinking age. If they could pay, they could imbibe.

Ending their daily canvassing with a few cold beverages

quickly became a regular habit for the pair.

As they settled in on the night of the twenty-eighth, Kyote took a measure of the establishment's clientele. Most seemed there only to ready themselves for a raucous night spent elsewhere. After a couple of drinks and a few words with people they knew, most went on their way.

The air was thick with perfume, smoke, and sweat. It took some effort to breathe in the dense atmosphere. On occasion, Kyote would cough in discomfort. There were brief respites when the front door opened and faint wisps of cold air rolled inside.

Across the booth from Kyote, Celene had slumped into the dark brown fabric of her seat. She stared off into the distance as she toyed with the half-empty glass bottle. After a few minutes of silence, she took another swig and set the beverage back on the table.

While the alcohol managed to numb the growing concerns she had, it also caused Celene to become more introspective. Going for drinks every night seemed like an unsustainable bit of self-medication. The brief lifting of spirits transformed into something else as the night progressed. They would leave either drunk or more discouraged than when they had arrived.

Celene was aware that their current search wasn't exactly advancing at an acceptable pace. Without new information or a fresh lead, there was only so far they could carry it. She began to wonder at what point Kyote had recognized this undeniable truth. Was that why he led them to drown themselves in booze?

As Kyote pounded down glass after glass, Celene felt the brew sour in her mouth. There was going to be a moment— soon she expected—when they would have to make tough decisions about their future. Would they head out of the city, to look for her relatives in Tir's countryside? Many smaller villages dotted the northern landmass of Isll'miahn. If nothing was uncovered, would they have the persistence to cross the Llonth'vriedj, the bridge which connected Tir's two main islands, to Issl'soeth in the south? Only now did she realize just how large Tir really was.

Celene was about to break the long silence when, surprisingly, Kyote spoke up. He raised his beverage and peered at it closely.

"Ya know, with enough alcohol, I think we show the person we've always been. On the inside. Hidden behind all the politeness. A man is only truly honest when he's filled with rage or drunk enough to shed all pretense. He speaks true when no longer shackled by civility."

When Celene gave him a cross look, he continued, but only after polishing off the last of his beer.

"Look at how we waste so much time and energy pretending to be courteous to each other. We hold our tongues and play just nice enough so that the others don't rise up and kick us out of society altogether."

"That's a pretty cynical view of people," Celene noted. It saddened her to think this was how Kyote saw the world. At that moment, she reached for her drink.

"Probably. Probably so. But, I've sat around and watched enough people, even when they don't think someone else is looking. Ya see, when they think they're out of the public eye, they let themselves relax because they don't have to keep pretending to be a part of the human race."

He paused to pour another glassful from the nearby jug. Once he had, there were only a few centimeters of the brew left. Celene was certain it wouldn't last long.

"In truth, if you give a man enough drink, loosen his tongue up but good, you're more likely to find out what he's really like. Find out his real opinions, not the filtered garbage he lets out in polite company. Find out that he has the hots for his friend's wife. Or something even worse. That he steals coins from the blind. That he only works a day job because everyone else does and he can't think for himself. Can't be bothered to. Lives in fear of his own choices."

"And you?" Celene asked as she watched him raise the mug. She looked at the young man who was once like a brother to her. He'd come back from the war with a haunted look in his eyes that kept growing darker with each beverage he swallowed. "What truths do you keep hidden?"

Kyote offered a toothy grin. Celene could feel a shiver run down her spine. To make the sensation go away, she downed the last of her own drink.

He never responded.

They paid their tab and stumbled back to the inn. Neither said much as they fell onto the bed. Kyote was fast asleep in seconds.

It was Celene's turn to be restless for some time, as she tried to sort the muddled mess that roiled in her head. At some point, the alcohol and exhaustion finally caught up with her.

Kyote swam up from the darkness of his liquor-induced slumber in a wooden shack lit only by a red lantern suspended from the ceiling. The previous few hours were a blur which left him with no recollection of coming here.

A quick glance at his surroundings did not help him understand where he was.

The interior was unlike anything he'd seen before. Details slowly came into focus as the lamp's flame grew brighter by the second. The wood-paneled walls seemed to pulse with a life of their own, as the throbbing in his head caused his vision to warp. The air around him was dense and hot. It clung to him like a damp cloth. He felt a growing desire to peel himself out of his clothing. He could smell the sweat collecting in the folds of the fabric.

Somehow he was simultaneously numb and burning up from within. The roaring fire in his brain flickered behind his eyes. At that moment, he badly wanted to douse himself in cold water. He knew that if he could just cool off, he'd feel so much better.

He sensed the presence of others in the room. His head swiveled back and forth as he tried to pick out their forms in the shadows. As the seconds passed, various silhouettes slowly took shape. Though he understood that these were human forms, he failed to recognize them.

While a few shuffled back and forth, none made an effort to approach him. In the flashes of lamplight that passed across them, Kyote only saw the movement of cloth. Their faces remained hidden as they lingered along the edges of the room.

He attempted to rise from his seat. He was no more than halfway up when he felt something pull against his limbs. He glanced at both wrists to find them tightly bound, lashed to the chair with leather straps. He gave them a second, futile tug before returning his attention to the formless figures.

Kyote opened his mouth to speak. A howl filled the claustrophobic chamber for a few seconds. Stunned, he recoiled as his jaw slammed shut. The lantern's glow grew in intensity. The inky shade that had covered the faces around him seemed to blow away like smoke in the wind.

Something was very wrong.

While he didn't recognize everyone there, those he knew looked like caricatures of themselves. Standing at the front of the crowd was Flynn, who towered over him with a bulbous forehead. The creases in his brow wavered as he scowled furiously at Kyote. Beside him, somehow, was Rolde, whose eyes bulged so much that they almost sprung from their sockets.

Chuckling softly to himself in the back of the room, Wallowrich waddled forth. The older gentleman was now a corpulent ball of flesh with only stubby limbs and a head to keep him from rolling away. His suit was stretched taut across his body.

Kyote's attention returned to Flynn, who remained in place with his arms crossed. From his gaping mouth, he muttered the same thing over and over again.

"Words words words words..." he droned endlessly. Only an occasional change in inflection hinted that he meant something else. Kyote tried to understand the man's diatribe.

At the center of it all stood Gohn, dressed in an ashen suit that matched the tone of his skin. At first, Kyote hadn't noticed his presence, but Gohn became increasingly prominent in his vision. Lanky arms, which reached down past his knees, hung at his side.

Unexpectedly, Celene stepped out from behind Gohn, looking the same as usual. She was the only person not warped by whatever madness had changed everyone else's appearance.

Kyote wanted to ask Celene what was happening to him. She, of all people, could tell him how he'd ended up here. Unfortunately, words failed him. His jaw hung open and only a whimper spilled forth.

For a moment, the image of Celene flickered, as if she was an illusion formed by quivering candlelight. When she reappeared, her hair had lightened to a reddish-brown hue and was trimmed to shoulder-length. Somehow, her skin had lightened. His eyelashes flickered as he shuddered. A second later, Celene reverted to her original form.

Hands came out of the darkness and grasped at Celene.

Long gray fingers coiled around her limbs as they yanked at her with brutal force. She lost her balance and fell backward as they dragged her.

As Celene was pulled away, Kyote felt rage flare up within him. His muscles tightened and his jaw clenched firmly. A burning sensation ran across his bare skin. Sweat began to stream down from his forehead and along his back. Sharp claws extended as they tore through the ends of his fingertips. His eyes cast a golden orange beam that lit the room with an eerie brilliance.

He howled, pulling one last time on his restraints. The savagery of his thrashing was enough to rend the straps and he tore himself free.

Kyote leapt across the room and tackled Celene's captors. These vague shapes that were once people he knew joined the brawl. As they did, Kyote lashed out at them with his long curling talons. Each time a hand grasped at his arms, he slashed at them. Blood sprayed into the air as extremities were laid open. More than one limb was rent from its owner.

From time to time, a familiar face would flash before him. There were Gendarmery soldiers, even members of the VRF 12th, who'd fought with him during the war. Dhu and Vergan, in particular, attempted to restrain him. For a moment, he saw Hammerfeuer and a handful of his lackeys. Seconds later, Gohn's men appeared, including the barrel-chested Effee.

Unexpectedly, Rolde slid across his path. Kyote hacked at him, and the horizontal swipe cleaved Rolde's head from his torso. His body stood like a statue as Kyote pushed past him. Still in the clutches of the disembodied hands, Celene remained just beyond his reach.

With one last push, he closed the distance. The impact of his haphazard dive knocked them all to the floor. Kyote hunched over Celene, who was pinned to the ground.

He peered into her eyes, but it wasn't Celene staring back at him.

Kyote dug his claws into Celene's face and began to pull. He was going to peel away the skin until he found his childhood friend buried inside. She screamed in horror.

And still, he kept tearing the flesh away.

Kyote's body jerked. His heart was racing as he bolted upright and placed a hand on his chest. Sweat had plastered his hair to his scalp. He was in the dingy, sweltering motel room that stunk of decades worth of sweat and nightmares

After some time spent staring at the darkness, he cocked his head to the side. He was overwhelmed with relief to find Celene sprawled out, face down on her side of the bed. Her breathing was soft and regular. During the night, her shirt had rolled up, exposing her lower back.

He reached out and touched the bare skin. The sensation of her flesh on his fingertips calmed him.

It would be some time before he slept again.

Though he kept the dream to himself, its visceral imagery haunted him the following day. Only when he swallowed a few drinks could he successfully push the dream to the back of his head.

Once again, he was on his back on top of the bed, but Kyote could not sleep.

Due to what was undoubtedly already a hangover, Kyote felt as if every nerve-ending was on fire. Two pitchers of the local ale with a few shots to wash it down had done a number on him.

The insistent banging at the door didn't help. He figured someone was looking for a patron in one of the motel's adjacent rooms. *Get outta the damn bed and see who it is before… ugh, shit.*

When the drubbing began to rattle the doorknob, he realized the visitor was not likely to give up. For a few seconds, he stayed still, hoping that if he ignored it long enough, whoever it was would eventually give up and go away. When the pounding became more violent with each blow, he knew he'd have to deal with it. At some point, they would wake—

"Huh, uh, who's that?" Celene muttered as she flipped over. Her eyes remained tightly sealed as she gathered up the blanket and pulled it up under her chin.

Fucking dick, Kyote thought to himself as rolled out of bed. He shook his head, which only made the throbbing worse. For a second, he wanted to vomit. He ground his teeth and opened his eyes wide.

"Just a minute," he called out. Dressed in boxers and a sleeveless shirt, Kyote grasped the knob tightly as he opened it. He leaned forward and peered outside to find a pair of men in well-tailored black suits, both of who were standing too close to the door for comfort. He was reminded of Gohn's goons. This caused his heart to beat faster and his muscles to tighten.

In the pale neon glow of the motel's sign, he noticed, even in his hungover state, a detail that doubled his already racing pulse. On their blue ties was stitched a red script that marked them as part of the local crime syndicate.

While he'd heard rumors of such groups before, it wasn't until they arrived at Issuhn on Tir that Kyote came to understand the reality. The Tirean capital was ruled by an organized syndicate of "businessmen" who dealt in numerous ventures of varying legality. Everything from prostitution, drug manufacturing and distribution, to even the simplest of protection rackets were under their direct control. Each of the city's districts was managed by one of the establishment's families and a cadre of well-dressed thugs. To signify their role to the populace at large, each member wore a distinctive piece of blue neckwear. Although the majority of the metropolis' citizens went about their daily lives without issue, the presence of this organization was part of the public consciousness. They were bogeymen who seemingly never ran afoul of the law. In fact, many in the public turned a blind eye to their activities. To Kyote, it seemed that Issuhn on Tir's governing administration and enforcement officials pretended they had never existed.

Kyote's shoulders dropped. He wasn't afraid of a pair of low-level thugs there to shake him down. Once sufficiently bribed, they would surely be on their way.

"We don't need any room service," Kyote said dryly before either could speak. That they'd stopped their incessant knocking was a relief. "Sorry, we're all good here."

When he began to close the door, the man on the right, who was nearly twice his width, reached out and stopped the effort. The man stood with the pompous self-importance of a bouncer. He crossed his arms over his chest and took a single step back.

"We're here to collect," the other man, a lean, sallow fellow whose slick black hair was pulled back into a ponytail, spoke as he moved in close. The musk of his cologne tickled Kyote's nose.

"I already paid at the front desk." At some point, they were going to make a threat and he would have to decide whether or not he wanted to be gracious about it. While he hated the idea of rewarding such behavior, tossing a little coin their way to avoid conflict might be worth it. Celene's heavy breathing hinted that she'd slipped back into sleep. He'd prefer for her to stay that way.

"You gotta pay us," Ponytail announced matter-of-factly. "Everyone who stays *here* has to pay the residence fee. For you, it's double."

Kyote probably wasn't going to be gracious.

"Why for?" Kyote scowled. He already knew the answer to his question: he wasn't Tirean and he had the looks of someone who might be trouble. They weren't wrong on either count.

With the blood pumping in his veins, his headache quickly faded. As he grew increasingly alert, Kyote began to feel good. His night vision had adjusted, and he could see that they were alone. The adjacent streets were surprisingly empty. Perhaps the locals had been forewarned.

Knowing that he was about to indulge, he smirked.

"Look man, you can either pay up or we—"

Before the threat could leave Ponytail's mouth, Kyote jabbed him in the throat.

As he let out a garbled grunt, Ponytail clutched at his neck and stumbled backward. His eyes bulged as his face became flushed. In between gasps, he let out a string of incoherent swears.

It took a moment for Bouncer to realize what was happening. He stared dully as the other man staggered from the open doorway. In that pause, Kyote charged out of the room. With one arm, he shoved Ponytail into a nearby pile of refuse. With the other, he pounded Bouncer in the solar plexus. The impact forced the breath from his lungs. A swift drive of Kyote's knee to the man's groin caused his eyes to cross. He fell to his knees with a whimper.

Hearing the sounds of movement behind him, Kyote turned around as Ponytail clumsily rose to his feet. While he gingerly rubbed at the red spot along his Adam's apple, Ponytail raised a single fist and slowly moved towards Kyote.

"Fine with me," Kyote muttered. With his bare heel, he kicked Bouncer in the side of the head and turned to give the goon his full attention. The blow dropped the big man for the count. He went facedown onto the paved walkway with an inglorious grunt.

Before he could raise his own hands in defense, Kyote had to retreat. The lankier of the two assailants moved quickly and landed multiple strikes to Kyote's chest and shoulder. One struck a nerve that momentarily deadened the surrounding muscle group. Ponytail bobbed and weaved in anticipation. Kyote quickly realized that his brand of savagery wasn't going to overwhelm the trained fighter.

Kyote considered letting his fury take over, but he knew that would only make matters worse. He really didn't feel the need to kill them, he just wanted to chase them off. Since one man was already unconscious on the ground, he knew that his time in Neyong would have to be cut short. Ripping the thug apart would only draw unwanted anger from a group with far better resources.

The fighters moved back and forth in a violent ballet. For every blow Kyote landed, Ponytail got in two. Kyote was starting to feel the fight. His left shoulder was numb and he had at least one cracked rib. Much of his mental energy was spent resisting the urge to throw himself at Ponytail, take him by the skull, and repeatedly bounce it off of the street until he stopped moving.

Instead, he had to use his head for once.

Tired of the dance, Kyote shifted his posture and leaned forward. His jaw jutted outward, providing an enticing target. Clearly feeling sure of himself, Ponytail took the bait as he whipped his back leg around. Kyote ducked the roundhouse kick and drove a foot into his plant leg. Ponytail's knee buckled and he collapsed.

He screeched as he tumbled forward. Before Ponytail could do more than grasp at the damaged joint, Kyote jumped on top and began to pummel him.

As he drove bloodied knuckles into the man's face, Kyote used his head again. He pulled Ponytail, who was stunned but still conscious, in close and spoke.

"Question and answer time, jackass. Gohn. Do you know him? Tall, skinny weasel. Skin like ash. What was his first name?" He attempted to dig the fact out from the trash heap that was his memory. He briefly recalled a conversation with Flynn about the servant on one of their trips across Verenigen. "Artis! Artis Gohn. You know anything about him? You ever work for the man?" With every pause, he shook Ponytail.

Still dazed, his captive mumbled.

"What? Speak up, asshole!" He reared back to slap him across the cheek.

"No," Ponytail eventually replied. "Ain't never heard of no man. Nobody named Gohn. I work for… work for B-bupati Diento'va."

Either Ponytail was being truthful or the head injuries he'd sustained made him useless and unreliable. To reward the man, Kyote hammered a fist into his head a few times until he eventually went limp. Though bloodied and bruised, Ponytail would live. He'd be uglier for a time until the swelling receded.

"Kyote?" Celene's called out nervously from inside the room. "Kyote? Is everything… are you okay?"

"It's all good, babe," he said as he stood up and brushed his hands on his thighs. "Just taking care of a problem."

He paused for a moment.

"And creating a whole new one," he eventually muttered to himself. He looked back and forth between the pair of well-dressed bodies.

Kyote only had minutes to settle on a course of action. He couldn't leave them here, out in the open, and moving them would only delay the inevitable. They would eventually wake and come looking for him with both renewed vigor and a pack of their compatriots.

He eventually dragged the unconscious pair into a nearby alley and dumped them in the shadows. After removing their ties, he used the cloth the bind their hands. He again thought of killing them, and again he decided against it. After a beating, they might hold a grudge that would have them looking for Kyote during their usual rounds. If the pair were found dead, though, more of their kind might make pointed inquiries. He and Celene had made their faces well-known while questioning the locals about her family.

They had to pack up and move before sunrise. Though they'd yet to exhaust all leads in the district, he didn't want to hang around. The extorters certainly reported to someone, and once whomever that boss was saw what was done to his men, there would be even more trouble with his name on it to avoid.

Chapter 19

The Thirty-first of Sehbienimond
Ilkabari District, Issuhn on Tir

In the northern acreage of Ilkabari District, just south of its border with Neyong District, stood the Majira estate, one of the city's oldest structures. The mansion, built nearly seven hundred years ago, hailed back to Tir's imperial roots, before Issuhn on Tir swallowed up the surrounding countryside. The single-story wood-framed abode, topped by angled, red-tile roofs, sat on a sizable estate that was protected from the rest of the ward by a two-meter tall security wall.

Within this overbearing barrier was a series of reflecting pools, ponds filled with local fish and well-manicured gardens. A ring of golden lamps was strung along the outer walkway that surrounded the main building's exterior. Two additional structures, which housed the servants and security guards, were tucked behind copses of colorful maple trees.

Despite its historical value and the excellent care that had been taken to keep it maintained, the Majima estate rarely saw visitors. With two armed men posted at the front gate and another six patrolling the interior, one could not simply walk about the aged property like a tourist. Only invited guests were permitted. The locals knew well who lived within and discouraged the interest of newcomers.

Deep inside the manor, Hojo Majira quietly sat as he

meditated. The smell from recently-lit incense filled his nostrils with each breath. As the longtime head of Ilkabari's organization, it served him well to separate the stress of the day from his own nightly relaxations. Though, as of late, things had been fairly peaceful.

Most of the tasks and arrangements between his crew and that of the other district heads were managed by underlings, many of whom were under the command of other, more seasoned personnel. Rarely did anyone bring concerns to Hojo. A few of the more old-school operatives occasionally asked for his blessing on more significant operations. He began to wonder if he'd become a leader in name only.

His office was a simple room, the walls covered by ancient artwork hailing from a time when Tir was a less industrial nation. Many were aged watercolors of maidens in proper attire and landscapes of the shoreline from the 1700s, when Issuhn on Tir was but a tiny port town. Along the back, a pair of matching decorative screens flanked his desk, hiding the entrance to the master's personal quarters and bath.

Since an old friend and recently-arrived guest waited for him in the dining room, Hojo pushed his concerns aside. It was a poor host who brought personal concerns to the dinner table.

In truth, Hojo was relieved to entertain company of any kind. He had two sons, both married with their own children, neither of whom he'd seen in years. They wanted no part of his business and chose to live a normal, lawful life. After his passing, the mansion would undoubtedly go to one of them. At that point, they would have to make arrangements with his associates, since the venerable locale served as a base for the organization's criminal activities in the district.

The sliding sound of a door panel caught his attention.

"Sir?" a voice hailed from the open entrance on the far side of the room. Hojo looked up to find his head of security, Daino

Kuijairos, framed in the doorway. Daino was an older man, with short silver locks, who always treated him with the respect due to the proper leader of Ilkabari. From the creases in Daino's brow, Hojo knew that something was amiss.

"Yes? Please, come in." Hojo beckoned to him. Surprisingly, Daino remained where he was.

"Sir, there are visitors who wish to have an audience with you."

"Is that so? At this late an hour?"

"Men from Neyong. Diento'va's crew. Said they were sent to speak directly with you. A formal request."

Hojo was quiet for a moment. Most of Ilkabari District's business was handled without his direct involvement. His lieutenants were capable men who kept the proverbial gears well oiled. None of them attempt to seize control of the district for themselves because they all respected the old ways.

"Send them in."

Though he didn't let it show on his face, Hojo was excited. It had been months since he'd heard appeals from his business partners. It had been longer still since he'd traveled to the Chōratsu-tō-neu, the golden highrise at the heart of the city where the district heads convened.

A few minutes passed before Daino returned with two men who immediately bowed once in Hojo's presence. Bruised knuckles and off-the-rack suits told Hojo that they were low level, more used to hustling for tribute than meeting with the upper hierarchy of the organization. A glance at their ties confirmed this; the distinct emblems stitched into the blue silk told him their rank.

Both men kept their heads lowered, kneeling to ensure that they were lower to the ground than the master of the house, who remained in his seat. Hojo nodded. Someone had taught them well.

Hojo flicked his hand, motioning that they should rise.

"Tell me why you've come here," he spoke as he watched the pair. "I am late for dinner with my guests."

"Sir, all apologies for coming at such a late hour, but we've a formal request to, uh… well, *request* of you." The man stumbled over his words. "Our associates have tracked a man into Ilkabari who beat up two of our own only a few nights back. We spoke with Master Diento'va, and he ordered that we confer with you directly on the matter. Ask your permission to enter Ilkabari proper to find the man before he escapes Issuhn on Tir altogether."

"You've come to find a man? A single man? Seems a bit much, no?"

"A savage one, sir. Someone from Verenigen, not even a Tirean. Described him as crazed and violent. More beast than man. Attacked some of our fellows without provocation. Put them in the clinic but good. Signed into the inn's guestbook by the name Kurttsen. Arrived on the ferry from Eithos Los with a girl earlier in the month and they've been making inquiries with the locals ever since. They're looking for someone by the name of Kaize. We think they ran off from Neyong after the fight."

The mention of the Kaize surname caught Hojo's attention. A smile curled at his lips.

"And you would send hordes of your own men into Ilkabari to find this man?" Left unspoken was the implication that Hojo didn't wish to invite what might be the start of a coup by Bupati Diento'va. Allowing a dozen of his men free reign could start a steady stream of even more into Ilkabari. Before long, Diento'va's crew would be so entrenched that it would be easy for the other head to add the ward into to own.

"Well, uh, no, sir. Not legions. We just wanted to—"

"Might I offer some aid?" a voice from the open door interrupted. His guest, having waited long enough, had come to investigate. "I think my services can draw out your prey."

Hojo stifled a chuckle. His evening promised to be most entertaining.

Chapter 20

The Thirty-second of Sehbienimond
Ilkabari District, Issuhn on Tir

Though being dragged from their bed in the middle of the night had been inconvenient, Celene wasn't too put out by having to abandon Neyong District. In fact, when Kyote explained the situation to her, she was surprisingly agreeable.

While a few dangling threads still needed tending, she felt that their investigation in that ward had all but ran its course. Though it was premature, their departure would have been inevitable.

Though she never admitted it aloud, there were other reasons she felt glad to move. At some point, she'd begun to develop the beginnings of mysophobia. The nearby Akayásen and its seedier clientele caused an irrational obsession with cleanliness to form. Celene hated the sensation that walking amongst its crowds left. Though most weren't visibly dirty, she thought of herself as increasingly befouled the longer she remained outdoors. Direct contact was an anathema to her. Back at their lodgings, there was never enough soap to make her skin clean.

Her growing uneasiness was also fueled by the fact that Kyote was drinking an unhealthy amount. Many of the local bars sold dirt cheap beer, and Kyote had indulged far too much as of late. If relocating curbed that particular habit, she'd considered it a boon.

What concerned her most, though, was the real reason for their flight.

Even as she washed up and packed her things, Celene prodded Kyote for details. Kyote's account of his fight with the thugs seemed to be missing some vital facts. He claimed that petty crooks attempted to barge in and rob them while they slept. Kyote made sure to downplay the incident, calling it a mere scuffle that ended when the potential robbers ran off.

The bruises on his arms and the way he favored his left side hinted at something more.

Although she wanted to grill him, there was only so much she could ask before he shut her out altogether. Learning how far she could push him was a precarious game at which she was becoming adept.

They checked out and began their trek through the streets. It was still dark and only a few of the locals were out.

For a time, the conversation between them remained strained. Kyote was still tired. Celene was saddened that her trust in Kyote was wavering.

Their transit took a half-day, a portion of which was spent getting directions. Since many of the streets were unmarked, they occasionally found themselves in dead-ends or alleyways that led along circuitous paths back to familiar locales. Before sunset, they finally arranged for new lodgings at a hostel on the eastern edge of Ilkabari District.

For Celene, Ilkabari District was a surprising breath of fresh air. Unlike the more centrally-located boroughs, which were overpopulated and grimy, this area proved comfortable and spacious. The paved roadways were arranged in a simple grid pattern, and people moved at a slower, almost lackadaisical pace. They regularly stopped to gossip idly before they headed on to other locales. These were not people in a frantic rush.

Ilkabari's territory ran along the southwestern portion of the metropolitan area, just beside the outer city limits. As such, there was a more rural character about the construction and inhabitants. A number of produce markets allowed growers who hauled their crops in from distant farmlands to offer their wares.

A few days after their relocation, Celene thought about her relationship with Kyote, which had become increasingly tense. It wasn't so much that they were in conflict, but that their goals differed now. While Kyote continued to give lip service about aiding her in the search for her family, his mind often wandered.

Since he deflected all attempts to discuss her concerns, she observed Kyote in the times when he wasn't keeping up the ruse. With his guard down, he grew anxious. His gaze often snapped about, as if he was tracking something she could not perceive.

Celene suspected phantoms of the past events lingered around him. His time spent away from her and Dulton had cost him a dear friend and, despite his assurances to the contrary, he was still obsessed with the man he blamed for Rolde's death.

Celene felt no anger towards Kyote because she believed that he was coping as best as he could. She only wished he would cut back on his indulgences, as the regular alcohol consumption was not helping his condition. His complexion had grown pale and his eyes were constantly bloodshot. Between the shortness of his temper and a constant restlessness, he seemed to be burning himself out.

Since Ilkabari had far fewer drinking establishments than

Neyong, Kyote was forced to find a local market that peddled wine and liquor. His recent issues with sleep, which was often plagued by vibrant nightmares, had driven him to medicate himself with local spirits. A half-bottle of rice wine or whiskey tended to do the trick.

While this didn't sit well with Celene, she held her tongue. It was better than having him return, stumbling drunk, to their room every night. Even if his mind was elsewhere, at least she knew where he was, physically. Celene had long ago grown tired of Tir's nightlife. Her own dalliances with alcoholism had dredged up an unhealthy darkness. Now, even though she hoped to lead Kyote away from trouble, she wanted little to do with Issuhn on Tir's bar scene. That the nearest public house was almost an hour's trek into the adjacent ward was a small comfort.

In reality, the situation was far worse than Celene knew.

Kyote continued to see visions of Gohn on the streets of Ilkabari District. The gray man would appear on the periphery of his vision only to fade into the crowd as Kyote looked around. Kyote became progressively exhausted as the encounters persisted.

To make matters worse, every night he fought increasingly-bizarre dreams filled with feelings of loss and a lust for violence he was unable to satisfy. No amount of self-medication could silence these terrors.

The last time he felt like himself had been when he beat up the two thugs. He'd slept well the following evening after the activity provided some sick form of release for his bedeviled mind and tense body.

This realization made him place his head in his hands in shame.

Sometime during the night of the thirty-second, Kyote stumbled out of bed and kicked over a pair of empty bottles. They noisily rattled as they skipped across the tiled floor. From behind him, Celene muttered incoherently. Though he was barely awake and even less sober, Kyote looked over his shoulder to where she still rested on the mattress.

When it was clear she would not wake, he shuffled on to the bathroom. As he stood over the toilet, with a hand pressed against the wall for support, thinking about his current situation.

How much longer can we keep this up? Sticking around this city's gonna get to us eventually. Either Celene loses her trail and gives up hope or some thug picks a fight that really puts us in a bind. Really pisses me off enough that I tear him open. I'm trying to play nice. As much as I can, I guess. Keep my shit to myself. Only so much booze I can down.

He chuckled dryly to himself as he flushed.

Got to keep the monster numb to keep it in its cage, I guess.

After washing his hands, he stomped back out and stood bedside. Celene had rolled over on to her side. At that moment, she appeared truly at ease.

Only when she's out like a light can she relax about me. Kinda sad, it is. I was supposed to come along and we were gonna do this adventure. I'm supposed to be the one to keep her safe. It should be us doing our thing, free of the drudgery of everyday life. But, she ain't happy. She ain't even good at hiding it. Not from me, at least. My being here hasn't made things any better for her. If I left—just walked right out that door and never came back—she'd be sad, but, eventually, things'd turn around for her.

The weight of the knowledge sat in his stomach like a lump. He stayed, silently contemplating the idea for some time. His legs ached from immobility.

Eventually, he slipped back under the covers. He wouldn't leave her, yet. He'd already been apart from her for far too long once. Kyote wanted to have her nearby for just a little while more.

Just before they headed out for the day, Celene gathered up a knit sweater. The pale blue garment was well-worn, with a few loose seams and some discoloration along the sleeves. Now that they were out in the city's more rural areas, there was a distinct chill in the air. Though it was still the harvest season, Celene noticed a drastic downturn in temperatures now that they were so close to the Dwyr Sea. She wondered if they were in for a particularly harsh late season.

After stopping for a breakfast of rice porridge and hot tea, they journeyed southward. She was anxious to follow up on a few leads. Two, in particular, pointed to local businesses along the outer-lying neighborhoods where the Kaize family might have once been patrons.

While Kyote wasn't particularly gregarious that morning, to Celene it seemed as though he was at least attentive. He responded to her comments with more than occasional grunts. His eyes weren't bloodshot and he didn't reek of booze.

As they moved along the main thoroughfare, Celene heard the cries of a young girl. The child stood alone on a street corner, hands pressed against her face as streams of tears ran down her cheeks. Celene stopped and scanned the courtyard.

"Hold up," Celene announced to Kyote, who only gave her a strange glance. When he noticed Celene's sudden interest in the girl, he shrugged. During her time at the orphanage, she'd mothered the other wards, so it came as no surprise that Celene was drawn to the frantic youngster.

Celene slowly approached the child, who had to be no

older than five. She had long black hair and was draped in a floral print dress that was too light for the weather. That she wore neither socks nor shoes shocked Celene.

As he slumped against a lamppost, Kyote watched Celene carefully draw near and go down on one knee. Even through his jacket, he could feel the cold steel, which satisfyingly soothed the burning in his lower back, near his kidneys.

"It's… it's okay," Celene began as she held a comforting hand just above the girl's left shoulder. "You'll be fine. I'll help you find your mommy."

Since the young Tirean did not shy away from contact, Celene touched her arm. Though the girl continued to sniffle, her sobs quieted.

While Kyote made no move to join Celene, he did remain within earshot. He expected that this would either end one of two ways: in a heartfelt family reunion or with an angry mother reading Celene the riot act in Tirean for messing with her child. Sometimes even the most innocent intentions could be misconstrued. For Celene's sake, he hoped for the best.

Out of the corner of his vision, he spotted motion in the distance. The lanky silhouette just out of sight annoyed him like a splinter in his skin.

His eyes flicked to the side, just to ensure that Celene was okay. She still knelt in front of the girl, attempting to dry the child's tears.

Kyote shifted his weight from one foot to the other as he spun his head about. For the most part, he spotted nothing out of the ordinary. People milled about, on their way to the market or their homes. Men loaded down with crates pushed through. A few shoppers paused to converse with acquaintances.

Through the loose assembly of locals he spotted Gohn. This time, Wallowrich's former butler remained in place. Plain as day, the ashen-hued man stood on the far side of the square talking with two elderly ladies. Gohn was now dressed in a cream button-down shirt, charcoal-hued slacks and matching blazer. His collar was unbuttoned, and he wore no necktie. Kyote was shocked by his relaxed, casual appearance.

Though he couldn't hear from this distance, Gohn's conversation with the older women appeared congenial, as if Gohn was catching up with old friends.

Kyote remained in place against the lamppost and shook his head.

When the vision of Gohn remained, Kyote's brow furrowed. Gohn's figure had always disappeared into wisps of smoke before Kyote could reach him. He waited pensively in place.

With each passing second, Kyote's heart rate accelerated. He bit at his lower lip, resisting the urge to charge across the court.

Gohn waved goodbye to the ladies, turned, and met Kyote's stare. Their gazes locked and Gohn sneered. Gohn's dull eyes glimmered. While Kyote was well out of earshot, he could read his lips.

"Follow me," mouthed Gohn before he retreated into the adjacent alley.

Kyote was off.

Celene didn't notice his departure until a pair of ladies cried out in distress at being pushed aside. With the girl's hand still in hers, she stood up and watched as he cut a sharp path through the morning crowd.

"Kyote, gods damn it!" Celene barked at Kyote. He gave no sign that he'd heard her. Almost instantly, she covered her mouth and glanced at the surrounding throng, scared that her outburst might be considered blasphemous. When no one reacted, she turned to watch Kyote disappear into the darkened backstreet.

Though she wanted to give chase, Celene wouldn't leave the child until she found her guardian. As she swore about the timing, Celene knew she was better off where she was. Kyote would eventually find his way back to her. He always did.

An older woman finally came out of the crowd and collected her child without a word to Celene. While Celene protested, the pair scurried off, leaving her by herself in the courtyard.

Kyote chased Gohn into the murky network of back alleys that led away from the main thoroughfare. He didn't stop to consider how he'd gotten there. As far as he was concerned, this was a bit of good fortune. All the time and energy he had wasted jumping at specters was finally going to pay off. If he had to chase him out of the city, he would.

Gonna catch you, motherfucker. Gonna catch you and kill you. Make sure you know why this is—

As Kyote rushed headlong into the approaching intersection, he spotted a trio of well-dressed men lurking in the shadows. Each sported a necktie with a simple pattern of interconnected chevrons in primary colors. They all brandished weapons as they stepped forward.

Gohn shimmied past the goons and backed into the adjacent alley.

"Ay'hola," one called out in an old Tirean greeting.

Once Kyote skidded to a stop, another two thugs slipped in behind him. They'd been hiding between the closely-packed buildings, waiting for the moment that he'd burst onto the scene. Before he could turn, someone struck him in the back of the knee with a steel baton and dropped him to the ground.

As he stumbled to the pavement, sharp shocks ran up though his hips and into his torso. Kyote barked out in pain as he winced. While he doubted anything was broken, he couldn't get to his feet just yet.

This concern proved to be irrelevant.

Two men were on him before he could react. He raised an arm over his head, a weak defense for the hail of blows that rained down on him. Kyote collapsed into a pile. Once down, boots began to kick at him.

As they continued to bludgeon Kyote, his mind shut down.

They were waiting for me. Expected me to walk right into this. Didn't break out the guns 'cause they wanted to take me alive. I don't think they'd care if the locals heard the gunfire. Maybe Tireans have gotten used to looking the other way.

These assholes… they're gonna do a number on me. I only hope that Celene has the sense—

One blow struck him just right. He slipped into unconsciousness before his head bounced off the pavement.

As he went under, Kyote heard a female voice calling for him from somewhere off in the distance.

Chapter 21

The Thirty-third of Sehbienimond
Ilkabari District, Issuhn on Tir

Kyote's head hurt something fierce. It wasn't the sharp, burning ache of a hangover that poked at the back of his eyes; the dull throb radiated from multiple locations. While unpleasant, he'd certainly felt a lot worse.

Then again, when your bar for pain was set by having been set on fire, launched from a tower, and thrown into a neighboring mansion, anything else seemed pretty minor. Kyote smiled with his eyes still closed. It was perspective few others had.

A voice, which floated somewhere off in the distance, spoke up. "Wake him. I don't have the time to waste."

Ugh, this isn't gonna be pleasant.

Cold water splashed across his face. The shock of the icy fluid caused him to gasp. The muscles along his shoulders clenched tightly as his body went rigid. Kyote's eyes flashed open as his head flung back.

At first, he couldn't see anything. Before long, his eyes adjusted, and he was able to pick out the chamber's details. Bare walls were marred by scratches. Though the only light came from a lantern hung somewhere behind him, Kyote noticed a dark splatter on the stone floor near his left boot.

He wondered how many victims exited the facility's back

door wrapped in fabric and rope to be dumped off elsewhere.

A few meters away, standing with his arms crossed behind his back, was Gohn, who watched with interest as Kyote returned to consciousness. Beside Gohn was a pair of well-dressed thugs, each armed with a baton and brass knuckles. Their suitcoats hung from hooks on the far wall.

"Kyote Kurttsen," Gohn started from a few paces away. Though Kyote had been lashed to the chair, Gohn remained well out of his reach. "I hadn't bothered to find out your full name before. It wasn't of import at the time. The only one that mattered was Mr. Earrele, and that was because of his prior relationship with my mark at the time. You and the other one were but associates."

Gohn motioned toward the men waiting in the wings. "It appears that you've made a nuisance of yourself among some of my acquaintances. While many people would like to think they can just disappear into the city at large, this could not be further from the truth. A canvassing of Neyong made it easy to uncover who you and your female friend were and where you'd been. Once they tracked you to Ilkabari, it was only a matter of time before they trapped you."

He turned to meet the stern visages behind him. Before he could continue, Kyote spoke up.

"You've been here all along, ain't you? I knew I saw you in Neyong. It wasn't just in my head."

One of the men charged and drove a fist into Kyote's jaw. Gohn reached over to the man's shoulder to draw him away.

"So sorry to ruin your delusions, but I've been a guest in Ilkabari for some time now. Reconnecting with old friends. Visiting with Hojo Majira, the head of the district's operations. Imagine my surprise when someone of your description was brought to Master Majira's attention. Subordinates from Diento'va's crew came asking for permission to enter the ward and track you down. I will admit that I saw an opportunity. Offered my own assistance as payment for Master Majira's fine hospitality."

Gohn's associates shifted restlessly. Noticing this, Gohn changed course.

"Well, it seems that our time together is short. Before my friends take over, I do have some inquiries of my own. This whole *event* serves a dual purpose, as I need some information from you. Purely a matter of sating my curiosity. If they get to rough you up at the same time, well…" He paused for dramatic effect. "Where might be your friend, Flynn? Flynn Earrele? Did he come with you?" Gohn inquired. Though he tried to seem aloof, his eyes showed concern.

"Fuck if I know where he is. Last I saw, he was cleaning up *your* mess in Norte'wald."

Gohn rubbed at his mouth. "Though it's a shame, I knew you'd be obstinate. I would have liked for this to be a quick process. I so need to wrap up loose ends. Should have tended to it at the time, but I was on a tight deadline. That and you fools have the gods' good fortune to get out of scrap after scrap. Now, your friend, the fat one—"

"Rolde! His name was Erich Rolde," Kyote barked as he tried to rise from the seat. The bindings dug into his skin as he strained against them. "If you kill a man, at least know who he was and why you had to end him!"

Gohn recoiled, alarm causing his eyes to bulge. Then his mouth curled in a faint grin. The color in his cheeks faded to its usually-ashen hue.

After stepping back a few paces, he motioned for the two thugs. The one on the left, who'd already delivered a blow, moved in and threw a hard right across Kyote's jaw. Kyote tasted blood in his mouth. A sharp pain in the side of his face made him think a tooth had broken.

Usually, I can heal broken bones. Wonder what happens if they pop a tooth out.

A few more punches landed on his face. The first man rubbed his bloodied knuckles and stepped back to let his ally have a turn. The shorter thug produced a thin wooden cane, with which he delivered a few quick lashes to Kyote's arms and upper back. With each blow, the switch cut into his skin.

Kyote was shocked by how much it hurt, considering how thin and light the reed looked.

"Wa-ho-o-o-o shit," he bellowed as the second man backed off.

Gohn, who remained at the back of the room, waited and watched, showing no reaction.

"That... that tickled some," Kyote sputtered as his head rolled back. Swelling around his mouth caused his words to slur. As his hair fell back away from his face, the orange glow in his eyes shone in the dark room.

Though blood oozed in small patches on his skin, the wounds began to close. Before long, only a few bruises and traces of undried fluids remained. As they watched him heal at an impossible rate, the torturers looked at one another in confusion. Gohn let out a sardonic chuckle.

Kyote wondered if he would be able to free himself from the restraints. Though giving into his rage allowed him to fly carelessly into any fray, he'd never seen evidence that it gave him enhanced strength. The leather shackles might hold him. If they did, he might destroy his hands in a frantic attempt to pull himself free.

He decided to play the waiting game. Given enough time, his captors would slip up. Whether he would be in the condition to capitalize on the opportunity was a different matter.

After another round of thrashings, Gohn stepped in and addressed his subordinates. Coarse lines creased his brow; Kyote's resilience had put a wrinkle in his plans.

"Do you have an answer now?" he asked. "Flynn. Where might he be? I'm sure you know enough about him to tell me something."

The Library, probably.

Kyote snorted and offered a pursed smile. "Sorry. We went our separate ways. Got no clue where he is."

"You may take your leave," he ordered his men. "Send for Hessen. Tell him to bring in the girl. I think his particular brand of persuasion is required here to really leave a mark. That, and our friend needs to understand the stakes. Playing coy will do him no good."

While neither seemed thrilled at leaving their work unfinished, both men collected their jackets and departed.

At the words "the girl," Kyote's heart beat violently in his chest.

I swear by all the gods that if he harms Celene, I will paint the walls with his blood.

Gohn stepped in close and began to speak softly.

"You might have been able to hide in Tir—unknown to me—for some time had you not picked a fight with those men in Neyong. Imagine my amusement when I heard the tale of a man with your particular *fighting style*—one much like a man Effee described from the melee at Wallowrich's home—who thought to thrash a pair of low-level grunts. 'A savage man,' it was said. Stirred up a hornet's nest, did you, and as such they put out the word for your capture. Even sent their own into Ilkabari to track you down. When I heard your physical description, I knew it could be no one else. So few non-Tireans head this deep into the city's western wards. Rare are the Verenigen natives, even mutts like yourself, who visit the country's rural regions. Most stay near the harbor or around the business sectors. I will admit that a part of me expected you to be with Earrele, but it appears you've upgraded your traveling partner."

The mere mention of Celene caused Kyote's pulse to flutter again. Any hope that she'd steered clear of Gohn and his men was quickly squashed.

"What do you get out of this?" Kyote asked as he sagged in his bindings. "Having your men whale on me like I'm a heavy bag? I ain't got no info you need to beat out of me, and you know it. You want Flynn? I ain't got no idea where he is after I left him behind."

"You're very much correct in that regard," Gohn noted. "Once Flynn handed over the Ocellar—the World's Eye as you know it—the three of you became merely a loose end to address. Still, you must know something about Flynn. A place, besides Norte'wald, where he might find lodgings. Any piece of information would benefit you greatly. But make no mistake. These thrashings? This whole tiresome *event?* That, my good man, I do for *them.* These associates, some of which belong to Diento'va of Neyong. Others report to Hojo Majira, the master of Ilkabari. A few work directly for me, in a technical sense, towards other, non-cartel related goals. This little situation is a payment for their continued cooperation. A perk, one might call it. Many of the present acquaintances are in the local syndicate, as you know it. Or, they know men who are. Personally, once I've wrung every piece of information from your brain, I'd have you executed and be on my way. Lengthy torture is something in which only the mentally ill indulge."

"Sounds right up your alley, then," Kyote snarled. This caused Gohn to laugh to himself, though it was a soulless sound, without mirth.

"At first, my allies thought to have you tortured and broken," Gohn continued. "But, it appears that maybe those efforts would be wasted. While I'm sure they would enjoy roughing you up over and over again, they would only injure themselves in the process." He pointed at Kyote's eyes, which had only recently returned to their natural dark brown.

"You have a very unique gift. Something in you that allows you to endure even the worst of thrashings. One that might be useful to a footsoldier. To my master, Tah'Coscienier Grhahnth? Not nearly so vital to his long term designs. He made no mention of any need for your existence. As such, I have no use for you. You are a thorn to be removed and nothing more…"

Gohn trailed off as he tapped at his chin thoughtfully. In that pause, Kyote wondered what Gohn might have meant about his "master." After the numerous blows to the head he'd suffered, he was struggling to piece together more than one coherent thought at a time.

"Also, you're a crafty enough individual that eventually you might slip free of your bonds and make problems."

Kyote was surprised by what might have been a compliment. Before he could respond, his attention was drawn to the entrance. The knob rattled for a second before it turned.

The doors opened to an older man dressed in a drab tan shirt and gray slacks. A pair of workman's boots clopped dully on the stone floor. He propped the entrance ajar and pulled in a metal cart loaded with various tools. A number of the steel implements were stained with blood. Amongst a collection of thin knives sat a saw and two mallets.

When Hessen stopped to arrange and clean some of his equipment, Kyote saw that the man's pudgy face was covered with pockmarks and scars. Blue eyes had gone dull, almost to the point of being gray in hue. At some point, a sizable chunk had been taken out of his jawline, leaving a gnarled cluster of pink tissue.

Hessen grabbed a balled-up clump of leather cloth. With a flip of his wrist, he unfolded an apron that he quickly slipped over his head. Once tied off, the apparel covered his outfit. Dried brown splotches discolored the front.

Unexpectedly, Hessen walked back through the doorway. The sound of something scraping on the floor could be heard.

Kyote's eyes locked on the leather-clad man as he dragged Celene, who was strapped to another chair, behind him. Unlike Kyote, who still thrashed against his bindings, she sat still. Though there was no sign that she'd been harmed, she was pale with terror. Her mouth was gagged, and streams of tears ran down her cheeks. Her eyes were bloodshot.

Hessen arranged her directly across from Kyote. Once he felt she was properly placed, he dusted off his hands and looked at Kyote.

"I will tell you my rules, of which there is only one. She will be taken to another room, where my men will watch over her. If you make a sound, at any point during my time with you, I will have her killed. What I do to you after that will be worse," Hessen announced. When Kyote failed to respond, Hessen reached in, grabbed him by the chin, and forced Kyote to meet his gaze. "Strong of will does not mean strong of flesh. Your stubbornness will only make me enjoy the breaking all the more."

"Now that we've established some incentive for you—" Gohn spoke from the back of the room. "—I would hope you might be a bit more compliant. Hessen will take time in between sessions to see if you're willing to divulge anything you'd like to share about Flynn and his possible whereabouts. Is that not correct, Hessen?"

"It is true. Every now and then, you will be permitted to speak. Not scream. Not beg. But answer. About this man,

Flynn. When you are ready to tell us everything, then it will stop. The torture, that is."

"Yes," Gohn continued. "Whether you do it sooner or later, makes no difference to me as the end result with certainly be the same, for you. For her… maybe she gets out of this alive. You would do well to consider that."

Though he bit his tongue, Kyote sneered. He looked at Celene, who was paralyzed by fear. There was no message hidden in the tear-soaked eyes. He doubted that she felt anything other than panic.

Gohn snapped his fingers. Two men, a different pair, entered almost instantly.

"Take her out," Gohn ordered with a flick of his hand. "The kind of work Hessen's about to perform might be too much for the delicate flower. Wouldn't want her to faint. Or worse. Hessen doesn't like unnecessary distractions as he goes about his duties."

The duo followed their orders and pulled Celene, whose gaze never left Kyote's face, out. In the distance, another door creaked open.

"Well, as much as this might have been entertaining, I do have other appointments," Gohn spoke as he headed for the exit. "I do not expect we will ever meet again. Later today— maybe tomorrow—Hessen will relay unto me what you told him. Maybe, in passing, he'll tell me if the girl was set free." He motioned to Hessen, who nodded with grim joy.

As Gohn departed, Kyote caught a glimpse of the room beyond. Waiting for Gohn was a black-haired man of pale complexion with a thin, curved scar along the left edge of his jawline. He was dressed in a three-piece suit, and a long wool jacket was cinched tightly around his waist. Dirty green eyes almost glowed in the dark pits between his high cheekbones and his dense brow ridge. In his hands, he cradled the World's

Eye. Upon spotting Gohn, he beckoned to the gray man.

The door closed behind Gohn.

Kyote knew this wouldn't end well. Hessen had been ordered to brutalize Kyote and would probably enjoy doing so. Hessen might occasionally pause to ask about Flynn, but that wasn't the primary reason for his efforts. What little he could tell them about Flynn was unlikely to satisfy them. It certainly wouldn't end the long and painful session. The fact that they had Celene somewhere nearby was the only reason Kyote kept in control. If he could take the agony on all his own, it might just save Celene's life.

But for how long? Reason nagged at him. *Eventually, they're gonna kill me. Gohn made that much clear. Hessen might tear into me for a while until he just decides to start pulling out organs. Once they do, why would I think they're not gonna do the same to her?*

Hessen looked at Kyote.

"And now we tend to the problem that is you," Hessen announced as he reached for a curved knife. With a fingernail, he scraped at a flake of dried blood. "Gohn states that you will be hard to kill. That you must be watched at all times lest you free yourself. That you are too *wild* to act like a normal man should. I like to think of that as a challenge." As he turned around, there was a coarse grin on his lips.

While running the cutting tool along a strip of leather, Hessen continued.

"Not a word, you must speak until I ask a question of you. They—" He pointed to somewhere outside the room. "—have orders. If they hear you cry out, they are to put the gun to the girl. Is that enough to hold your tongue? To keep you in your place? Nod once, and only once, if you understand."

Begrudgingly, Kyote did so. The skin of his palms creaked

as he gripped the arms of his chair. This response pleased Hessen.

"Are there any revelations that you would like to voice before I begin?" Hessen inquired as he stopped within arm's reach.

Kyote's ground his teeth as his jaw clenched tightly.

At first, Hessen looked him over, evaluating the canvas before him. Hessen flicked his wrist, and the blade slipped across the top of Kyote's forearm. Though the pain was immediate, Kyote bore it. His nostrils flared as blood leaked from the wound. A flash of orange lit up his eyes, and the slash resealed.

Seeing this, Hessen smirked. He made the same move, striking the same flesh with the honed edge. Before the injury completely reclosed, he struck again. Sanguine drops dripped to the floor as the flesh healed.

After some time, Hessen nodded to himself. He leaned in and spoke, his breath rank.

"I will let you in on a secret," Hessen whispered as he swiftly plunged the weapon into Kyote's thigh. Despite his desire to scream out, Kyote bit his tongue as his eyes bulged. "Your death is inevitable. You *will* die. I suspect so will she. The longer you chose not to confess, the more likely my friends will grow bored. They may take it upon themselves to indulge." Hessen began to chuckle. "You may not be the only one screaming tonight."

This, more than the tool buried in his leg, caused Kyote to buck against his restraints. The edges of his irises flickered a bright orange.

"Good, this is what I wanted from you," Hessen noted with a smile as he turned the blade inside the wound. Kyote's mind blanked for a second, and his nerves flared against the excruciating pain. When the steel scraped against bone, Kyote lost the fight to hold his tongue.

"I'll fucking kill you!" he roared. Hessen grinned as he continued to twist the handle. At this, Kyote added, "KILL YOU!"

Hessen released his grasp and backed away to his tool cart. A low chuckle rumbled within his thick chest.

As he screamed incoherently, Kyote heard a gunshot from somewhere nearby. Kyote abandoned any pretense of control.

The bloodlust called to him from within.

What else did he have to lose?

His eyes glared orange and his muscles clenched tightly. Preoccupied with the selection of his next tool, Hessen did not notice.

"You failed far sooner than I would have expected," Hessen added as he collected a polished stiletto. "Did not even make it long enough for me to give you permission to speak. To be fair, *everyone* screams eventually. I was told you were tougher than that. A shame, really."

Kyote didn't hear the words. Everything around him fell out of focus. Colors faded to shades of gray. He could smell the stink of Hessen's sweat.

All he wanted, at that moment, was to tear him open.

Kyote yanked himself free of his bonds. He writhed with such force that they creaked in protest. Before either could snap, both of Kyote's thumbs dislocated as they folded inwards under the strain. Large patches of skin peeled back as the restraints dug into the meat of his wrists. Blood poured freely from multiple lacerations, providing unexpected lubrication. With one last heave, he pulled his arms loose just as Hessen turned around to face him.

"Your noisy flail—"

"Kill you," Kyote seethed as he grabbed Hessen's arm and yanked him off his feet. Hessen did not fall to the floor, but stumbled closer to his would-be victim. Before he could regain his balance, Kyote twisted the man's hand, breaking three fingers in the process. Hessen dropped the blade into Kyote's grip.

Kyote flipped the knife and plunged it deep into the man's dense abdomen. Hessen grunted for a moment as shock painted his pudgy face. A gurgling cough slipped out of his open mouth. Kyote yanked upwards, and before too long, Hessen's bowels slipped out of the gaping wound.

As he clutched futilely at his innards, Hessen stumbled backward. His arrogant speeches were now replaced with whimpers. He tried to speak, but his words came out in a scrambled mess.

Kyote had the presence of mind to cut the remaining restraints. After some furious sawing at the dense hide lashings, he was finally free. He dropped the stiletto and propped himself up. Once out of the chair, Kyote struggled for a moment, feeling woozy. He reached down and pulled the curved blade from his leg.

Bloodied and limping badly, Kyote barreled shoulder-first into Hessen and knocked him to the ground. Before the torturer was entirely flat on his back, Kyote straddled him and quickly plunged the weapon into his chest. Kyote's grinned maniacally as the steel easily slipped into the man's flesh.

Within seconds, Kyote stabbed Hessen a dozen times. Two blows struck the heart, which caused Hessen to bleed out almost immediately. By the end, Kyote was jabbing at a lifeless sack of fluids.

He howled in the dead man's face. Kyote rose from the body and looked for the exit as he wiped both hands on his pants. He left the gore-coated weapon in Hessen's torso, just below the left collarbone.

With his eyes still glowing brightly, the cuts on Kyote's arms began to close. Both thumbs popped back into joint. The hole above his knee grew smaller with every clumsy stride.

By the time he reached the door, he was almost entirely healed, physically.

Kyote flung the door aside and charged into an abandoned kitchen. He'd been brought to an empty restaurant and held in a storage area.

For a moment, he paused as he tried to gain his bearings. His head snapped about like an animal's at every sound. Soon he heard the muffled conversation of two men from the next room.

"Throw some bones to decide it."

"Fuck that. You always win at dice *and* cards. I say leave her."

"That ain't gonna happen. Hessen don't want no trash left about his place. And you know Gohn and his pal don't want no evidence left behind. Already too many people got an idea of what side hustle he's been getting into as of late. Sneaking out of the city like he's got meetings elsewhere. We leave it like this and the Master's gonna catch word, and shit's gonna roll downhill and eventually hit us."

At this, Kyote rushed through the double doors on the far side and into the restaurant's dining area.

While there were a number of tables and chairs, most had been pushed aside. At the center of the empty space sat a lone seat, its occupant slumped and lifeless. On either side stood a single gunman, still in the midst of banal conversation, as if the body was of no importance.

Kyote saw Celene sitting there, her eyes open but unseeing. There was a single bullet hole in her chest. Her shirt was soaked in blood. Her pale blue sweater had been torn off and cast aside.

His heart sunk. Any rational thought slipped away. Honestly, he didn't want reason anymore. He only wanted to destroy these monsters.

Noticing his arrival, the thugs turned to Kyote with their guns out. Until the first one shot him in the shoulder, he barely noticed.

Kyote rushed forward. He was on the first man with such ferocity that there was no time for retreat. Now on the floor, he impotently flailed as Kyote grabbed his head. As he howled, Kyote twisted. A few cracks later, the man was dead. His limbs went limp, and his pistol spun away as it slipped from his hand.

For a moment, there was nothing else in the world as Kyote peered into the Tirean's empty eyes. His breath blew raggedly through his open mouth. A fine mist of crimson came out with each exhale.

Kyote's body jarred as another round popped him in the back. This one glanced off a rib and exited at an odd angle. At any other moment, he might have yelped in agony. Kyote rose and turned towards the remaining thug. On the second stride, he leapt into the air and tackled him.

Kyote climbed the gunman and grabbed him by the temples. He jammed his thumbs into the man's eyes and began to squeeze. Frantically, the man slapped at Kyote's hands, but to no avail. His screams only spurred Kyote, who slammed the back of his head into the flooring.

Soon, the carpet was soaked by a red smear.

Kyote had no idea how long he kept at it, but, eventually, he stopped pummeling the dead man's head. The features were a grisly mess that was now unrecognizable.

For some time, Kyote sat there, panting in ragged heaves. Bullet holes slowly sealed shut. Perforated organs healed. A fractured rib would take longer to mend, but none of his injuries would last.

He couldn't look at Celene. Not just yet.

The glow in his eyes faded and his humanity resurfaced. As nerve endings returned to life, he could feel the pain of his recent injuries. Freshly-healed muscle fibers twitched.

For a while, Kyote sat there, hunched over. Finally, he struggled to his feet and stumbled towards Celene. Though limp, with her head slumped backward, she was still tightly lashed to the chair. He removed her bindings. He pulled the gag from her mouth and pitched it aside. Streams of sorrow ran down his rugged face, where the droplets collected in his beard.

For a moment, he ran his fingers over the skin of her arms. While there were abrasions along her wrists, she didn't appear to be marred otherwise.

Gingerly, he lifted her up and walked her back into the kitchen. Once there, he looked for an exit. Just beyond Hessen's torture chamber was another unmarked door. He pushed his way past that into a small, poorly-lit stairwell.

By now, his body demanded payment for the extensive use of his healing gift. He only had so much time before he gave out entirely. He needed to be somewhere else when this happened.

As Kyote's limbs grew weak, he bumped into a wall. Despite her diminutive frame, Celene weighed heavy in his arms. A dull throbbing pounded at the base of his skull and his eyes were on fire. There was a metallic taste in the back of his mouth. The smell of baby powder on Celene's body, once a comforting scent, now did little to settle either his head or stomach.

After a few deep breaths, Kyote pushed on. Around a turn in the corridor, he found the exit to the adjacent alley. Once through the doorway, the stench of rotting trash was almost too much for him. Kyote gulped hard as he looked at his surroundings.

Not too far ahead was another door. With Kyote's body near collapse, he moved towards it. His boot batted an empty box aside, which sent a pair of rats scurrying.

Kyote was relieved to find the building unlocked. Though the interior was dark, it had once been a warehouse. Now, it was a nearly-empty space that reeked of spoiled food and mold. A few rotted crates still littered the main floor.

Kyote didn't care what the place used to be as long as it provided shelter.

No longer capable of supporting him, his legs gave out and he collapsed. His shoulder bounced off of the concrete floor. His head spun for what felt like minutes as his eyes struggled to focus. The depository's darkness pulsated.

He slumped there, almost lifeless, with Celene's body still wrapped in his arms. He tucked her head into his shoulder as he caressed her back. He could feel the last embers of warmth as they died within her.

Before he lost consciousness, Kyote wept.

Chapter 22

The Ninth of Iefimond, Year 2063 BAE
Palicosta

Flynn was done with his former existence. The war had worn on him in ways he couldn't have predicted. The people he'd killed still populated the worst of his nightmares. Even now, he occasionally dreamt that the Moa'rehnzan general's terrified eyes stared lifelessly at him. To make matters worse, the time he spent with the LIO had not prepared him for civilian life back in Verenigen.

Joining Kyote and Rolde had only made things harder. Instead of returning to the introspective life of an Evisran, he'd become a for-hire killer and thief. Rather than delve into readings and meditations, hoping to find the man he once was, he'd indulged in a lifestyle that ultimately only brought him pain.

One of his biggest regrets was that he couldn't revisit Norte'wald, not even if he felt compelled to see his dying father one last time. He couldn't show his face there. The fact that he failed to see the red flags around the mission left him wondering how far off the path he'd strayed.

Flynn had to simplify his life and focus on his Evisran faith. He planned to take up residence in a small township where no one would know who he was and what he'd done. Once settled, he would make regular visits to the Library to continue the educational pursuits he'd once enjoyed.

Before he could set this plan into motion, Flynn made a stop in Scae'hale. With Rolde's possessions in hand, Flynn traveled to the family's farm to let his parents know that their son had passed. In the short discussion he had with the eldest Rolde, Flynn tried to be truthful. He explained that their son was killed during a contracted mission. Flynn admitted that, even though they'd been betrayed, he was culpable for not heeding warning signs.

He departed the following day on a stagecoach bound for Kit'abana. As he reclined in the back of the vehicle, Flynn attempted to sort out his thoughts. Though he'd done what he set out to do, Flynn felt no better. While he doubted he would ever truly be over Rolde's passing, he hoped that in time the grief would fade.

Kyote was another matter. While Flynn's anger with the man had lessened, he had no interest in continuing their association. Flynn couldn't trust his safety around Kyote. If he never saw Kyote again, he might consider himself fortunate.

Flynn's visit to Kit'abana offered a brief respite. The Library employees who knew him were pleased that he'd returned safely from the war. They brought him into their homes and fed him well. During his time at the Library, Flynn was invited to join fellow Evisrans for a short visit to Ierija'roca in the south. It was there that he spent a few days in meditation, trying to clear the past few years from his head.

No matter how hard he tried, Flynn struggled to reconcile himself to the violent nature that lurked within him. It was firmly anchored to the well of energies at his core, the spark that fueled his gift. Every time he considered it, he remembered being surrounded by dead bodies in Fort Biaa. Flynn hoped that someone could teach him to channel the ability safely and stop that uncontrollable violence.

After some months, he obtained a new home. Flynn discovered a small cottage for sale in the fishing village of Palicosta. It took every last coin he'd earned over the past three years, but he purchased the two-story abode from a gentleman who needed to offload his recently-deceased mother's house. Since he and his family had no use for the inherited property, Flynn was able to purchase it for far less than it was worth.

On one cold day in Iefimond, Year 2063 BAE, Flynn moved in with a few crates.

The furnishings were sparse. In the upper bedroom were an uncovered cot and a bedside table. In the sitting room waited a timeworn couch, and the kitchen held a small table with two matching chairs. A set of old dishes gathered dust on the cabinet shelves.

Still, Flynn was relieved to have anything. In his boxes were a few personal effects, but nothing that might be considered décor. It would be some time before he would have the coin to purchase additional amenities.

Smelling mothballs and ointment in the air, Flynn opened the windows. Hours later, he'd unloaded everything and was arranging his meager possessions.

While wiping at the sweat that dotted his brow, Flynn looked over the objects scattered across the bed and nearby table. Painful regret quickly crept into his chest.

After the fight, Flynn had pocketed two imbued ores from the ravaged display room. He'd then returned to Wallowrich's office and his dense library. Flynn didn't want the more obscure works to be lost.

On Wallowrich's desk, he found more documentation about the World's Eye. To the side lay an unlabeled book; its purple exterior was ragged with age. He picked it up and was a few pages in before he understood what it was about.

Now, standing alone in his new home, he held the same hardback before him. He opened it and flipped through a few pages of densely-scribbled handwriting at a time. Judging by the yellowed pages and faded ink, Flynn assumed that the uncredited author was probably long dead. In what few passages he could read, there wasn't a coherent timeline to follow.

In the margins of one page were the words "anchored to Aetrhe'month?"

After a short while, Flynn was overcome by a growing anxiety. He'd taken the ores and the book on a whim, and, now that he was alone with himself, he felt nothing but guilt. Flynn gathered the various items and slipped them into a footlocker, which he placed in the shadows at the back of his closet.

Once his evening meal, vegetable soup and bread from the local baker, was done, Flynn went outside to take in his new view. By now, the distant pier was packed with fishing vessels anchored for the night. At least there was the prospect that he might get work as a stevedore. Perhaps, he might even sign on with one of the captains. He was a quick learner and not opposed to physical labor. With a little training, he was certain he could manage the nets and cages.

Flynn drew in a deep breath of the crisp, briny air. Within seconds, the cool breeze dried the perspiration along his brow.

Flynn rested against the fence and let out a satisfied sigh. Palicosta was just the type of village Flynn had envisioned. Once he'd settled into a daily routine, he might start to feel at ease.

The sound of pebbles rolling across the nearby alley caught his attention. Flynn's body tensed as he spied movement on his left. He shifted his stance. With a flick of his head, he looked at the young woman who was walking down the lane. She wore a flower-print dress over which was draped a teal-colored sweater.

He still expected Gohn or one of his men to come out of

the dark for him. He wondered how long would it take until he stopped jumping at shadows.

The girl looked to be in her late teens. Dense blonde hair was pinned back with clasp, and a braid was tucked behind each of her ears. As she neared, he noticed the aqua color of her eyes. As their gazes met, she blushed and offered a smile.

"Hello," she said as her pace slowed.

"Hello," he replied with a nod.

Flynn's gaze returned to the horizon, where orange slowly faded to blue. He was surprised when she spoke again.

"Ar-are you related to Mrs. Falkjen?"

"Hmm?" He turned to face her. She had stopped in the middle of the lane. "Oh, uh, no. Her son, uh, Willem, recently sold me the house," Flynn sputtered his reply.

"Ah. It's a shame she passed away. Mrs. Falkjen was a nice lady who didn't give anyone any trouble. Loved her flowers." She motioned toward the bushes that had clearly gone untended for months.

Flynn nodded. He didn't exactly know what to say. He'd only met Willem once, and the man had said very little about his mother.

Just as he thought the girl was about to walk off, she reached out and offered a hand.

"Well, welcome to Palicosta."

He took her soft fingers in his and shook.

"Thank you. The name is Flynn."

"Jori."

Chapter 23

The Twelfth of Oadimond
Halong District, Issuhn on Tir

Kyote was facedown on the table, surrounded by a number of empty beer bottles and the remains of a fifth of whiskey. A glass stein rested just within reach of his left hand. A rim of suds clung to the interior. No one dared to clear the display after he'd bribed the wait staff to drop off the drinks and leave him be.

As drunk as he was, Kyote wasn't out cold yet. He would've welcomed unconsciousness, but his brain wouldn't rest.

How long had it been since Celene's death? He vaguely remembered carrying her from the abandoned restaurant. Her limp weight had felt so heavy at the time. Eventually, once he was strong enough, he'd stumbled from the warehouse. Did he take Celene with him? He had no recollection. He couldn't imagine leaving her. Still, there was a void in his memory, a span of darkness. He only hoped he'd arranged for her burial.

Scenes flickered through his mind like an out-of-focus slideshow. Celene's murder had not pushed him towards revenge. Instead, it had pulled the last thread of hope, unraveling anything but his urge to crawl inside a bottle.

Eventually, he stumbled into the south side of Halong District and took up residence. Some nights—or were they days—he only sobered up enough to go out and procure more drink. While the older couple that ran the hostel gave him looks, the huge stack of coins he'd handed over kept them silent.

Kyote no longer felt human. The portion of his heart that had loved Celene that had once grieved over her loss was dead; the anger inside him had exhumed it, set it on fire, and scattered the ashes for good measure. In its place sat a soul-crushing ennui that urged him to lie down for good.

His ruminations were interrupted by a belch. When nothing else followed, he reached out to continue the night's consumption.

Drinking from the bottle of whiskey that sat before him, he noticed that the room was too loud. And too vivid. Why was it so bright in here? The gold and crystal décor seemed to reflect every ray of light, brightening each surface with a brain-searing luminescence. Maybe it had been this way before he started drinking and he just hadn't noticed, or even cared, but it certainly was now that that last mouthful of booze was sloshing about in the bottom of the bottle.

A well-dressed goon stood beside him, barking in his ear, pounding the flat of his fist into the tabletop. Each blow threatened his carefully-arranged display of bottles.

Kyote shook his head.

"Ay'hola, asshole." The Tirean greeting certainly wasn't meant to be polite this time around. "Hey, you filthy bum, this here booth is reserved for Mister Jianotti. You gots some brass balls sitting here. You gots ta get up *and now*. I'm only gonna give you this one chance. Damn table's gonna stink of bum as it is."

Kyote grunted as one hand flicked upwards. A middle finger was his answer.

"Hey, get up!" A thick, stubby digit poked him in the

shoulder. "I ain't fuckin' kidding. You're makin' the boss wait." After a second, the muscle added, "And you're pissin' me right off!"

Well, whoop-e-dee-doo.

The goon placed his hands on Kyote's arm. He had a grip like a vice as his fingers curled tightly.

Kyote was tired.

He grabbed the nearest bottle and smashed it on the corner of the tabletop. Before his assailant could react, Kyote jabbed it into his forearm. The broken shards sank into the meat of his limb.

The henchman bellowed a string of swears with a hand clasped over the bleeding wound. Streams of blood leaked out through his fingers.

Despite his inebriation, Kyote moved quickly. He collected the half-empty mug and launched out of the booth. A swift uppercut drove the tankard into the thug's face. The impact was fierce enough to shatter the glass, which turned the curved handle into a shiv. Kyote pounded the new implement into the man's face, quickly reducing it to a gooey mess.

Kyote climbed onto the man's chest and rode him to the ground. With one hand on the man's collar, Kyote kept driving the remains of his glass into the savaged countenance.

He didn't even notice that two pairs of hands grasped him by the shoulders. He did feel a cudgel strike him across the back of the head.

Kyote spun about and hissed like an animal. While this caused his assailants to recoil briefly, they renewed their assault. They were quickly joined by a quartet of the establishment's own bouncers.

While he struggled against them, the six men eventually subdued him.

Well, this isn't the worst I've ever felt…

The thought dragged Kyote out of unconsciousness.

Kyote's eyes flickered open to a sight that was pretty familiar. He was alone inside a storeroom, strapped to a chair with leather and chains. From the ache in his face and chest, he knew he'd been worked over pretty good.

Some really unimaginative assholes we have here. Probably got a playbook they go by. Instead of doing me a favor by putting a bullet in my head, they want to torture me. He shrugged as he let out a snort. *Might as well see if anyone's about. Get this ball a rolling, as they say.*

Kyote cleared his throat, drew in a deep breath, and began to yell. His voice cracked for a second.

"Hey! Hey, assholes! Is there anyone around? I'd like to get whatever bullshit you have planned started, okay? I don't have all day! If you're not gonna kill me, go get me a coffee!"

Sounds of movement from an adjacent room brought a smile to his lips. The scrape of chair legs on the floor was followed by the scurried stamping of boots. Seconds later, the door opened, and a pair of henchmen dressed in the usual apparel barged into the room. Both briefly brandished their firearms. Once they saw that Kyote was still secured, they holstered their weapons.

"It's clear," one called out over his shoulder.

A third man entered, this one much smaller than the others but with sharp eyes.

He'd always assumed that those who lorded over the Tirean crime syndicate were older men, who'd spent decades either running the business or working their way up through the ranks. This man, with his bright eyes and slicked-back black hair, looked to be in his thirties. His light gray suit was well-tailored and modern in design. On the dark blue tie that hung from his neck was a Tirean character stitched in golden thread.

He eyed Kyote for a few seconds.

"Usually, one would expect you to bow politely, but I think I can ignore your lack of manners, considering the circumstances," he spoke. "Musaboru Jianotti, soon-to-be head of business interests in Halong District. And your name is?"

Considering the ache in his bones, he decided against sarcasm. "Kyote Kurttsen."

At this, Jianotti's brow rose.

"Well, Mr. Kurttsen, I'd thought to have you beaten for a while until my men were sufficiently tired. And then we'd shoot you and hang you from one of the nearby lampposts. Send a message to anyone else who might raise a hand against those who run Halong District." Jianotti leaned in close to examine his face. "But, it seems that you've thrown a wrench into such plans."

Kyote chuckled softly. *Didn't stay properly busted up, I guess.*

"In light of the stories that have made their way up from Ilkabari about a man of your… *nature* and your unwillingness to remain bloody and broken, I think I might have other uses for you. Not too many on the streets of Issuhn on Tir can take such a thrashing and shrug it off so easily. Maybe you're more than a drunken punching bag." Jianotti placed his hands behind his back and straightened out his shoulders. "I lost a good man last night. Heddo's family is closely associated with my own. His father worked for mine until his retirement. There is history there, as you can imagine. Father would want this handled. I will have to deliver bad news to his relatives before tomorrow is out. I'd thought to let them know that their son was avenged. Now… now, I think I might find other, better uses for you."

"You…" Kyote coughed. "You talk a lot, ya know."

As one of his men moved in, Jianotti waved him off, chuckling.

"You, my friend, are amusing." Jianotti took a few paces back. "While I would love to continue having you make me laugh, my men are chomping at the bit for some payback. Heddo was their friend, you see. They won't kill you—though, I wonder if they can—but they will get their fill of beating on you before you see the light of day again."

At that, one moved in and landed a right cross on his jaw.

"Of course. So, is this your go-to thing?" Kyote said as he spit some blood from his mouth. "You *businessmen?* 'cause this isn't even the first time I've been tortured since I got here."

"I hear. Stories at least. Of a bogeyman who escaped Majira's finest. They won't give out any details, but they were quite insistent about relocating their lost captive. Now, how exactly did that play out?" Jianotti inquired as he tried to hide a smirk. "I only ask so that I might lord it over Majira the next time we meet. Stick it to the old man one last time."

"His finest? Heh. Let's just say that I got pissed off enough at having my time wasted, killed the shit out of them, and walked out." Kyote then looked at Jianotti's men. "Doesn't bode well for you, I think."

This caused one man to reach for his gun.

"Maybe, maybe not. But I think that I might be convinced to offer you the opportunity to walk out of here. Not to freedom, mind you. You still owe a debt to me. A man's life does not come cheap."

"Some come cheaper than others."

"If I were to find some other use for you, what would that be? What might you be proficient at? I think I might have the answer, but I'd like to hear it from your lips."

"I'm the killing kind. That's all I'm good for."

"You don't say." Jianotti smiled with perverse joy. "I think I can find some use for you in that regard. Perhaps, though, I shouldn't let you roam about the city without an escort and a leash. You have the smell of a man who might just wander away."

"I might." Kyote tugged at his restraints for a moment. "Gotta say that I didn't realize that this was a job interview. I might have worn something nicer."

"I'm a flexible, open-minded employer. Your apparel is not a deal-breaker."

"And what do I get out of this? Why should I say yes?"

"I don't have my men unload their guns on you. Set you on fire. Drown you. Bathe you in acid. Whatever it takes. At some point, I think even your body might have its limits. If you say yes? I set you up with a place, an endless supply of booze, your drugs of choice, and women—"

Kyote cringed for a second.

"—or men, if that suits you. All I ask is that you occasionally put your skills to use. For me. There will be a changing of the leadership in years to come, and working for me will have its perks."

Kyote remained silent. He couldn't go back to Verenigen. Maybe if he was lucky, the work would kill him.

"You will, of course, be under guard until you're not a flight risk. Can't have you skipping out, can we?"

I ain't got nowhere else to go. No one else to see.

Kyote nodded. If this city was to be his prison, at least his sentence came with an endless supply of booze. He hoped that he could drink the memories of Celene away.

"Let's get this over with, then."

Jianotti walked out of the room, smiling. Over the next few hours, his men broke Kyote's nose and most of his fingers. Both of his eyes swelled shut. A few days later, under the watchful eye of a bodyguard, Kyote moved to a safe house further north.

Seven long years spent serving as Jianotti's assassin would be his sentence.

Epilogue

The Thirty-fourth of Oadimond
Vertegarte

As O'mas had predicted, his cottage was the topic of local gossip for months following its completion. While the carpenters hadn't objected to O'mas' non-traditional abode, older residents were less accepting. On the rare occasion when he went into town, he could feel their judgmental eyes as they watched him go about his business. When the calendar changed years, the interest of Vertegarte's natives eventually waned.

O'mas focused on more important matters. While the study of imbued ores and gifted individuals provided a pleasant diversion, his thoughts regularly returned to the Grymore Foundation's recent activities. This work often kept him up late into the evening.

Feeling a bit groggy, he got a late start to the day.

With a book in one hand and a half-eaten apple in the other, O'mas wandered from the kitchen back to his living quarters. A cot was tucked away in the back corner, but most of the room was set up as a study, with bookcases and chests arranged efficiently in the limited space. Mementos were tucked away in every nook and cranny. Just inside the lone doorway was his desk, atop which sat stacked letters, both opened and unread.

Some were missives sent to him by old contacts in the

VMF, who kept him apprised of events that should no longer concern a retired spymaster. Others were inquiries from friends from throughout the continent, including a few from members of the Library in Kit'abana and the Byraelian Assembly in Gold Flats. Off to one side was a letter from Willem Ethvarth of Port Hadley. O'mas wanted to give his dear friend's writing his undivided attention. Distracted as he was, now wasn't the time.

Just as he was about to slip into the desk chair, O'mas heard a knock at the front door. He cocked his head to one side. He'd not had a caller in almost a month and wasn't expecting one. The next mail delivery was ten days away.

He reached for his pistol and held it at the small of his back as he crossed the room. O'mas paused as his hand fell to the knob. His gaze went to the lintel, where the Rhepelles, one of his imbued ores, was placed. Its protective aura cast a comforting warmth over him.

One day, someone who will want to shoot me is going to be on the other side, he thought to himself. *With the Rhepelles, I might actually survive. Hopefully, today won't be the day.*

He was both surprised and relieved when he opened the door. Just outside was a girl, draped in a huge green cloak, in her early teens. There was sweat on her brow. Long reddish-brown hair fluttered in the faint breeze and fell past her shoulders.

She stood silently and looked up at the space above the doorframe.

"Can I be of some assistance?" he eventually inquired as he slipped the pistol into his waistband.

"I… uh…" Her gaze fell to his face.

"Did you come out here for a reason?"

She nodded as her feet shuffled nervously.

While he didn't want to pull the information out of her,

O'mas wanted to know why she was here.

"Do you have a name?"

"It's… uh, Jehn," she revealed with a shy smile. "Jehn Brumal."

"Good. My name is Marianus O'mas." *That's a start, at least. I can't exactly berate her, asking why she knocked on my door, now can I? Well, I could, but I think that it would only send her off in tears. That would mean a visit from concerned parents.*

When she said nothing else, he let out a sigh and continued. "And how old are you?"

"Just turned eleven, sir," Jehn replied as a warm blush lit her pale cheeks.

Sir? At least someone instilled politeness in her, he thought to himself.

"And you came out here, why? Shouldn't you, oh, I don't know, be playing with friends?" O'mas was not one for children or uninvited guests. His cottage was far enough away from Vertegarte that she didn't happen upon it by accident.

"I, uh, I heard about the man who lives outside the village. An outsider from the north. The adults talk about you—"

Still?

"—I just wanted to see what made you so special. I figured you had to be special to get so many people interested."

Interested? Outside of the short-lived gossip generated by my moving here? I doubt they care so much.

"Well, here I am." He made a sweeping wave down the length of his body. "Did your parents mention me?"

"They were Vale'vigia," she replied as her face sagged. He well knew that the Vale'vigia had suffered untold losses at the onset of the war. The Moa'rehnzan military's attempt to breach the Vale was a bloody affair. If he'd visited Vertegarte years ago, he might have been witness to a much livelier hamlet.

O'mas had always regretted that the Verenigen Congress made no effort to provide assistance to Vertegarte and the Vale'vigia. There were a few token attempts at humanitarian aid, but no sign of military support. Politicians far more interested in respecting arrangements chose to ignore a clear danger to the village. In the end, all but a few of their warrior class were wiped out.

Now that he was reminded of the recent past, O'mas quickly recognized the oversized cloak that was draped over Jehn's shoulders. Its circular brass clasp was a familiar symbol of those who'd served.

"Well then, who tends to you now?"

"My aunt, Marcel. I live with her now."

"And she wouldn't mind you being out here?"

"She might." A coy grin curled the corners of her mouth. "If she knew."

O'mas tried in vain to stifle a laugh. It was clear that on some level, she was either precocious, willful, or both.

"Well, before I can talk to you any further, you might want to ask your aunt for permission." He figured this would put an end to her curiosity. If she was like anyone else in Vertegarte, Marcel would put a stop to her interest. "Just so that she knows where you're at and with whom you're talking."

"H'okay," she said as she lingered at the bottom step.

"Now would be as good a time as any," he suggested as he pointed to the dirt pathway behind her.

"I'll see you later," she called out as she scurried off.

O'mas was certain that he'd never have her darken his doorstep again.

Ten days later, she arrived with the mail, claiming that she had permission to be there. It would be months later before he met Marcel only to discover that Jehn hadn't spoken about her visits. By that time, though, he'd come to realize she was sensitive to his imbued ores, the Rhepelles in particular. Any initial objection to her presence was supplanted by curiosity about how someone so young was already showing signs of being gifted.

That, over the coming years, he would grow to enjoy her company proved to be a surprise.

ABOUT THE AUTHOR

Author of *Not Gods But Monsters,* Joshua Banker was born in Greece in 1973. He grew up in the San Francisco area before moving to Chattanooga where he attended the University of Tennessee at Chattanooga and received a BFA in Graphic Design. After moving to Charlotte, NC, he ran an independent entertainment review website from 1999-2006. Now living in Greenville, NC, Josh is a writer, painter, and illustrator, loves all things H.P. Lovecraft, is married and has two cats and a dog.

Visit **http://www.joshuabankerbooks.com** for updates.

Follow the author on social media at **https://www.facebook.com/joshuabankerbooks/** or **https://www.instagram.com/joshuabankerbooks/**